THE WOLF WHO WOULD BE KING
VOLUME ONE

WOLF IN SHADOWS

— ROBERT POYTON —

THIS IS AN INNSMOUTH GOLD BOOK

ISBN: 978-0-9956454-4-8 Paperback
ISBN: 978-0-9956454-6-2 E-book

Cover design: Innsmouth Gold
Wolf chapter heading graphic courtesy of
https://lupas-deva.deviantart.com/

Published by Innsmouth Gold.

www.innsmouthgold.com

Cover art by Shelley De Cruz
Copyright@2023 Graveheart Designs
www.facebook.com/graveheartdesigns

To the memory of Robert E Howard

"To run with the wolf was to run in the shadows, the dark ray of life, survival and instinct. A fierceness that was both proud and lonely, a tearing, a howling, a hunger and thirst."
— O.R. Melling

PROLOGUE

The young thief slid through the open window and, unhooking the grapple from the ledge, wound the rope swiftly up behind him. He glanced outside but all was quiet, save for the distant whisper of the sea and a soft night breeze that carried the scent of jasmine up from the garden below. As he was returning the rope to his backpack, the soft chink of harness and a low cough alerted him to the approach of the Palace Guard. The thief moved quickly into a darkened alcove as two armoured figures strolled slowly by, talking softly as they went. Fortunately for the thief these weren't the elite Talons but older City Guard nearing retirement age, given easy duties to see out their service.

The thief waited until the corridor was quiet once more then, with a quick glance at the rough map he'd prepared earlier, set off with slow, silent tread towards the Royal Chambers. The time spent wooing one of the Palace maids had not been wasted and had been far from unpleasant, a most agreeable way to prepare for tonight's excursion.

The youth was tall and lithe, his long blonde hair restrained by a plain cloth headband. He wore a simple dark blue tunic, breeches and sandals, carrying nothing except a dagger and the pack slung over his shoulders. Two turns, another check of the map and he found himself outside the large door of what should be one of the Royal treasure rooms.

Holding his breath, he tried the handle and gently pushed the door. It moved to his touch, the door was unlocked, swinging silently open on oiled hinges. The room interior was dark and the youth paused to allow his eyes to adjust from the soft torchlight of the corridor. Then, keeping his movements careful and deliberate, he crept forward, closing the door behind him. He almost immediately froze, some sixth sense warning of him of impending danger; was there was a slight smell of burning, perhaps? But nothing moved, the room was still.

He crouched and, reaching into his pack, brought out a flint and candle, lighting it after a couple of strikes. Holding the candle aloft, he looked around, taking a sharp intake of breath as he noticed two things. The first was the light reflecting back from a heap of jewels in an open, wooden chest. The second was the figure of a man, half hidden in the shadows. No features were visible, just the vague outline of a wide shouldered frame. A gruff voice spoke with a lilting accent. "And who might you be, boy?"

Quick as a flash, the thief responded. "My name is Laertes, I'm a serving boy. It's my first day here, I got lost in the corridors."

There was a low rumble of laughter from the dark.

"Bel's balls, you are no serving boy. You are a thief!"
The youth shifted nervously, hand automatically seeking the hilt of his dagger.

"Are you a thief also, then, come to steal the Royal gems?"

The figure moved forward into the dim light, the youth gasped and his hand dropped away from the dagger. The powerfully built man wore a plain but finely tailored, knee length white tunic. At his belted waist was a poniard in an ornate green sheath. Cold, grey eyes regarded the thief from a scarred face, framed by long, dark hair and silver-shot beard. "I'm no thief, boy. I'm the King..."

The thief stood uncertainly, glancing at the door.

"You wouldn't make it," the King smiled, eyes narrowing. "I may be old, but I'm still fast."

The youth swallowed nervously, weighing up his odds but before he could come to a decision, the King moved. Like a striking snake, his hand drew the poniard and threw it in one easy motion. All the young thief saw was a blur as the long blade whistled past him to bury itself with a thud in the heavy door. The youth's shoulders sagged and he raised his hands in surrender. Even though he was still armed and the King was not, one look at the corded arms and broad shoulders of the man bespoke of great strength... and the cold grey eyes held grim purpose.

"Am I to be executed then, Your Majesty?" The youth's voice quavered. To his surprise the response was laughter, a deep chuckle that developed into a hearty peal.

"Executed? No boy, a wolf doesn't prey on mice. Besides, you have courage in attempting to rob the Palace and courage is a quality I admire!"

The King strode to the door and reclaimed his dagger. As he did so, there was a noise outside, then a knock. The King motioned the youth to step away and he opened the large door slightly.

"Is all in order, Sire?" It was the voice of a Palace Guard. "We were passing and heard voices."

"All is well, Argades, just your old King talking to himself. Be on your way, good fellow, have no concern for me."

The guards moved off and the King closed the door. Picking up the candle, he used it to relight two sconced torches on the wall, their warm glow revealing the whole room. There was little furniture in the room, save a couch and a high backed chair stood next to a small table. On the table an ink pot, quill and rolls of parchment sat next to a large wine pitcher and a plain, silver goblet. The walls were bare apart from a few weapons and shields hung as decoration. The King sat at the table and indicated the parchment.

"Sometimes, when sleep is elusive, I come in here and write." He closed the lid on the ink pot. "Stories of old, tales of the past. None shall read them, I imagine, but it helps pass the time in this marble barn. I was writing when I heard you outside."

"Heard me, Sire? But I was silent!"

The King shook his head. "Silence to you city folk is as of the blundering of oliphants to anyone raised in the forest".

The King waved a hand towards the couch. "Sit, boy. Have some wine."

The bemused youth sat, taking the proffered goblet and gulping nervously - it was good wine! The King sat back in his chair and surveyed the thief.

"So, what brings you robbing to my house? And the truth this time. I admire courage, but despise liars!"

In halting words the young thief told of his life. Of his upbringing in one of the poorer quarters of the city, the imprisonment of his father, the death of his mother. Of falling in with a gang and of learning the art of hand to mouth survival. Of bigger and better jobs, until this one, and of the fact that no other thief would dare accompany him. The King stayed silent throughout, occasionally taking a swig directly from the pitcher. He rubbed his chin and grunted.

"Hmm, a not uncommon tale in this city. Life can be hard, boy, but you seem to have developed the skills to
survive. You remind me a little of myself at your age, long ago though that was."

"Surely not Sire, were you not born into this? Are you not of noble birth?"

The King rumbled with laughter once more.

"Far from it, boy. I was born in a simple hut in a small village far to the north of here. It was there I learnt the ways of survival in the wild, hunting, tracking and use of the blade for battle. But it was here in Adelphis that I learned of other ways to survive. In fact, at one time I was a thief like yourself."

"A thief, Sire? But how, then, did you become King?"

"Well, that is a long tale, indeed. Let me first tell you how I became a thief..."

CHAPTER 1

The youth paused, silhouetted in the lurid flare of torchlight that cast flickering shadows about the murky street. Two sounds had alerted him, a barked command and the jingle of harness. He faded back into the darkness of an alleyway as a squad of Militia stamped by. The youth had no particular reason to hide but his short time in the city had already taught him to be wary of officialdom. One good thing with the Militia, you could always hear them coming. But then, the youth reasoned, stealth was not so important when you were part of a squad of a dozen armoured men. Besides which, he had heard tell of certain arrangements in some areas where an appearance of patrols was maintained, though these patrols were hurried and well advertised in advance. The youth shook his head, such ways were alien to his way of thinking, a far cry from the customs of his own people.

Satisfied that the squad had passed, the youth moved back

into the torch-lit street, though street was a somewhat grand title for what was little more than a muddy alleyway between the buildings. The stench of offal and waste was ever-present, the youth wondered at how so called civilised people could live amongst such filth.

He had been in Adelphis for barely a week. The vast, ancient metropolis exerted a powerful pull on travellers and wanderers from across the Kingdom and beyond. His own origins lay far to the North, his people one of the many clans that populated the Far Reaches, as the City people called that land. His clan had their own name for their country but none in Adelphis was interested in the opinions of a Northern outlander, the discovery of which had led him into more than one dispute already.

He thought back to how he came to the city; firstly leaving his own land with a group of traders, then variously walking and riding with merchant caravans journeying south. Although bandits were rare in the Kingdom, an extra sword hand was welcomed by most traders and within a matter of weeks he had reached the city.

The final approach to Adelphis had been on foot, along the dry and dusty Great East Road that followed the track of the sparkling blue River Geryos. The sun beat down on his bare head, as it always seemed to in this place. It was hot, damned hot, much hotter than his grey, frozen homeland. He had long discarded his heavy bearskin cloak and woollen garments, wearing instead a simple lightweight tunic and breeches, his road-worn boots traded for high sandals. The plain scabbard holding a heavy broadsword and the leathern cord wolf tooth necklace were the only items still remaining from the start of his exodus.

The outlander was perhaps eighteen summers in age, tall and strongly built, just over six feet tall, wide of shoulder and narrow of hip. Black hair, tied back against the heat, framed a pale, narrow face with high cheekbones. Cold, grey eyes gave a dispassionate mien to the youthful features, offering no clue as to the thoughts within.

Cresting the hill that overlooked the approach to Adelphis, the youth shielded his eyes from the glare and took in the panorama below. Small figures worked in shady olive groves; golden crops waved in the soft breeze; sheep and cattle grazed the sparse pastures that lay around farm buildings. Through the centre of it all, road and river wound ribbon- like towards the city. A blue haze hung above the far horizon and the soft wind carried a faint salt tang as it cooled his sweating face.

From his vantage point, he saw how the metropolis straddled the river Geryos not far from its estuary and was built in three concentric rings. The outer ring, protected by a wooden palisade, was a sprawl of shacks and huts. These housed, he guessed, the various workers of the city and outlying districts, or those who could not get into the city proper. Beyond the huddle, a high, white stone wall circled the city itself. Within that ring, another wall at its base, loomed a high, craggy promontory with a white fortress sat atop it. This was The Rock, and if Adelphis was the heart of the Kingdom, then The Rock was the heart of Adelphis.

With the Old City at its feet, The Rock housed the Citadel, the Royal Palace, the Senate and The Temple and was home to the Kingdom's rulers. The youth squared his sun-burnt shoulders, wiped the stinging sweat from his eyes, took a swig of warm water from his flask and set out on the last leg of his long journey.

Passing the unmanned palisade, the youth tramped the wide, dusty road through the squabble of huts and people. His senses were immediately assaulted by the sheer numbers of people squeezed into this space, more than he had ever seen gathered together before in one area. The stench alone was incredible, a potent mix of human and animal and everyone seemed fixed in some feverish activity, except for the numerous beggars squatting or lying in the roadside dust.

The crowd was a mix of a dozen races and a hubbub of languages and accents filled the air. Blond haired Bavarii haggled with dusky, white robed Sahki traders; a group of Khaluk riders thundered through on shaggy war ponies; an ebony Nibian dignitary, resplendent in animal skin cloak and head plumes, was carried past in a palanquin. Few had the dark curly hair and olive skin of the native Adelphians; those that did were mostly officials, or traders and artisans travelling to and from the city .

Eventually, the youth arrived at the East Gate. Set in the high stone wall, flanked by guard towers, the large archway was manned by a squad of Militia, clad in light leather armour and armed with long staves and short swords. Most people appeared to come and go freely, particularly merchants and their trains of goods. The youth strode forward with confidence, assured he would enter with no hindrance. As he went to pass under the archway, however, a stave barred his way.

"And where might you be going, boy?" the Militia man sneered in the trading tongue. He took in the youth's dusty appearance, the pale skin burnt red in the hot sun, the poor cut of the clothing, which did little to conceal the powerful build and heavy arms. There was something of the wilderness about the youth, a wolfish quality to his movement and mannerisms. Indeed he looked as out of place in this setting as one of those wild creatures would look in a kennel of hounds.

The youth replied in an unfamiliar accent. "I seek entrance to the city, I am here to make my fortune."

The Militia man glanced again at the cold eyes and the heavy broadsword in its plain, worn sheath. His comrades, sensing trouble or sport, gathered close. The guard spat into the dust and replied.

"We have beggars and penniless wanderers enough, be on your way!"

The youth's nostrils flared and his eyes narrowed, his right hand twitched.

"I'm no beggar, I am a warrior!"

This brought a peal of laughter from the guards.

"A warrior?" one cried. "More like worrier! A sheep worrier!"

His colleagues laughed heartily at the jest and the youth felt confused and angry. His hand twitched once more, aching to draw the sword and run these fools through. The first guard caught sight of the movement.

"Think again, boy." He nodded his head upwards. The youth followed the gaze to the top of the guard tower where another Militia man stood, crossbow trained directly at him. Growling a curse in his own tongue, the young man span on his heel and walked swiftly away, the laughter still ringing in his ears.

For the remainder of the day he roamed the outer circle, buying some food and ale with what little coin he had left. His experience was a far cry from what he had been led to believe. Travellers spoke of Adelphis as being a place of wonder, of marble paved streets, of precious gems in abundance, of wanton and lascivious women, of opportunity and reward. So far he had experienced nothing but rabble, stink and noise.

He slept overnight in a crude tavern, little more than a large shack by the main roadside. In the morning he enquired of the barkeep how best to get into the city. The man made it clear that unless he could bribe the guards, show he had rightful business in the city or be a trader of some sorts, the prospects of entry were dim. It was as he sat eating cold gruel for breakfast that the youth saw a merchant train approaching along the Great East Road. As he watched it draw near, a plan formed in his mind.

The caravan was led by an escort of four mounted Kingdom soldiers, their bronze armour dusty from travel. Then followed a line of pack mules and attendant traders, some local, some of different nationalities. But what really caught his eye was the large covered wagon rolling slowly in the midst of the group. Beside it rode a short but powerfully built black haired man in a dark red robe. His copper coloured skin and almond-shaped eyes marked him a fellow outlander, though of the East rather than the North. A curiously shaped sword hung at his waist, its blade more reminiscent of a cleaver than the straight swords favoured locally. The youth left a coin on the table and sauntered, with apparent disinterest, closer to the caravan.

As the train approached the gatehouse it slowed and the youth made his move. With a final glance to ensure no one was watching, he ducked, dropped to the floor and rolled quickly and smoothly under the wagon. Most eyes were fixed on the gate ahead and the bold move went unnoticed. Once under the wagon, he gripped the front axle with both hands, then pulled his feet up into position. The rear axle was not quite close enough to reach with his feet but by pressing them to the sides of the frame and tensing his body, he found he could hold himself up off the ground. For what seemed like an age he remained in place as the wagon trundled slowly forward. Stinging sweat ran into his eyes and his muscles began to quiver and burn with the strain. At long last he heard the voices of the gate guards and the wagon rolled on. Seconds before his cramping muscles gave out, he dropped, sword digging into his back as he fell, and rolled swiftly out to the side. If anyone saw him, none gave cry.

Rising to his feet, now even more dusty, the youth moved quickly into the cover of a shop awning. The street here was no less crowded than outside the wall, but most of the buildings were of stone and everything looked somewhat older and more established. He followed the caravan along the main street, which led him directly into the heart of Adelphis' bustling commercial district, plazas and squares housing a collection of stores, traders and open and covered markets.

Each square seemed to cater to a different trade. In the first the coppery smell of blood hung heavy in the air, pale animal carcasses hung from the stalls, young children waved fans in an attempt to drive away the flies. The second square was alive with the cries of many types of vendor, from rabbit-puller to knife sharpener. As the youth moved further into the district the traders and goods became more select, there were more craftsmen, more expensive produce.

In the final square exotic silks flashed red in the bright sunlight, yellows spices poured from earthenware jars as men haggled and the cries of exotically plumed birds accompanied the low murmur of trade. Above all, gulls wheeled in the azure sky and the scent of sea was heavy in the air. Beyond the rooftops lining the opposite side of the square the youth could just make out the topsails of ships in the main dock. This was more like it he thought, now he could begin to seek his fortune!

That had been two days ago, during which the youth had gone from place to place, seeking in vain for some kind of work. The people of the city, while accustomed to travellers from many far-flung lands, seemed little inclined to offer work to outlanders He tried getting access to the dock area but was again turned away by the Militia.

Taking advice from a market trader, he decided to cross the Geryos and try his luck in the neighbourhoods on the south bank of the river. A short walk from the commerce area brought him to Pergares Bridge, so named for the large marble statue of the ancient warrior king that guarded its northern approach. Lofty and noble stood the mighty stone warrior, sword held aloft and stern gaze turned out over the sparkling blue water. The bridge itself, of the same white stone as the city walls, spanned the river in five wide arches, trafficked by ponies and carts as well as people on foot.

The youth paused halfway across the bridge to take in the fresh air and the view to the west. Small boats and skiffs passed under the bridge and further along, to his right, he could see the larger vessels berthed at the city's main docks. On the opposite bank, to his left, were what appeared to be older docks, empty apart from a few decrepit looking vessels. Beyond, lost in a blue haze, he could just make out where the Geryos widened into its estuary. Above all hunched the gleaming white walls of the Citadel, like a watchful bird of prey atop The Rock. From here he could make out flags flying atop the high towers, the Royal Eagle standards fluttering in the hot, summer breeze.

Crossing the bridge, the youth found that the district on the south bank was much more run-down than the commercial area he had just left and the further he ventured into it, the more down-at-heel it became. His wanderings took him through a cluttered market area and into a large square. A tavern sat on one corner, on another was what appeared to be some kind of burial field or cemetery.

Taking the other main exit from the square, the youth soon found himself wandering a maze of narrow streets lined with slum dwellings and old warehouses. Small creeks criss-crossed the area and the stench of open cesspools filled the air. The youth walked at random, noticing that the poorly dressed locals eyed him sullenly and with ill-favour. A scrawny dog ran out into the centre of the street and started barking at him. Uncomfortable, he turned and made his way back to the market area, eventually finding a cheap flop house at which to stay.

A burst of drunken laughter brought the youth back to the present. The patrol now passed, he moved out of the shadows and strode with an air of confidence through the streets, making his way into the Old Market. The crowds were thick here, the cry of merchants filled the early evening air. Cooking smells assaulted his nostrils and his mouth began to water. As dubious as the meats on the stalls looked, their odour was enticing. The youth had not eaten a decent meal for days now, his meagre coin almost gone. Charity to the hungry and homeless was not a local custom, it seemed. He growled as his belly rumbled and he shook his head again. No hungry stranger would be refused board and hospitality in his home village, yet here people starved in the streets as the rich stepped, or more often, were carried over and around them.

He girded his belt and strode on, keeping his gaze

downward. A feminine call made him look up. A small group of scantily dressed women stood in provocative postures around the well at the centre of the main square.

"Hey there big feller, need some company?"

"Ooh no, choose me, young man," said one of the older ladies in the group, "I bet you could use an experienced hand, special rates for first timers!"

The harlots laughed and the young man felt his face flush. He had experience of girls back home, of course, but little more than youthful fumbling in darkened corners. More laughter caught his attention as he turned a corner and, seeing a crowd gathered up ahead, he moved forward to investigate

"Another winner!" announced a voice. "Come friends, will no one else roll the skulls? Try your luck against old Sullo! Our friend here just won a pouch full of coin!"

A gaunt man with an eye patch raised a bulging money pouch triumphantly and shook it in the air, grinning. "It's true, twenty silver dina!"

The youth shouldered his way through the crowd. At their centre a short, wiry man stood behind a street barrow, lit in the orange glow of two suspended lanterns. The man, glanced up at the newcomer and displayed crooked teeth in a wide smile.

"You, young sir! You look like a man who enjoys a challenge! Roll the skulls, try your luck against old Sullo! Is Lady Fortune with you tonight?"

The man made a flourish with his hand and rolled five ivory dice along the table. They bounced against the raised edge and came to rest, two showing a carved skull on their faces.

"Skulls to win, lad. All bets go in the pot, most skulls takes the money."

The youth rubbed his chin.

"I have only a few copper coins."

"Copper is fine lad, lay one down, let's begin!"

The youth took out his money as the crowd gathered around. Unseen by anyone, the one-eyed man slipped the bag of coin back to the dice-man before drifting away.

The youth won the first three rolls, lost the fourth, then won the next two. Each win brought a huge cheer from the crowd and lots of backslapping. The youth began to feel that perhaps city-folk were not so bad after all. Someone even pressed a flagon of ale into his hand, then, when that was drained, another. Soon, flush-faced and laughing with his new friends, he had amassed a tidy pile of copper and silver coin. Sullo paused and cracked his knuckles.

"Lady Fortune is indeed with you young man. How about we play for some real stakes? At least give me a chance to win back what I've lost?"

The crowd cheered again, several encouraging the youth on.

"Aye, why not?" he nodded, then roared to the crowd, "Why not!". Another cheer was raised and the dice-man grinned.

"Well now! How about we roll for, say...ten gold sovereigns?"

The youth was taken aback. "Ten gold? That's many times more than what I have here. I can't match the bet."

"Not to worry lad. Tell you what, you look like an honest man. I will lend you the money. If you win, you win. If I win, well you can pay me back, with a little interest. Look, tell me where you are staying and put your mark here."

The man produced a sheet of parchment from below the table. "These good folk can witness it. Now I can't say fairer than that, can I?"

The youth furrowed his brow, uncertain at what to do. The thought of ten gold coins was a strong lure, more money than he'd ever possessed in his life. The crowd urged him too and so he nodded assent, taking the offered quill and making a simple rune mark at the bottom of the scroll. The crowd cheered, then fell into expectant silence as the youth rolled the dice again - three skulls! More back slaps and congratulations followed, then the group fell still to watch the dice-man.

With a smooth twist Sullo scooped up the dice, made a flick of the wrist and threw the dice tumbling along the table. Five skulls! The crowd groaned as one as the dice-man laughed.

"Bad luck son, that's the way of the bones. Looks like you owe me ten sovs. I'll start by taking this back." He moved to scoop back the pile of coins in front of the youth.

"Hold!" cried the youth. The flush had gone from his face and his grey eyes glittered coldly. "You switched dice."

The subtle movement would have passed unnoticed by most, but not the keen eyes of a hunter. Sullo was indignant.

"I did no such thing, how dare you!" His protest was

interrupted by the youth grabbing his wrist. The man cried out as, with a sharp twist, his hand was forced upwards and open, revealing five dice. The youth then picked up a die from the table, weighing it in his palm.

"This one is heavier on one side!"

Sullo protested loudly again, but as he did so, nodded to a figure in the crowd. The youth, suddenly aware of a presence at his shoulder, released the cheater's wrist and turned. Before him stood a slab of a man, taller even than himself. He took in the heavy belly, large chest and huge, hairy arms. Atop a thick neck sat a face bristling with whiskers and menace. Small, piggy eyes regarded the youth with contempt.

"Pipe down, boy, or I'll take that girl's sword you carry and shove it sideways up your shitter," he growled.

The youth grinned broadly. Here was a language he could understand!

"By Morrg," he replied, "I learned something here today."

"What's that, boy?" the large man sneered.

"Well, I learned what comes out when a bear swives a pig!"

The large man's nostrils flared and he raised a scarred fist to punch, but the youth was quicker. Reacting to the man's intention rather than his movement, the youth swivelled from the hip and swung a balled fist directly into the giant's mid-section. With a loud *Ooof!* the man doubled over, straight into the thunderous uppercut that the youth unleashed. With a loud crash, the giant was flung back, knocked out cold.

A woman screamed and the crowd scattered, or most of them at least. One figure moved towards the youth, a knife blade glinting in the lantern light. The youth lithely shifted his torso aside, easily avoiding the thrust. Grabbing the knife hand, he twisted sharply. There was a grinding crunch followed by a high pitched scream and the knife-wielder staggered away, ashen faced. The youth wheeled back towards Sullo, who was hastily gathering the coins. He took one look at the murderous gleam in the youth's face and shouted, "Ragnor, Tassim, Brend!"

The youth made out three figures, including the one-eyed man, moving towards him through the crowd. All had swords drawn. Someone else was shouting for the Militia. He made a snap decision. Spitting a last oath at the dice-man, the youth turned and ran.

CHAPTER 2

The youth fled until the sound of pursuit was no longer in his ears. He had no fear of facing anyone in a fight but the rules of this place were unknown to him. Killing a man in open combat was accepted in his clan but who knew what punishment it might bring in this madhouse? Sharply turning a corner, he bumped full into a man coming the other way. The unfortunate let out a groan and slumped back against the wall. He was a short, elderly man, a lined, sun darkened face framed by close cropped grey hair and a dark, curly beard. He wore a plain cloak and carried a long walking staff and looked angrily up at the youth, eyes flashing in the torchlight.

"Watch where you are going, you clumsy oaf!"

The youth raised his hands in apology, he had been taught always to honour his elders.

"Apologies, here, let me help you up." He reached forward and assisted the man upright, dusting him down. "There, I hope you are all right now, old man?"

The youth made to walk off, but the old man's walking staff barred the way across his chest.

"Just a second, young man," the bearded face tilted up at the youth. "I believe you have my purse in your hand?"

A flicker of emotion betrayed the conflict in the youth's mind. He sighed and put out his hand, the purse in his upturned palm. The old man took it back.

"Thank you. If you are going to dip purses, boy, you need more skill than that. Oh, and also, take more care choosing your targets, best not to try robbing a thief!"

"You? A thief?" The youth laughed and slapped his thigh. "A sad old man who can't walk without a stick?"

Suddenly, the youth was on the ground looking up. His legs had been taken from under him with a single sweep of the staff.

"Apologies, here, let me help you up." The old man offered a hand. The youth snarled and sprang up unaided, right hand moving to the broadsword hilt. The staff caught him sharply on the back of the hand, then again on the forehead. The youth found himself sat in the dust once more.

"Didn't you hear me, boy? Choose your targets! By Zantus, you are a dumb one, aren't you?" The old man smiled then began laughing. To his surprise the youth found himself laughing too, all anger gone in the shock of his defeat.

"From your accent and appearance I'd say you are not from round here? You obviously don't know who I am. Why did you try and rob me, in any case?"

"Money for food, old man. I've not eaten in days and

I just lost all my coin at the dice table."

"Fleeced by Sullo were you? Let me guess, you objected and met the rest of his gang?"

"Knocked one down, made another squeal, didn't hang around to chat to the rest."

The old man raised his eyebrows in appreciation. "Good for you, lad." He cast an experienced eye over the youth and made a decision.

"I tell you what, come with me, let's get you fed. After that, we will talk! My name is Stanler, by the way."

"And I am Llorc."

"Lurk? What sort of name is that?"

"No, Llorc. Llorc!"

"Ah, I've got it now. Alright Lurk, follow me."

Llorc sat back and gave a belch of appreciation. His belly was full, he had a mug of beer in his fist and he was sat in the enclosed courtyard of a slightly run down tavern called The Bearpit, situated on the edge of the square he had previously explored. Stanler seemed well known in the inn, many greeting him with a nod and moving aside for the pair as they moved through the crowded main room to take an outside table at the rear of the building. The clientele were a villainous looking bunch, shifty eyed, taciturn, many of them scarred or displaying the cropped ears or missing fingers that Llorc learnt was the punishment here for thieving.

Street urchins occasionally darted in and out, acting as messengers and runners for some of the rogues. Coarse voices and ribald jest mingled with smoke from the cooking spits that, combined with the reek of garlic, ale and unwashed bodies, formed the tavern's heady atmosphere. In the corner of the courtyard birds cooed from a dovecote, a distant snatch of drunken song floated in on the warm night air

By the time the pair reached a table, two large jacks of foaming ale had been set down for them by the landlady, Megaera. Stanler explained that the tavern could be a dangerous place for the unknown or unwary but was run with an iron hand by Megaera and her son Hespero. Meg, as she was known, was the widow of a former local enforcer, a man feared and respected in the neighbourhood. Dark curly hair tied back from her round, open face, buxom and broad shouldered, Meg was not above stepping into the heart of a fray in order to sort out the miscreants and had been known to reduce even the toughest of villains to tears. Her foghorn voice would cut above the tavern din if anyone got too boisterous. Hespero was a quiet, studious looking young man who seemed content to help serve around the place.

Stanler watched as the youth downed the beer and wiped his arm across his mouth.

"Better?" he asked.

"Much. My thanks, old man. I have no coin to repay you, though."

"Don't worry about that, there are other ways you can settle your debt."

A sudden look of apprehension crossed the youth's face and his shoulders tensed. The old man hooted with laughter and slapped the table.

" Your face! Don't worry, I'll leave that sort of thing to the priests. No, Lurk, I'm talking about work! Well, a kind of work anyway. You are a stranger here so will not have heard of me but I run this neighbourhood. Nothing happens here without my say so."

"You run it? What do you mean? You are some sort of chieftain?"

"You could say that, lad. See, this is how it works. There's the City Authorities, round here that's the Militia. Above them are the magistrates. Over the river in the Old City, there's the City Guard. Above them are the judges and senators but they have nothing to do with the likes of us. The Militia tend not to bother us too much, we are left to run our own affairs. That means keeping order over this rabble." Stanler grinned and swept a hand around.

"And your people here, what do they do?"

"Thieves, blackmailers, beggars, for the most part. Some run gambling and vice dens, some are involved in smuggling and contraband. Duty is high on goods going into the North Docks, our rates are a little more flexible"

"And the authorities allow this?"

"They tolerate us, as long as we don't overreach ourselves. A bribe here, a payment there, it all helps grease the wheels. They would rather these things were controlled than have this lot running loose round Adelphis. Besides, the high and mighty sometimes call on our services."

"They do? But why would a rich man need a thief?"

Stanler laughed. "You are new here, aren't you Lurk! There are many things they may wish stolen. Legal documents, incriminating letters, family treasures, all manner of things. Beside which, the rich have unusual tastes, they seek fine drink, exotic drugs and other, more fleshly pleasures."

"You sell all these things?" Llorc's eyes grew wide.

"Not me, lad," Stanler shook his head. "Well, some of these things. You see, there are different gangs in different parts of the city. We here in the Ratteries are the lowest of the low, though when it comes to thieving and burglary none can touch us. Other gangs run drugs, some run prostitution or gambling. Some organise assassinations."

"Who agrees all this?" Llorc was fascinated by this aspect of civilisation, totally unlike his simple clan culture.

"It's just the way things have developed. The gangs meet occasionally to settle any disputes. However, like anywhere, it's the strong that prevail at the end of the day. It's easier to seek forgiveness than permission! Which is where you come in, Lurk."

"What would you have me do, old man?"

"Well, most of our non-thieving activities revolve around shifting contraband and protecting local businesses. Other gangs sometimes try and muscle in, so a strong arm and a keen eye are useful, added to which you are an outlander. You have no local ties or loyalties, I can trust you... I hope?"

Llorc nodded, looking grave. "My word is my bond."

"Yes, I had heard that about you Northern types. So, most of your work will be local protection but there may be thieving too. I'm not talking about picking pockets or the like for one such as you, I mean those special jobs I mentioned earlier. They are often on another gang's patch and they are not always happy to see us. You are a big lad and, despite me putting you on your arse earlier, I imagine you are useful with that sword, no?"

Llorc was on more familiar territory now. "I was taught by some of the best warriors in my clan. I went on my first raid at twelve and was blooded at thirteen. But I am no thief, my people are hunters and warriors! Ours is the Wolf Clan, we do not skulk in shadows, we confront our enemies in open battle, face to face!"

Stanler sighed. "Listen, Lurk, that may be the way you settle things in the North but it's different here. No one will stab you from the front, they will always attack from the back. They will work in numbers, like a pack of rats. People will lie to you, cheat you blind and, if you are a poor outlander, the law will always side with them, not you. This is the way of civilisation."

Llorc reflected on recent events. "Then civilisation stinks, in more ways than one!"

"That's as maybe. Tell me though, what is a hunter but a thief of life? And answer me this lad, how rich would you get fighting dimwits such as yourself in frozen fields? What does the winner get? A few mange-ridden sheep? A handful of copper coin?"

Stanler took another swig from his mug. "Listen, Lurk, play it clever here and you could make a fortune! Imagine returning home like a King, you could buy your village ten times over with what you can make here!"

Llorc pondered for a moment. "It's true enough. I journeyed south because of my Grandfather's tales of his wanderings and the lack of anything at home. All there is to do is fight, drink, marry a cousin, fight and drink some more."

The youth smiled at a memory. "The most exciting thing was when the Njordir raided our borders! Aye, we had some good battles there! But once we had defeated them we settled back to fighting amongst ourselves, in the time honoured tradition of our Clans."

Pausing for a moment Llorc nodded and banged the table with his fist. " Alright, it's settled. I will work for you and you will teach me the ways of civilisation!"

Stanler extended a hand and the two grasped forearms and shook. Stanler grinned in approval and roared. "Excellent! Now, more beer!".

CHAPTER 3

Llorc awoke next morning with a sore head. He lay on a straw pallet covered with a thin blanket and struggled to remember where he was. Sitting up quickly to look around brought a sharp stab of pain. He groaned and brought a hand up to cover his eyes.

"Bad head?" A cheerful face topped with brown curly hair popped around the curtain hanging in the doorway of the small room. "Come get some food, that will help!"

With a chuckle the face disappeared. Llorc stood unsteadily, splashed his face with cold water from a bowl in the corner and stepped through the curtain. He found himself in a long open room with various doorways leading off of it. The floorboards were partly covered in straw and the room was dominated by a long wooden table lined with benches. A group of people, many of them children, sat at the table eating from wooden platters. At one end a suspended pot bubbled and steamed in a large open fireplace, stirred by the owner of the ruddy, cheerful face. The youth appeared to be about Llorc's age but was more rotund and much shorter. He ladled some stew from the pot onto a wooden platter and brought it over to the table, moving with a pronounced limp. Llorc noticed how one leg was dragged slightly behind. The lad placed the platter on the table and smiled again.

"I'm Trant. Stanler said you'd be joining us. Sit, sit, have some food!"

Llorc sat and began wolfing down the hot stew

"Ah, the leg," Trant responded to Llorc's obvious stare. "Trampled under a horse when I was a kid. Never was fixed right!"

Llorc nodded and looked around as he ate. Some of the group stared at him, others ignored him as they ate their own food, two argued noisily. He reckoned their ages ranged from eight to fourteen, with a couple of older lads there too. They were a mix of hair and skin colour, representing half races of the world.

The main door to the room was suddenly flung open and a young man entered, carrying a bulky sack over his cloaked shoulder. Lank, straw coloured hair framed a pinched, pale face. The mouth seemed fixed in a down turned sneer and a pair of brown eyes regarded Llorc with contempt.

"Trant!" the man shouted, holding out the sack. "Take this loot will you and put it in with yesterday's. I'll sort it later. And I know exactly how much is in there!"

Trant took the sack and hobbled away. The newcomer wiped his nose with his sleeve and stood near

Llorc, drawing aside his cloak and puffing out his chest.

"So you're the new boy, are you?"

Llorc continued eating and mumbled with a full mouth. "I reckon so."

"Well, I'm Draccus. I'm second in charge round here. So just do what your told and watch your step, right?"

Llorc shrugged and tore a hunk of bread to dip in his stew. Draccus clipped one of the young lads around the back of the head and took his place at the table.

"On your way, you lot, you should be out working by now."

The children grumbled but one by one, got up and traipsed out of the room.

"Try The Spice Market," Draccus called as they left. "There's a new caravan just in from the South, should be rich pickings!" With that, he produced a knife from inside his cape and, staring at Llorc, began cleaning his nails with it.

The sound of raised voices and laughter drifted in from outside, then Stanler entered the room, closely followed by slightly built cloaked and cowled figure.

"Ah, Lurk, so you are up then! And I see you've met Draccus and the others!" Stanler walked over to clap Llorc on the shoulder.

"This is most of our merry company. There's a few out collecting already, you'll meet them later. And this is Galenna."

The hooded figure pulled back its cowl to reveal spiky blonde hair and an intense emerald eyed stare from what Llorc thought was a very attractive face. The girl looked to be not much older than himself.

"Galenna is my niece and my right hand. Draccus is my left hand. Along with all the other rascals we are one big, happy family Isn't that right?"

Draccus shrugged and speared the loaf on the table with his dagger. Galenna swept her cloak back, revealing a curvy figure, though the short sword and dagger at her belt did not go unnoticed by Llorc either. She sat at the far end of the table as Trant returned with more bread and a jug of wine. Galenna smiled at him in thanks and took to eating and drinking, casting not one glance at Llorc. Stanler took of his cloak and hung it on a peg in the corner. He then turned to Draccus.

"Draccus, I'd like you to pay a visit to The Squid. Osgar is late with his payment again, feel free to remind him why he pays."

Draccus grinned and sheathed his dagger, nodding. "I'll see to it, chief." He rose and left. Stanler sat next to Llorc, waving away the offer of a platter from Trant.

"So this is our home, sweet home. We call it The Den." Stanler gestured around. "It's an old warehouse. This was once a busy district, all the shipping trade came through these docks. They were good times for us, the gangs ran most of the docks and markets. But a few years back they built a new dockyard and commercial district over on the north bank. All the trade has moved there now, it's all within reach of the City Guard, we can't get a look in."

The older man reached into his tunic and took out a small flask. Raising it his lips, he took a pull and sighed with appreciation. Then he turned back to Llorc and continued.

"This whole area has been left to rot and fester, that's why they call it the Ratteries. Still, it serves our purpose, the place is like a maze. No one can get close without being seen and, in any case, the plodders rarely venture this far in."

"You all live here? Who are all the children?"

"The little ones all live here, this is a large building. They are waifs and strays, orphans for the most part, or abandoned. I give them a place to stay, some security, a hot meal. In return they act as eyes and ears for me, run errands and carry out a few jobs. I fence anything they dip, as long as they don't work too local. Trant is our cook and housekeeper. The older gang members take care of heavy work or special jobs, they all live close by."

Stanler rose and clapped Llorc on the shoulder.

"Anyway, when you've finished your meal meet me outside. I'll show you around and take you through our routine. Time to earn your keep, young man!"

For the rest of the day Llorc accompanied Stanler as he visited various inns and other businesses in the local neighbourhoods. At each, a small pouch would subtly change hands while pleasantries were exchanged.

"They pay you?" Llorc asked after one of the visits.

"Yes, they pay for a service. I see to it there's no trouble in their taverns or at their stalls. In return, they pay a weekly amount. It's not a lot but it adds up over all the places we protect. That's the secret you see, keep the amount reasonable then they don't object to paying."

"And what if they don't pay? Or what if there is trouble?"

"That's when you get to work, Lurk." Stanler grinned. "You are there to either start trouble or to stop it. Understand?"

Llorc nodded. He understood, though shook his head again at this difference between city folk and his own people.

"I know, I know," Stanler chuckled. "Back home everyone protects each other, I'm sure. Well, community is an admirable thing, but there's precious little of it round here. And believe me, if I didn't do this, someone far worse would!"

They began walking again. Ahead, a middle-aged bearded man stood atop a box. Dressed in a plain brown robe, he was making an animated speech to a small crowd. Clustered around him were half a dozen others in similar garb, palms pressed together as if in prayer.

"Who are they?" Llorc gestured towards the group.

"That's Guryon and his flock, followers of The Prophet. It's a new religion, come up from the south. They call themselves Sharers or *Lachalokim* in their own tongue. They preach equality of all, rich and poor alike, that all wealth should be shared." The pair strolled past the group and Guryon and Stanler exchanged nods.

"They worship one god as opposed to our several and claim this god once took human form in order to guide and give example to us." Stanler explained.

"Why would any god relinquish their power and take frail human form?" Llorc shook his head, bemused. "What else do they preach?"

"Chastity, temperance and forgiveness of enemies."

Llorc roared with laughter and clapped his thighs. "Why

only a fool would follow those teachings!"

"My late wife did." Stanler cast his eyes downward. Llorc was flustered, his face reddened.

"My apologies, old man, I meant nothing by it. I'm sure she was a most wise and kind person."

Stanler looked up, his eyes sad, but his lips smiling.

"Lurk, it seems your skill with words matches that of your swordplay. Gratitude, lad, yes she was both of those things, and more besides. For her sake I allow Guryon use of a building in the Ratteries for his ministering. I see his flock is growing."

"No surprise, if they teach sharing of wealth. I've never seen such riches and poverty so close together as within these walls. My own people would not see a clan member destitute."

"Do your own gods preach such things then? Do your people even have gods? "

"Aye, we have them. Dubh, the God of War, Nuada the Huntress, Greum Judge of the Dead. And above them all Morrg, Father of our people. Old and grim as the mountains he is, and little concerned with the ways of his children. We do not pray to our gods, as you civilised folk do, though. We seek to please them with our actions, in battle or in the hunt, in raising our children well and in maintaining the strength of the clan. We have no priests as you do here, though each clan has a *Druacht*, a wise woman or wise man to advise the Elders, or to wed couples."

"Much simpler than our city gods then. For Father Zantus is forever meddling in the affairs of mortals, they say. Often in rivalry with his wife Ophara, or in some scheme with Karnos, our god of war. There are gods for everything here, Uldona the Sea goddess, Ilios the Messenger, Kyros for love, Bel for thieves, Dinos for wine. There are city gods, household gods and revered ancestors worshipped as gods too. Perhaps that is why the priesthood here is so large and the rites and rituals so complex. None may approach the gods directly they say and, it seems, money and sacrifice ease the path of communication!"

Llorc grunted. "If a god can be bought for coin, it can't be much of a god! I'll rely on the strength of my arm and my wits, if it's all the same."

Stanler smiled, then paused to cough. He motioned to the tavern ahead. "Here endeth the lesson for today." He made an elaborate bow. "Enough talk, my throat is dry. Come, let's take a drink."

CHAPTER 4

Over the next couple of weeks, Llorc got to know the circuit and was eventually sent out on his own for collections. He encountered no real problems, most vendors appeared happy to pay and Stanler was respected, if not entirely liked. In any case, a glimpse of those cold, grey eyes and a hand moved to sword hilt was enough to overcome any reluctance. During that time Llorc saw little of Draccus, which was no hardship, and even less of Galenna, which he hoped to change.

He got a chance to talk to her one night in The Bearpit. Stanler had called Llorc in for a meeting and Galenna was with him. By fortune, Stanler was summoned away on some errand and saying he would be back soon, he left the two young people alone. Llorc coughed and swirled his beer in his mug. Galenna looked bored.

"So... you are Stanler's niece then?" He ventured.

"Not really. But he knew my parents. When they

were... gone, Stanler took me in. I had no other family in the city."

"Very kind of him. And did he... does he ...?"

Galenna glared at him and spat angrily. "No, he's not like that! His wife died a few years back, he's never had eyes for another woman. He's a good man!"

Llorc beat a hasty retreat. "Apologies, I never meant to offend. It's just that in my tribe it's unusual for a woman to be unmarried, especially such a beautiful one."

With a roll of her eyes Galenna groaned, "Oh, please, save it for the tavern wenches. So your tribe, they live in huts, grow turnips and herd sheep, right?"

Now it was Llorc's turn to bristle. A cold gleam entered his eyes. "My people are Clannacht! We are warriors! Ours is the Wolf Clan, the tribe called on to defend our lands. Boys and girls are trained from childhood to fight and when battle calls, all stand in the line!"

Galenna seemed unimpressed. "Let me guess. You were born on a battlefield, your coming was foretold by the sages and your father was King of the Barbarians."

"I was born in a hut. My father was a bard."

"A bard? What the hell is a bard?"

"A teller of tales. One who holds all the clan stories and sagas to pass on to the next generation. He knows all the songs of old heroes, of great wars and battles."

"A singer, then?" Galenna laughed. It was the first time Llorc had seen her smile. His scowl softened and he laughed too.

"Yes, a singer, a skald, but still a warrior! In battle he would lead the warrior chant."

"So do you sing then, mighty warrior?"

"Me? No, I did not inherit my father's skills. My cousin was trained to take on my father's mantle. I was trained by my mother's father, now there was mighty warrior! He wandered far and wide as a mercenary before returning back to the Clan. It was he who told me tales of Adelphis and taught me the trading tongue. He was here in the city once, many moons ago."

"And now here you are. Made your fortune yet?"

Llorc stretched his powerful arms out and shrugged. "Not yet. Early days. I hope to learn."

"Well Stanler is a good teacher, you can learn a lot from the old man."

"Before then, perhaps we could-"

"Oh, so you two are talking now, are you?" Stanler had returned. "Come on Lurk, no time for chat, I have a job for you."

The job turned out to be a rival gang causing trouble at a nearby inn. The appearance of Llorc and a couple of Stanler's other heavies soon solved the problem. On the way back, Llorc broached the subject of other, more lucrative work, the thievery that Stanler had mentioned before. The old man nodded. "Soon," he said, "soon."

It was a few nights later that Stanler called Llorc to his chamber in the Den. The old man was seated behind a well-worn and marked desk, sorting silver coins into three piles. He smiled as Llorc entered. Draccus and Galenna were already there, sat at a small table in the corner of the room. Llorc joined them, still chewing on a beef bone.

"I've an important job for the three of you. Word has come in that a caravan arrived from the East a few weeks back, carrying an expensive gift for some Senator. My source tells me this gift is currently being kept in a town house in the Old City. It's a straightforward in and out, first floor. No guards, as far as we know, apart from any local plods, of course. Any questions?"

Llorc spoke first. "What's a Senator?"

Galenna rolled her eyes, but it was Draccus who replied. "A Senator, barbarian, is a member of our governing chamber. You see, there is the King, Thelios the Second. He rules over all and has command of the army and navy. The Senate is a group of politicians elected by the great and the good to advise the King and to serve as intermediaries between the King and his people. The third body is the Priesthood, who serve as intermediaries between the King and the Gods. Got it?"

Llorc hadn't really but nodded anyway. It all sounded confusing and unnecessary to his mind, back home things were decided by simple show of hands or use of force.

Stanler unrolled a parchment. "Here's a map of the place. We don't know exactly what this valuable gift is but we do know it is held in this room here." He indicated the rough drawn map. "Little Vasil will take you up to the Old City in the cart. Galenna, you'll be going in, I want you to take Lurk with you. Draccus, you're on watch."

"Him?" Galenna protested. "What does he know about

thieving? He's just a lump with a sword!"

"Girl, I was hunting and climbing while you were still crawling on the floor. Have I not proved my skills these last weeks?" Llorc retorted. Then he turned to Stanler.

"Did you not say yourself that a hunter is a good thief?"

"I did, lad." The older man replied. "And that is why I am giving you this opportunity, so don't let me down!"

Galenna snorted and folded her arms but Stanler was unmoved. "It's settled then." Stanler rolled up the scroll. "You go tomorrow night, I'll put the arrangements in place."

The next night the trio assembled again in Stanler's room. Draccus and Galenna both wore light leather jerkins and were armed with daggers. Galenna had two empty sacks hanging from her belt. Llorc strode confidently into the room, broadsword strapped to his hip.

"What in Bel's name have you got that for?" exclaimed Galenna, pointing to the sword.

"It's my sword," shrugged Llorc, "As it's an important job I'll take it with me in case there's a fight."

"We are going thieving not fighting, barbarian." Draccus said. "Get rid of it, just bring a dagger!"

Llorc sighed but complied with the request. Stanler unrolled the plan once more and made suggestions as to approach and escape route. Wishing them a final good luck, he saw the trio on their way.

One of the young urchins, Vasil, was outside waiting for them with a pony and covered cart. The trio clambered aboard and the boy nudged the pony on with a soft click. They crossed Pergares Bridge and, sticking to quiet back streets, were soon close by the inner wall and gateway to the Old City. The three slid out of the cart and crouched in the shadow of a nearby building, Vasil leading the pony off to wait in a nearby alleyway.

From their vantage point, they could see that the large iron-studded wooden gates were closed, just a small single doorway set within one gate was open. Torches set in sconces around the arch reflected off the armour of the guard on duty.

"Shall I creep up and kill him?" offered Llorc.

"By the Gods," muttered Draccus, "No, you dumb ox, kill a City Guard and we shall have the whole force down on us! We sneak in, follow me and keep your silence!"

Draccus led them to a shaded area of the high, white wall and moved along it, away from the gateway. They soon came to a secluded garden, bordered with short olive trees that grew in the shadow of the wall. The wall itself was covered in vines, Llorc gripped one and made as if to climb up.

"What are you doing?" hissed Galenna.

"I thought we were to climb?" Llorc replied. "It would be easy enough with these vines."

Galenna shook her head in disbelief. Draccus let out a low, three toned whistle, at which a rope ladder dropped down from the top of the wall towards them.

"See, barbarian, a ladder! Easier still to climb," he sneered.

Llorc's face flushed angrily in the dark. He decided from now on to keep his mouth shut and proffer no more suggestions. The trio climbed one by one up the ladder to the battlements above. Llorc climbed last. As he reached the top, he saw Draccus slipping coins to an indistinct figure who pulled up the ladder and promptly disappeared into the night.

"Who -" Llorc began, already forgetting his earlier decision.

"A night watchman." Draccus whispered. "We pay him and he sees us in and out."

"By Morrg," Llorc muttered. "Is there no one or nothing in this place that can't be bought?"

"Everyone has a price, barbarian, remember that!" Draccus responded, then he turned away to guide them down the steps and into the Old City streets.

At that time of night the wide streets were deserted, though they kept to the shadows in any case. Once, they heard the approach of a guard patrol but the soldiers passed by along another street. Soon they reached their target. Set back a little in a quiet side street, a two story town house, surrounded by a wall just over the height of a man. There was an iron gateway across the front entrance, behind which a fountain tinkled softly in the dim moonlight. Galenna led them around the perimeter wall to a narrow alleyway at the rear of the property, overlooked only by the shuttered windows of the neighbouring house. Moving silently and with care, the three by turns lifted and hoisted each other up and over the wall.

Once over they crossed a small paved courtyard and were quickly at the rear door of the house. Galenna cautiously tried the handle. It was unlocked, their inside man had done his job.

She glanced at Llorc, nodded to Draccus, then slowly pushed open the door and slid inside. Llorc followed, Draccus stayed outside on watch.

Inside was dark and the two thieves stood motionless, letting their eyes get accustomed to the gloom. A passageway led into the house, with an open arch to their immediate right. Llorc glanced quickly through it, making out a large kitchen in the pale moonlight that filtered through the window. All was quiet and still.

Galenna tapped him on the shoulder and motioned to the youth to follow. She glided along the passageway, Llorc following closely, hand on dagger hilt. They came to the stairway, exactly as it was positioned on the map, and began to ascend, pausing at any creak underfoot and listening for any movement from upstairs.

By and by, they reached the upper floor and trod softly along the length of the upper hallway leading to the room containing their prize. Passing two other doors, the pair soon reached the end room, pausing once again to listen for any sound. All remained silent, so Galenna lightly pushed the door handle. The door swung open and the pair entered slowly, Llorc closing the door softly behind him.

It was a large chamber, containing a writing desk and chair, a cabinet and a chest in a corner. Atop the writing desk was a small, finely carved chest that Galenna motioned to Llorc to pick up. He did so, it fitted easily enough under his arm and was not particularly heavy. Galenna, in the meantime, kneeled and opened the larger chest in the corner, smiling at the coins contained within. She began filling the bags she carried. Llorc moved to the door and opened it ajar, listening intently.

Satisfied that she had enough, Galenna rose and moved to the door. Llorc opened it fully and the two thieves trod softly back to the staircase. It was as they were almost there that something caught Llorc's eye. On a pedestal in a small alcove was a finely crafted statuette of a female figure, probably one of the local gods. Llorc thought it would fetch a good price in The Bearpit. He paused and turned to tell Galenna to pick it up. As he did so, the chest under his arm caught the plinth and the statue tottered, then fell to floor with a crash, breaking into three pieces.

Galenna spun towards him, eyes blazing in fury, hissing.

"What the-"

Her curse was interrupted by the sound of movement behind one of the doors. Llorc thrust the small chest into Galenna's hands and whispered "Go!"

Without waiting to see if she obeyed, he drew his dagger and turned back to face the door. It flew open and a figure emerged, sword in one hand, lit candle in the other. Llorc immediately recognised him as the foreign man he had seen riding alongside the wagon he had hidden under. With a scream the man charged at him, the heavy cleaver-like blade in his hand. There was little room in the corridor but somehow Llorc twisted aside, the sword nicking his knife arm as it descended. As the man lifted the blade to strike again, Llorc punched him in the ribs, feeling the give of bone under his heavy blow. The man staggered back with a curse but still held on to his sword.

Llorc moved to bring his dagger into play, as he did so the Easterner brought his sword up with surprising speed to block the movement. Again Llorc tried, again the man shielded himself with his sword. They were at an impasse, Llorc could not get past the blade, the man had not room to wield it properly and was injured. With a curse Llorc flung the dagger full at the man's face, then turned and sped down the stairs, hoping at least to have bought his colleagues time to escape. The man batted the missile aside with his sword and followed haltingly, grimacing and clutching at his side.

Llorc took the courtyard in three strides and with a mighty leap swung himself up and over the wall. The others were already ahead, he caught them up with a sprint. Behind, they heard a hue and cry as the alarm was raised. Fortunately the two experienced thieves knew the district well and by way of back streets and shadowed alleyways, were able to regain the top of the inner wall without further incident. Not daring to wait for the watchman and his ladder, they took Llorc's previous advice and climbed down the vine-clad wall in flurry of slips and slides and desperate clinging. With the ground firmly beneath their feet, the trio quickly found Vasil and retreated back to the safety of the Ratteries.

Stanler was waiting for them, mugs of brandy at the ready. The trio burst into his room and a furious Galenna at once began to berate Llorc.

"You idiot, you ape, you brainless bumpkin, what the hell do you think you were doing? Straight in, straight out, that was the plan! Never change the plan!"

She swallowed the fiery drink in one gulp and hurled the beaker against the wall. Dumping chest and sack onto the table she said, "I'm going to bed, we can sort out the split in the morning!"

Draccus was quietly laughing to himself. Stanler looked bemused, then pleased as the contents of the sack spilled out across his desk, a glittering pile of coin. Then he turned his attention to the small chest. After checking for any unpleasant surprises, he took a pick from a drawer and within seconds had the chest opened. Within, underneath some papers, lay a book. Bound in plain, dark leather, the book had an air of antiquity about it, a hint of mustiness as if from the tomb. Stanler flicked it open with the tip of the pick and quickly scanned a few pages.

"Don't have a clue what language that is. There are some pictures too though...ugh what in Zantus' name is that?" He quickly closed the book as if repulsed.

"Right, I'll see what I can find out about this book. It is obviously valuable to have merited its own caravan and guard. These papers may shed some light. I'll divvy up the coins tomorrow. Good work, you got what we are after but Lurk, be more careful next time!"

Llorc grunted his assent but quietly seethed, his frustration obvious. Draccus, still laughing, clapped Llorc on the back before leaving. Stanler lightly punched the youth on the shoulder.

"Don't fret lad, get some sleep, you'll get your coin tomorrow."

Llorc's mood was improved the next day when he received his cut of the haul. The coin alone had brought in a tidy sum, with the prospect of the book sale still to come. Later that evening Stanler returned to The Den and took Llorc aside.

"Well, Lurk, for a first job you didn't do too bad. Now I know you are handy with your fists and sword and you move well for a big lad but you need some extra training. So I'm sending you over to Terris Four Fingers for a few days."

"Terris Four Fingers?" asked Llorc.

"One of the best," Stanler replied. "Retired now but the best break-in man in Adelphis in his day. There's not a lock old Terris couldn't get through."

Llorc nodded his assent.

"Here's directions to his house, he is expecting you first thing tomorrow. Study well, lad, your life may depend on it one day!"

The next day saw Llorc at Terris' modest town house in a pleasant southern district of the city. A short, extremely wrinkled old man with a wide, bright grin greeted him at the door and showed him to a small room at the rear of the property. It was filled with all manner of tools, locks and similar items that the wizened man, who did indeed sport only four fingers on each hand, began to explain and demonstrate to the tall youth. Llorc proved a fast learner and in short time was picking locks with ease. Terris also advised him on ways of approaching and gaining entrance to different types of buildings and how to be alert for different types of trap or alarm.

On his return to the Den, Llorc was allowed to accompany Draccus and other gang members on simple jobs. Robbing warehouses mostly, with Llorc acting as look-out or, on one occasion, climbing up and through a first storey window to let the rest of the crew in through the main door. Llorc's natural stealth and athleticism, honed by years of hunting in the forests and mountains of his homeland, transferred well to thieving activities, forcing even Draccus to nod with approval at his abilities.

Soon he carried out the first of a run of solo thefts, the retrieval of a certain locket, a gift from an aged merchant to a young courtesan. The merchant paid well for the return of the item and word of Stanler's new protege began to spread.

CHAPTER 5

It was one warm evening in late summer that Stanler asked Llorc to walk with him to the nearby Old Docks, where the two of them hunkered down in the shadows of a deserted wharf. The evening was still and quiet, the rising moon reflecting in the river, the only sound the faint lapping of the dark water against the aged, green pier heads.

After a short while, Llorc heard the drip and muffled knock of oars. Stanler let out a narrow beam from his shuttered lantern and a light skiff pulled in to the dockside. Stanler motioned for Llorc to move forward and catch the rope that was thrown from the boat. As he did so, he made out three figures in the skiff. While Llorc tied the rope to a bollard they disembarked. By the gleam of moonlight and the single lantern beam, Llorc got an impression of earrings, gold teeth, shining white eyes and dark, bearded faces. Each man was dressed in bright, gaudy silks, wide belts held numerous daggers. Two wore large hats, all had buckled boots and carried short, thick cutlasses.

Stanler greeted them with a grin and playful punches to the chest. "Kagas, you old bastard. Makhali, Daahir, you sea dogs, good to see you again. This is Llorc, my new bodyguard."

The three men exchanged nods with Llorc then, heaving a chest out from the small boat, carried it into the shadows along the wharf.

"It's all here," the man called Kagas opened the chest to reveal it tightly packed with wine flasks. "Two score bottles of the finest Narva brandy. A nice little bonus we found on a recent merchant ship."

"Beautiful," smiled Stanler and handed over a heavy coin bag. "And here's what I got for your last haul, plus some extra for the brandy."

Kagas took the bag and lobbed it to Makhali, who caught it and immediately tucked it away inside his brocade jacket.

"Any problems on the way in?" asked Stanler.

"None." Kagas replied. "'Tis easy enough to slip past the naval patrols, they stick to the same old routes. The Cygnus is anchored aways off the coast, with this moon the lads'll see any patrol coming from a mile off. In any case, we'll be beaching up along the coast for careening come autumn. There's a secluded little cove I know of and with a few bribes here and there we'll be safe enough for a time. How's business here?"

"Fine enough," Stanler shrugged. "But times are changing. I can feel it in my bones. There's unrest in the air, too many eyes are turning our way, it will lead to no good I fear. Still, for now the pickings are good."

"So, lad," Kagas turned to Llorc. "This old dog no doubt has you duffing up innkeepers and robbing fat old merchants. If you ever feel like some real man's work let me know and we'll take you to sea."

Llorc grinned uncertainly. Although he had seen the sea he had never been on board a ship and the prospect filled him with some foreboding.

"My thanks," he replied "but I prefer the feel of solid earth under my feet when I swing my sword."

The pirates laughed, Kagas clapped the youth on the shoulder. The ebony skinned Daahir spoke "Cap'n, the tide, it will be on the turn soon."

"Right you are, lad." The men strode back to the skiff and they pushed off back into the river. As they faded into the gloom the last sight was Kagas' white grin as he raised one of the flasks he had quietly lifted from the chest to toast them.

"Here's to the breezes that blows skirts above kneezes!"

Seconds later the boat had vanished and Stanler motioned to Llorc to help him with the chest.

"Who were they?" the youth asked as they carried the chest back to the Den.

"Freebooters, lad. They ply the trade routes to the south. We keep in touch through carrier pigeon. I occasionally fence goods for Kagas. Him and me grew up together, we ran around these wharves as kids. Most of us in the Ratteries are descendants of sailors, pirates, and the assorted driftwood of a dozen nations. That's why we live here in the slums and not up in the Old City. Never be fooled lad, the people here will trade with you, they will take your coin, they will tup your sister, but they will never accept you as one of them. Kagas saw that years ago, he preferred a life at sea to these stinking alleyways. Perhaps he made the right choice, the air here is foul."

With that Stanler fell in to a contemplative silence. Llorc merely nodded and tried to put to the back of his mind the thought of rolling waves and mysterious, green depths.

As he began to earn more coin, Llorc bought finer clothes, including a vivid red cloak, a fine white shirt and a bright green silk sash, though he kept the the wolf's teeth necklace and simple worn scabbard that housed his broadsword. He got a name for generosity, buying drinks wherever he went and enjoying being the centre of attention. Women began to gather round him, though he always had an eye for Galenna, as she sat drinking alone in a corner. What he didn't notice were the eyes watching him.

He was well in his cups one night when a ragged urchin tugged at his sleeve.

"What's that? You want some coin, little one?"

"No, I have a message. Stanler says to meet him now at the old warehouse, south end of Pergares Bridge."

The boy turned and hurried off. Llorc belched and rose, somewhat unsteady on his feet. Fastening his belt he strode out into the night. The cool air cleared Llorc's head a little and he wondered why Stanler should call him out at this late hour, some contraband to shift perhaps? Making his way through the quiet streets and squares of the Old Market, he was soon at the south end of the bridge, where the squat outline of the old warehouse loomed over the street. As he approached the large wooden entrance, a small inset door swung inward with a low creak, revealing nothing but darkness within.

Llorc paused and sniffed the air. Something wasn't right. Nevertheless, he strode purposefully through the door and into the dark. There was little to be seen in the gloom, he could just make out the bulk of large crates in the shadows. Suspicion grew in his gut and he grasped the hilt of his broadsword, when suddenly the door slammed behind him and two torches flared into life. Momentarily dazzled, Llorc lifted a hand to shield his eyes. A figure stood silhouetted in front of him.

"Well now, take a squint at this fine dandy! It seems our young man found Lady Fortune after all." It was the dice-man, Sullo, and he was not alone. A huge figure loomed over his shoulder. Another two moved into view from behind the crates, Llorc sensed another behind him.

"Did you forget, friend, you still owe me gold sovereigns? Fifteen, wasn't it? Though there is interest to add, not to mention compensation. You broke Firka's wrist, you knocked out two of Beorthe's teeth and you drove away my customers! So, let's call it fifty sovs shall we? Oh and a mild beating! Seems only fair!" Crooked teeth shone in the torchlight.

Llorc's head cleared instantly. His natural instincts came to the fore, now he was in his element. No skulking, no intimidating fat innkeepers, this was battle! He laughed, eyes glittering in the orange light.

"I'll keep my gold, but you are welcome to my steel!"

Even as the thugs advanced, Llorc had drawn his sword in a whistling cut that sent the nearest man back, blade flashing inches from his eyes. Llorc moved into the space, continuing the swing from high to low. His blade cut deep into the calf of the second man, who let out a howl and fell, clutching his leg. Sullo hurried back, pushing the giant in front of him. Beorthe hefted a huge mace in his ham-sized fists and gave gap-toothed grin.

"So boy! You won't catch me by surprise thi-"

Llorc made a sudden lunge. With lightning speed he extended his lead arm in a wave-like motion from the hip. He judged the distance perfectly, the tip of the broadsword biting into Beorthe's left shoulder. Grunting in pain, the giant took a step back.

Instinct caused Llorc to duck and roll. The third man, the one with the eye-patch, hit only air with his swing. Coming up out of the roll, Llorc neatly kicked the crouching rogue with the leg wound in the face. One down. He then wheeled instantly, his back pressed to one of the large crates. The three attackers formed a semi-circle and closed in, Sullo lurking behind them, the torch he held aloft casting distorted shadows across the old stonework.

The man called Firka moved first. What he lacked in skill, he made up for in anger. Lifting a large cleaver to head height, he charged in screaming, and hacked down. Llorc twisted, deflecting the blow with his sword. His other hand instantly grasped the man's still-bandaged wrist and twisted sharply.

"You must like this," he hissed, as Firka screamed and fell back, face white with shock and pain. Llorc followed up with backhand slice that cut deep into the man's side. Bone crunched under the impact and Firka fell like a hewn tree.

Llorc immediately sprang back as One-eye's sword whistled past his face. The manoeuvre put him in the path of Beorthe's mace, and Llorc could only twist aside slightly, turning a solid hit into a glancing blow on his upper arm. Glancing, perhaps, but his entire arm was numbed by the impact.

The pain roused him to fury. A song of his father's came to him and he began a low chant that echoed eerily around the cavernous room. One-eye was upon him again and Llorc blocked one strike, two, then three. He saw his opening with the instinct of a hawk catching a hare. A small gap, a second's opportunity and his heavy sword thrust forward and up, catching One-eye in the lower belly. The upward thrust opened the man's jerkin, skin and muscles, his innards bulging obscenely from the wound. In fear and desperation, One-eye dropped his weapon and grabbed Llorc's sword arm with both hands . His one good eye stared hatefully into Llorc's as blood poured from his mouth and his life ebbed away.

Failing to wrench his arm free, and mindful of the giant behind him, Llorc instead went with the man's pull and used it to suddenly pivot, placing One-eye between himself and

Beorthe. His timing was immaculate, the heavy mace came down with terrible force and One-eye's skull exploded under the impact. Fragments of gore covered Llorc's face, lending him an even more terrible aspect in the torch's fiery glow.

With a shout of joy Llorc back-swiped with his now freed sword, cutting Beorthe deeply on the upper arm. The big man was strong, but the two wounds hampered his movement, blood ran freely down his tunic and he was breathing heavily. With a huge roar, Beorthe summoned a reserve of strength and lifted his mace for a killing blow. Llorc let him lift, a downward swing was more predictable, easier to dodge. As the mace fell, Llorc sidestepped, just far enough to be safe but still close enough to stay in range. He put the full power of his broad shoulders into a terrific swing and with a sickening thwack his blade bit deep into Beorthe's neck. Dark, venal blood seeped down Beorthe's torso, the giant staggered back, a confused look in his eyes. He slumped to his knees, dropping the mace, hand fumbling weakly at the gaping wound.

Llorc was about to deliver a final blow when a sharp pain brought him up short. Sullo had struck him from behind! Snarling, the youth wheeled, the movement causing blood drops to rain from his sword. With a shriek, the dice-man hurled his dagger full into Llorc's face, turned and ran. Llorc knocked the knife aside with his sword and pursued.

By the time he got to the door the man had vanished into the darkness of the surrounding streets. Llorc wiped, then sheathed his sword and set off back towards The Bearpit, his left arm still numb, a dull pain spreading in his back. He could feel wetness inside his tunic and his breath started to come in ragged bursts. In short time he was back at the Old Market square, the few passers-by recoiling from the grim, blood-stained apparition. Llorc took a moment to pause in a doorway, grasping the wall for support as the world began to spin around him. He fell forward into darkness and knew no more.

Llorc was woken by the sound of a racking cough. Glancing round he found himself in his room at the Den. Stanler was bent over in the corner, recovering from the coughing fit.

"Welcome back to the land of the living," he smiled at Llorc.

"How long have I been out?" Llorc grimaced at the sharp pain in his back.

"Overnight. One of the lads found you and we dragged you back here. Your wound has been cleaned. You were lucky, it was deep but missed your vitals. See, I told you to watch out for back stabbers!"

Llorc shrugged and winced from the movement. "Well you can't expect to fight five men and come out without a scratch. That's my new shirt ruined though." He smiled ruefully at the bloody, holed shirt hanging in the corner of the room.

"You did well, lad. We found three dead and blood stains where one had crawled away. You killed Beorthe and Ragnor, both feared men in these parts. That won't go unnoticed."

"And the rat faced one?"

"Sullo, the dice cheat? Gone to ground but we are out

looking for him. You did me a favour, lad, that little gang has long been a pain in my side. We can move into the gap you've created."

"Maybe. All I know is it was good to fight again." The youth grinned. "I was rusty, though. Back home that rat would never have got the drop on me. I need to fight more!"

Stanler laughed. "Careful what you wish for, Lurk! In any case, rest up, get your strength back!"

Llorc remained room bound for a few days. Trant came in regularly and fussed around him like a mother hen. On the third day he had another visitor. The curtain was pulled aside and Galenna strode in, caped and cowled as always.

"So, how's the mighty warrior?" she asked.

Llorc smiled. "Fine. Another day, I'll be up and about. How's things with you?"

Galenna returned the smile, running her eyes over Llorc's bare upper torso. "Oh, while you have been lazing around here, I've been busy. See, I have a gift for you."

She opened her cloak revealing a sack hanging from her belt. She removed it and threw it to Llorc. He caught the sack and grunted at the weight and feel. The bottom of the sack was dark and sticky.

"Is this...?" he ventured.

"Open it and see." Galenna gave an evil grin.

Llorc untied the sack to reveal the rictus grin and glassy eyes of Sullo. With a laugh he tossed the head aside and returned Galenna's steady, burning gaze. She moved towards him, sitting astride him on the bed.

"One gift deserves another," she whispered in his ear, running her hands over his bare chest.

Llorc grunted in agreement and took her in his arms. They kissed deeply. Ignoring the twinge in his back, Llorc turned so Galenna lay next to him on the bed. As they embraced fiercely, the dull eyes of Sullo stared blankly into the corner of the room.

CHAPTER 6

Llorc was soon back on the circuit. Word had spread of his actions and he found a new level of respect from the people he was dealing with. This made his work much easier, though he began to feel a certain lack of challenge in this new lifestyle and was conscious that his broadsword rarely, if ever, left its scabbard these days.

After making enquiries about sword masters, he one day travelled to a neighbourhood near the Old City to seek out a former soldier called Gaios, a seasoned veteran who had served in the City Guard. Gaios had retired from active duty following injury and now filled his days teaching swordplay. His students were the sons of well-to-do merchants or minor nobility, most of them reluctant. In Llorc, he found someone completely different. A student already possessed of a keen fighting brain, natural instincts and a sword style at once ferocious and overwhelming.

Overwhelming, that is, to an inexperienced fighter. When they first sparred, Gaios weathered Llorc's fierce onslaught before picking his spot and tapping the young man on the heart with the wooden practice sword. A grin split Gaios' scarred, whiskered face. Although his youth had long since passed he remained a powerful man, iron grey of hair and beard, but equally iron of arm and willpower.

"You fight well Llorc! Truth tell, I've not seen a fighting style like yours before."

"You've not fought in the North then?" Llorc returned the grin.

"Nay, lad, I never wandered up that way. My father fought there though, some years ago. The Kingdom decided to expand its borders northwards, I gather your people took offence to the notion. It was one battle my father rarely spoke about. I imagine it was quite some fight."

"Ah, my people will fight to the bitter end to hold onto their lands. Nothing unites them like an outside threat. Course, when that threat is gone, they fall back to fighting amongst themselves. That's one reason I have come to you, Gaios. I'm finding this civilised life dull. I need to maintain my edge, to learn new skills. In any case, as good as you say I am, you just tapped me with little effort."

"That's experience, my friend. You are good, but you rush in like a mad bull. If someone can withstand your first charge, they may find openings. That's how experience wins over youth!"

"My grandfather told me as much. He learned many things in his time as a mercenary. Some he showed me, but I would learn more. The spear, the use of the axe."

"The shield? Armour?"

Llorc scoffed. "My people have little use for either. They are seen as unmanly."

"If you had stood shoulder to shoulder with a hundred brothers in a shield wall, you may feel differently," the older man chided. "And some armour may have prevented you being stuck like a pig in your last fight. But enough. Let's spar again, I'll show you how to cover those openings."

Many times after training, the pair would sit in Gaios' courtyard with bread and cheese and a jug of wine. Gaios would talk of past campaigns, explaining various battles and how groups of men could be controlled and ordered. Llorc listened attentively. His own grasp of tactics comprised of little more than hurling insults then charging headlong into the fray. Fascinated, he began to gain an appreciation for the use of cunning in battle, as well as bravery and brawn. The talk also raised other questions.

"Gaios," he asked one evening as the pair reclined in the warm setting sunlight, "Why is it that the Kingdom needs such a huge army? All seems at peace here."

"What do you know of the history of Adelphis, lad?"

"Very little save it is the largest city in these lands, rivaled, I hear, only by the great city of Sahkmet in the south."

"Adelphis is indeed large and ancient, too. For many years it has been the heart of the Kingdom. What started as a three city state has spread and expanded over the generations. Armies were needed for that expansion, to conquer and control new territories and to protect the borders."

"But there is no war, the borders are safe now?"

"Mostly safe, lad, but the further out you go the less safe things become. Trade routes need to be secure, or none will use them and without trade, the city withers and dies."

Gaios paused to take a swig of wine. "You mention war, Llorc. No, there is no open war, yet there are many foreign powers casting a jealous eye toward us. You spoke of Sahkmet, well, trouble has been brewing for years with the Southerners, small border skirmishes and the like. Who knows how that may develop? There has been war between us in the past, there may be again in the future."

"This city is old, then?" Llorc asked.

"Yes, it is old, very old. No one really knows how long there has been a settlement here, thousands of years according to some scholars. The city has built up over the generations, atop the older levels, some of which are still there. They say The Rock is riddled with tunnels and caverns and down here at ground level the older parts of Adelphis were built over the Catacombs."

"What are the Catacombs?"

"Tunnels under the ground; chambers, passageways. No one knows why they were originally built, or even where they lead. The older parts of the city are built over them. The upper levels are used as tombs for the wealthy, opened only to inter the remains of departed nobility in their family crypts."

Llorc's ears pricked up at the mention of nobility and tombs. In his own culture it was the custom to bury chieftains and the like with much wealth and valued possessions about them. Might that same custom be followed here?

"And these Catacombs, they are unguarded?"

"There are but few entrances, to which the gateways remain locked but no patrols enter in. There are stories and rumours, mothers frighten unruly children with tales of the dwellers within who will snatch a bad child and whisk them off to the deeps!"

"There are monsters down there?" Llorc's nape prickled at the thought of supernatural beings.

"Perhaps. There are many myths and legends but none has delved deeply there for many years, as far as I know. In any case," Gaios smiled, "there are more monsters up here on the surface! You have far more to worry about from the so-called normal people around you rather than tomb burrowers. Especially in your line of work," he added, with a wry arch of his eyebrows.

Llorc affected an air of injured innocence. It didn't suit him. Gaios continued. "Don't think I don't know, lad, I have eyes and ears all over the city, just like your boss."

"You know Stanler?"

"I've not met him but, yes, I know of him. He's not a bad man as things go, Zantus knows, there are far worse. But a life of thieving, Llorc? For one such as you? Join the Guard, lad! I could put in a good word for you! Earn an honest day's wage!"

Llorc paused mid sip. "Me, a soldier? I'm not sure it would work, Gaios, I'm not one for standing in line or shining my boots all day. No offence!"

"None taken, lad." Gaios stood, indicating their session was over. "But think on it. I know you think everyone respects you but it's fear, not respect. They fear you. You don't see it but mark my words, fear can drive people to do strange things. And it's often those closest to you that bear the most careful watching."

In the meantime Llorc's relationship with Galenna continued, but always on her terms. He found her infuriating at times, but all frustrations were cast aside when she came to him, wordless, but intentions plain. Their love making was fierce and passionate, primal in its urgency. Sometimes she would leave after, other times she would stay until dawn broke through the shuttered window. Often she would cry out in her sleep, waking Llorc. He had no words to comfort her and would not wake her, just hold her closer. Later, he would look back at this time as one of the most content of his life.

Toutatis jumped in spite of himself as he turned from pouring a goblet of wine to find the Easterner already in the room. *By Zantus, the man could move silently.* He indicated a chair close by his ornate desk. "Please be seated, Passang."

He felt a small measure of satisfaction when the squat man flinched slightly as he bent to sit.

"I trust your ribs are recovering?"

Passang nodded curtly. "They are. Our people have healing techniques which speed the body's repair." He declined the offer of wine with a wave of his hand. "Why did you summon me, have you news?"

Passang fixed the Senator with a stern stare. Toutatis was not a large man, his dark hair and beard were immaculately trimmed, his hands soft and unmarked by labour, his manner almost foppish. But there was a cruel intensity to his green eyes that few could match and Passang soon averted his gaze.

"I believe so," Toutatis smiled thinly. "My assistant, Phileos, has been conducting extensive enquiries. He informs me that there is new information come to light. Ah, here he is now."

A heavy set balding man dressed in an expensive toga trimmed with purple silk, glided into the room. His build and pendulous jowls bespoke of the glutton. The light glittered off the bejewelled rings on his pale, pudgy fingers as he made a shallow bow towards Toutatis, ignoring Passang completely.

"Well?" Toutatis demanded. "What news?"

Phileos eyed the jug enviously and sighed.

"We have found the villain behind the theft, sir." He paused, as if for dramatic effect.

"Well, get on with it! The name, man, the name!"

"The individual in question is named Stanler, sir, he runs a gaggle of thieves in the Ratteries. It was his gang that broke into your property."

"And the book, where is it now?"

"Still with this Stanler, as far as we know, most likely at his hideout. He has been making enquiries amongst certain scholars about the grimoire, which is how the news reached our ears. Promise of coin and threat of punishment also loosened the tongue of one of his street urchins."

"Good, now we have a starting point. And how is it that the thieves knew exactly where to look?"

"Inside information, sir, from one of the kitchen servants new to the staff. I have had him placed in custody. The arrival of the Eastern caravan did not go unnoticed, it seems, though I would guess the thieves knew nothing of what they were stealing."

"Guessing is not good enough, we need to be sure, Phileos! For all we know, thrice-dammed Oresus was behind the whole thing. I swear he is behind most of my ills. If he didn't have the ear of the Queen I'd have dealt with him months ago!"

"We are keeping close watch on Oresus too, sir, but as yet have seen no indication that he has the book in his possession."

"Very well. Continue watching Oresus and listen for any further news of the book."

"And Stanler, sir?"

Toutatis, steepled his fingers in thought. "Fetch Wulforr, I have a task for him."

Phileos bowed again and withdrew. Toutatis returned to his couch and addressed Passang once more.

" So, you see, the book will soon be back in our hands, a minor setback, nothing more."

The Easterner remained impassive. "Perhaps. My Master was not pleased to hear of the book's theft. Such a rare tome merits greater care."

Toutatis felt a brief chill run down his spine. It was not advisable to incur the wrath of an Eastern sorcerer, especially one with the reputation of the Dahkosh Khalsang. He forced himself to remain stern. It did not pay to show fear.

"Quite. Though you were its guardian and failed to prevent the theft. In any case, what's done is done. The important thing is that the book is recovered in time for your Master's arrival. Such a generous gift is appreciated and I look forward to your Master revealing its secrets to me. In return we will grant him the access to the Catacombs that he desires, though why he would wish to visit some dusty old tombs, I know not."

"He speaks not to me of his plans, I am but a lowly servant. In any case, he shall be arriving soon, I shall inform him of these latest developments."

"How will you do that?" Toutatis asked. "You have no messenger or runner with you."

Passang gave a patronising smirk. "The Adepts of Lheng have their own means and methods."

With that the Easterner stood, bowed and left the room as noiselessly as he had arrived. Toutatis took another sip of wine and wondered if aiding this sorcerer really was the wisest course of action...

CHAPTER 7

With his new found confidence, Llorc began to take on more thieving jobs and also became more daring, often venturing into the well-to-do areas of Adelphis. Rather than waiting for jobs to come in, he also began to actively seek out targets for his nefarious activities. It was in the low-ceilinged back room of The Squid one night that he overheard something that roused his interest.

He had just made a collection from Osgar, who now sported a scar down one cheek, and was taking a draught of ale before heading back north to The Bearpit. Two men were hunched over a table just behind him and his keen ears picked up their furtive conversation.

The first, a slightly stooped, weary looking individual, touched the second man's sleeve.

"Is the merchandise ready?" he asked."My master is keen to take delivery as soon as possible."

"Worry not, friend," the second man replied, moving his

arm away from the grip. "All is in hand." This figure was cowled, despite the warmth, his face concealed. He continued. " Tis the finest powder too, we have the best sources. A mere few pinches will suffice for a room full of people."

"I hope so. My master hosts an event not four days hence, some of the most important people in the city will be in attendance!"

"I understand. Give me half payment now and the goods will be delivered in the usual way tomorrow."

A coin bag exchanged hands beneath the table and the first man rose and made for the door, pulling his cloak around him. Llorc drained his mug and swiftly followed the man outside. Keeping within sight of the hunched figure, Llorc waited until they were in a quiet street before quickening his pace. Drawing alongside the man, he made a sudden move and pushed his quarry into a dark alleyway. The man protested loudly, but a forearm across his throat and the glint of a dagger in the moonlight quickly silenced his dissent.

"I have no money, I am only a servant!" the man squealed.

"Fear not, fellow, I wish only to talk. Will you cease your struggles?"

The man nodded and Llorc lowered his dagger and released his grip but still remained between the man and the alleyway entrance.

"Good! Now, this merchandise I heard you talking about, what is it?"

"Lotus… lotus powder," the man stammered, his aged face pale with fear. Then, seeing Llorc's puzzled expression, he explained, "It's a drug. The fumes induce dreams and visions. It's very much in demand by those in high society."

Llorc nodded. "And your master, who is he and what is this event of which you spoke?"

"I can't say!" the servant quailed. "If my master discovered I had talked of this, he would severely punish me!"

"Your master isn't here, I am. Now talk, I am not a patient man!"

"Miletas, my master's name is Miletas. He is a patron of the arts and a leading socialite."

"And this gathering of his, you said many rich people will attend?"

"Yes, sir, his masquerades are the most exclusive affairs."

Llorc grinned at the title sir and clapped the man on the shoulder. "Good, well done, see that wasn't so hard was it? Now I want you to tell me all about your master's house and when this masquerade is taking place, leave nothing out! What is your name?"

"Dalasi, sir. I am but a poor servant, please do not hurt me."

"You are in no danger, Dalasi, for you have been honest with me. I seek only information. You have been a servant for some time for this Miletas?"

"All my adult life, sir. My parents sold me into servitude when I was but a child."

Llorc was taken aback. "Your parents sold you? Morrg, what sort of parent sells a child?"

"Be not harsh on them, sir, it was their only option. Our family was very poor you see, selling me into a servant's life gave me prospects of work and shelter. Otherwise I would be starving on the streets."

Llorc swore under his breath at the increasingly strange ways of this society. The hapless servant dared a question of his own. "You plan to rob my master?"

Llorc laughed. "A house full of rich people in a drugged stupor? It would be a crime if I didn't. But what of you Dalasi, will you tell your master of my plan?"

Dalasi spat into the dust. "What do care I if you rob the old goat? For years I have worked for him and his family, I get no thanks and little pay or care. If I do a single thing wrong, I get beaten. My life is nothing to him, rob him all you like, sir, you'll get no objections from me!"

Llorc grinned. "Good man. Now, the details, tell me when, where and how the house is guarded."

Dalasi spoke quietly and urgently and the beginnings of a plan stirred in Llorc's mind. When the servant had finished Llorc clapped him on the shoulder once more.

"You have my gratitude, Dalasi. Now, be on your way, speak to no one of this. Here's a silver coin for your trouble."

Dalasi stared goggle-eyed at the coin in his palm. "A silver coin! Why thank you, sir! I won't let you down!"

With that he ran off into the night and Llorc chuckled to himself before setting off northwards and home.

Later that week Llorc was in the Artist's Quarter, a district in the south of the city. The buildings were a mix of artisan studios and well to do town houses, with the occasional larger mansion set back in its own grounds. Taverns and eateries were also prominent, the neighbourhood lively, the people finely dressed and well spoken. Llorc stayed to the shadows and moved quietly through the streets until he found the address he was looking for. Easily climbing the stone wall, he concealed himself in the foliage surrounding the large house and settled in to wait.

Several carriages and chariots steadily arrived at the front of the mansion. The masked and costumed passengers alighted, their transport and attendant servants disappearing around the side of the building. Two large figures flanked the entrance to the house and a well-attired footman could be seen greeting the guests and announcing their entrance.

Soon the murmur of chatter and high pitched laughter carried across the gardens on the cool, night breeze. Llorc shifted and, keeping in cover, drew nearer to the house. The hired muscle was still on duty at the door. No matter, he had planned a more covert entry in any case. In a low crouch he moved swiftly across the open ground and flattened himself against the side wall of the house, peering into an open window. Inside was a darkened room, so the young thief slid noiselessly over the sill and glided to the door opposite. Opening it a crack, he saw a lantern-lit passageway and an ornate staircase leading up, from which the faint strains of music could be heard.

Llorc reached into the bag he had bought with him and pulled out a mask of the type worn in the city at carnival time. Tying his hair back, he placed the mask on his face, straightened and brushed down his tunic and stepped into the passageway. He had little hope, he knew, of passing as a guest but could, perhaps, pass as a bodyguard or some member of staff if questioned. He carried no sword but had a dagger concealed in a sleeve. The wolf tooth necklace was also tucked away, out of sight.

The hallway was empty, so Llorc took a chance. He swiftly gained the stairs and went up, two steps at a time, trusting to speed above stealth. On the upper landing he saw two archways and two doors, one of which began to swing open. Llorc darted swiftly into the nearest archway and crouched in the shadows. He was in a dimly lit room, pegs around the wall hung with all manner of cloaks and coats. A servant carrying a tray passed the opening without so much as glance in Llorc's direction, so the thief took the opportunity to being rummaging amongst the clothing. The search yielded no valuables and he crouched once more as the servant returned without the tray, going back through the door.

Steeling himself , the Northerner trod once more onto the landing and peered carefully around the second archway. The dimly lit chamber within was like nothing he had seen before. The large room was luxuriously furnished, filled with sculptures, wall tapestries and a tinkling fountain. From an curtained archway on the other side of the chamber came the gentle strains of a harp. Around the room were scattered couches and floor cushions, all occupied by reclining figures. Here and there, thick vapours arose from large censers, the air was thick with a cloying odour. Many of the revelers had eyes closed, features and limbs lax. Those whose eyes were open appeared to be staring at vistas other than their immediate surroundings. All were richly dressed and Llorc's eyes were immediately drawn to the jewellery on display.

He ducked back into the cloakroom to consider his next move. It seemed a perfect time to strike, so, with no further hesitation he returned to the archway and strode into the large room, holding his breath against the sickly-sweet fumes. Steadily and without haste, he began making his way around the chamber, carefully removing necklaces, amulets, rings and brooches. None made any move to stop him, most of them did not acknowledge his presence at all, those that did merely smiled lazily or laughed at his approach and touch.

Llorc had covered much of the chamber when his keen ears caught sound of the door on the landing opening and he hid behind a large couch as the servant returned to place another tray of food on a side table. None in the room took any notice and the servant was soon gone again. Llorc grabbed a last few items, placing them in the large pouch at his belt, then stalked back out of the room. In doing so he suddenly came face to face with the servant, now carrying a large jug.

"Who on earth are you?" the servant asked imperiously.

"Merely a bodyguard," Llorc replied. "Just checking on my master."

The man scowled, unsure, eyeing the pouch at Llorc's belt. "And your master's name is?"

Llorc made a slight shrug, then without warning, tapped the man sharply on the chin. The servant dropped as if pole axed, Llorc seizing the jug as if fell. With a satisfied grunt he dragged the servant into the cloakroom. Placing the jug on a desk, he bound and gagged the man, covering him over with cloaks in a corner. He had just moved back into the hallway, when he heard voices approaching up the stairs from the floor below. Glancing around, he took the safest route of escape, gliding swiftly up the stairs to the next floor. The landing here was more dimly lit and he crouched, still as a statue, in the gloom as the voices below moved along the lower hall.

He was about to go back down the stairs when the sound of a sob caught his attention. It was coming from behind one of the doors a little further along the hallway. Curiosity aroused, Llorc moved to the door and placed his ear against it. There was a definite sobbing from within, a young person from the sound of it. He slowly pushed the door open and peered around it. Within, lit by a single lantern, was a plain room containing a desk and several couches. On the couches sat a group of young children, there must have been a dozen of them. One or two sobbed, some sat blank faced, others stared nervously around them. Each wore manacles at the ankle.

Puzzled, Llorc slid into the room and shut the door behind him. The nearest child, a girl, gasped in fear at the sight of him, so Llorc swiftly removed the mask.

"Fear not, little one, it's just a mask. I won't harm you. What are you doing here, why are you all chained?"

The girl turned a tear-stained face up to him. "The lady said we are to be nice to the people here. She said we are to do as we are told and not to complain, or terrible things would happen to us. Panares brought us here in a wagon, he said he would beat us if we made a noise."

Understanding grew in Llorc's mind and his face grew grim at this depravity. "Nothing is going to happen to you, little one, I will get you out of here, worry not."

"But Panares will punish us!" the girl cried. "He will punish you too if he sees you, he is very cruel!"

"Let me worry about that. Now, children, can you stand?"

Most of the group nodded and, one by one they stood, some helping their companions. As they did so a voice could be heard from outside and the door suddenly swung open.

"Come now, children, time for you to begin work!"

A figure in a plain, dark tunic entered, short and powerfully built. His ruddy face twisted in a snarl.

"What's going on here, who the hell are you?"

Llorc made no attempt at deception this time but launched himself at the man, grabbing his right wrist with one hand and his throat with the other. But Panares was no mild servant to be easily subdued. With a roar he twisted, grabbing Llorc in likewise fashion and pushing forward on powerful legs. Llorc winced as his back hit the desk behind him and he found himself bent back over it, the man's grip tightening on his throat.

"Thief are you, or worse?" the man snarled in Llorc's face. "Do you have any idea who you are dealing with? Who owns these children?"

Llorc made no reply, concentrating on tightening his own

grip and trying to regain his position. But time was running out ,white lights burst at the edge of his vision and the pulse pounded in his temple. Panares gave a sudden cry as the young girl jumped up and clawed his face in cat-like fury. The squat man cursed and hit the girl, knocking her across the room. It was all the help Llorc needed. Kicking out, he pushed the heavy man back and sprang after him, right hand going to left sleeve and drawing the concealed dagger. The blade was short, but long enough to do damage. Llorc slashed the arm that was thrown up in defence then plunged the blade into the man's eye. With a strangled cry Panares fell heavily to the floor, blood running across the patterned tiles.

"Quickly, children, follow me!" Llorc beckoned.

The young girl, lip bloodied and swollen, moved first to Panares' body. She gave the lifeless form a savage kick, then bent to retrieve a key ring from his belt.

"Here." she unlocked her own manacles and passed the key along. Soon the whole group were free of their chains. Llorc, meanwhile, had opened the door a touch and was listening intently. All was quiet, the gentle harp strings could still be heard below. Holding a finger to his lips, he bade the children follow him as they moved down the passageway to the staircase.

Looking below, Llorc could see no one on the lower landing. He decided speed was of the essence and whispered to the children "When I say, run down the stairs to the ground floor, then through the first door on the right. If I am not behind you, the window is open. Climb out and escape as best you can."

The children nodded and Llorc silently signalled one, two, three, before waving the children on. Like a small flood they poured down the stairs, the scuff of their feet and panting breath the only sound of their passing. Llorc followed close on, dagger in hand. None came out from the main chamber, though he could hear some low conversation, the revelers were coming round from their stupor it seemed.

Without pause, the group were soon in the downstairs room and Llorc lifted each over the sill, telling them to run and hide in the nearby shrubberies. The last one gone, he slid himself over the sill and faded into the dark. As he reached the foliage a cry arose from the house. Looking back he saw the two doormen run into the house, then back out. More figures could be seen moving inside the house, one looking out of the window they had escaped from. Llorc cursed and gathered the children around him. Their upturned faces, pale in the moonlight, looked up at him expectantly.

"I want you to run quickly, that way, in a straight line. I want you to help each other over the wall, do you understand? I will be following but don't wait. If I am not there soon, split up and hide as best you can. If you can, get to the Ratteries, do you know where that is?"

"I do!" one small boy raised his hand. "It's where my cousin lives, we visited once!"

"Good lad! Alright, follow this lad if you can. Now flee. Be off with you!"

The children scattered into the dark and Llorc turned back

to face the house. One doorman remained at the main entrance but the other was walking directly towards Llorc's hiding place. Llorc crouched in the shadows, quieting his breathing, dagger held low, eyes averted. He didn't need to see the man, he could hear his clumsy approach and his heavy breathing, could smell him as he drew closer. The man stepped within touching distance of Llorc but didn't even know he was there. The last thing he felt was a hand across his mouth and the deep punch of a blade into his back. Llorc lowered the man soundlessly to the floor and with a last glance at the mansion, headed for the wall.

The children were still helping each other over when he arrived and he swiftly gathered them up and virtually threw them atop the wall. Following them over, he was aware of more commotion from the house and also the rattle of carriage wheels. Risking a peek back over the wall he made out a chariot heading for the main gateway, presumably someone off to fetch the guard. As he watched the chariot turned out of the gate and towards the road in which they stood. Llorc grinned, at last some luck was coming his way tonight! He bade the children hide in the shadow of the wall, then waited as the chariot approached.

It had not had time to pick up a lot of speed, so it was easy for Llorc to leap out of concealment and grab the horse's bridle, dragging it to a halt. The driver shouted and drew a short sword but Llorc turned and smoothly threw his knife at the man. The knife caught him square in the throat, the man falling out of the back of the chariot, dead before he hit the ground. Shouting to the children, Llorc quickly gathered them around him, into and hanging onto the chariot before urging the horse off into the night.

Stanler was about to retire to his bed when a commotion from below reached his ears. Holding a candle aloft he went out into the main room to see a grinning Llorc amidst a group of laughing children.

"What in Bel's name?" the old man asked.

Llorc's grin grew broader. "New recruits, chief. New recruits".

CHAPTER 8

High Priest Oresus stifled a cough as the small, private temple in the Old City filled with the heavy scent of incense. In time with the low chant of the attending devotees, he intoned the appropriate words and made the required gestures with the sacrificial blade. The tall Hierophant loomed above the small, plain altar, his heavy purple robes rustling against the stone. Oresus was completely bald, the large bushy eyebrows, curved nose and glittering black eyes giving him the aspect of some huge bird of prey, an appearance accentuated by a slight stoop and the hunch of his shoulders.

The two assistant priests stepped forward from the shadows, one carrying a large copper bowl, the other leading a bleating goat on a short rope. Oresus raised his hands and turned his face skyward, intoning the offering prayer.

"Great Father Zantus, accept this meagre sacrifice as a token of our respect. We ask you watch over us, guide us and protect us. We ask your blessings for King Thelios and his family and we ask you grant your strength to our armies in times of strife."

The priest with the bowl held it in place on the altar, while the other brought the goat into position. With a smooth, practiced movement Oresus slit the animal's throat, being sure the resulting blood flowed directly into the bowl. Not one drop was spilled onto the altar or onto his resplendent vestments. The bowl was circulated among the well-dressed congregation, who each dipped a finger in the blood and drew the sign of Zantus on their foreheads. The goat's body was meanwhile taken to the augur for examination of its innards.

Oresus stepped back, raising his hands again. Another priest removed the knife and the temple boys began the hymn that signified the end of the service. Oresus stood in apparent contemplation as the congregation slowly shuffled out of the room, chatting softly amongst themselves. As the last one left, he sighed and called for wine. His assistant, Murion, hurried forward with an ornate goblet. The priest's dark eyes glittered fiercely in the torchlight as he took a deep draught and smacked his lips with relish.

"Gods blast this incense, it leaves my throat dry as a foot soldier's sandal!"

"It is the most expensive kind, Eminence. Shall I ask for it to be changed?" Murion offered.

"No, no, Murion, we can't let the good and great think we are cutting corners. Only the best will do, the more special we make them feel, the more they leave in the collection plate.

More importantly, now is not the time to be upsetting our ruling classes, the situation balances on a knife-edge!"

"We have possession of the Toutatis papers though?"

"Not yet, though they are within our grasp. I have been assured that letter and book are being kept in a safe place. I'll not take possession or reveal them until we are certain of their authenticity. Being implicated in base burglary would do little for the Temple's standing!"

Oresus allowed his assistant to drape a cloak over his shoulders. Murion ventured a further question as he did so.

"And then we take the evidence to the King, Eminence?"

"If evidence there be, then yes indeed. But we must time our movements to the minute. Toutatis is on the hook but he is a slippery fish, if we strike too soon he will wriggle free. The Queen favours us but she has little power. Prince Leonte is still just a boy and will have no real influence for years. His father grows old and more and more set in his ways. The information contained in these papers and book may or may not tip the balance in our favour. I am away to dine now, finish here and be sure the temple boys keep their fingers out of the collection plate!"

The short, dark Murion smiled and bowed, stepping outside to summon Oresus' chariot driver to take him back to the official residence atop The Rock.

Stanler cast a sideways glance at Llorc as they strolled through Old Market. The young man was eating an apple with gusto.

"Keeping your strength up, then?" he arched his eyebrows.

Llorc grinned, "Aye, that I am."

"With good reason, I hear?"

Llorc's grin grew broader. "There are no secrets amongst thieves it seems!"

"No, boy, there aren't. It's not just me in any case, everyone has noticed. Most of them are happy for you both."

"Most but not all? Draccus for one, I'll wager. He barely speaks to me as it is, he is always whispering to his little gang when I'm around. Is he jealous perhaps?"

"Jealous of your new standing and status? Perhaps. But jealous of you and Galenna? Hardly. Draccus' tastes run in different directions. Have you not noticed how much time he spends with Hespero?"

Understanding dawned in Llorc's face. "Oh, I see! I never realised."

"You have such things in the North, I presume?"

"Aye", nodded Llorc. "There are those who prefer the company of their own kind. As long as they fight for the Clan, none judge them for it."

"Then your people are wiser than many here." Stanler stopped walking and turned to Llorc, grasping his upper arm. He looked up and spoke quietly. "Just be careful, Lurk. You are in uncharted waters now."

"Very well." Llorc shrugged and threw the apple core over shoulder. "Is that why you asked me to accompany you today?"

"No, not entirely. I'm hearing things, Lurk. I'm hearing about servants attacked and murdered in rich men's houses.

I'm hearing of wealthy art patrons robbed of priceless items, I'm hearing rumours of a crackdown on crime, this is not good!"

Llorc looked confused. "But I brought in all that jewellery, it must be worth a fortune! It was just there for the taking, chief."

Stanler nodded to a passing acquaintance then turned to face Llorc, speaking low. "First off, the jewellery is very valuable but impossible to fence. Most of it is hand-crafted, easily identified and easily traced. The lot will have to be melted down, we won't get much for that."

"I didn't think." Llorc rubbed the back of his neck.

"No you didn't, lad, you jumped in feet first! Second, I thought I explained all this, there are rules in place! We thieve and beg for sure but we keep it low key, except in the case of a few commissions. Commissions, might I add, from clients influential enough to deal with any consequences!"   Stanler paused and ran a hand over his face. "As it is the law are up in arms, they are looking to nail someone to the wall for this! The Militia are out in force sweeping the streets. I've kept all the kids back at the Den today, it won't be safe for them, they'll get picked up, beaten and questioned. The plod will be under pressure to find whoever did this, they'll take any measures necessary."

Llorc's face fell. "You are right, I thought only of the jewels. Apologies if my actions have brought us hardship. But I could not leave those children there, I had to kill that man in order to help them escape."

Stanler's face softened. "Aye, lad, well I can't blame you for that. You have a good heart for a thief, though that has brought another problem."

"You mean because we now have more mouths to feed?"

"No not that, we have food enough. In any event we have returned most of the children to their families outside the wall. Many of them had been snatched from the streets there. No, the boss of the man you killed, the one who owned those children... well, he is not a man I care to make an enemy of. He runs the oldest crime gang in the city and is not known for his forgiving nature. Our one ray of light is that none know who it was that carried out the deed. I presume no one saw you?"

"Only a servant, but I was masked and cloaked and the light was not good."

"Well, we will have to trust to fate that the trail does not lead to our door. It's not as if we have no other problems."

"You speak of the book now hidden in your secret hidey-hole?"

Stanler laughed "By Zantus, you're right Lurk, there really are no secrets amongst thieves! Yes, I speak of the book and the letter with it. It is written to Senator Toutatis and is from an Eastern sorcerer. The book is an ancient grimoire, a gift in return for some unspecified favour. I am in negotiation, through intermediaries, with certain members of the priesthood over sale of the letter and book to them."

Llorc grunted at the mention of a sorcerer. This was something out of his experience. "Why would the priests want the book?"

"There is fierce rivalry between the Priesthood and the

Senate. Each vies for the favour of the King, each seeks to have the most influence and so strengthen their own position. Toutatis leads the main Senate faction, so anything that may embarrass him is of interest to the Priests.

Llorc shook his head, political intrigue meant little to one raised on straight talk and direct action.

"So this Toutatis is another man not to be lightly Crossed?"

"That is right. Perhaps I was wrong to send you out to steal it but the money we can get for the book... well let's just say it would secure a future for many of our people. Toutatis has people out searching for his property, we have been under observation recently. Good observers, but not good enough to avoid our own eyes and ears. So be careful, Lurk, in matters of business as well as affairs of the heart".

The next morning, dressed in a smart, blue knee length tunic, hair tied neatly back and, for once, swordless, Llorc moved with confidence towards the Old City Gate. The large stone archway marked the entrance to the quarter of Adelphis populated by the older families, minor nobility and rich merchants. Sunlight glinted brightly off the polished, sculpted cuirasses of the sentries at the gate, their bright red helmet plumes nodding above the crowd. Each was armed with a spear and short sword and carried a medium sized round shield displaying the three headed eagle of the City Guard. These were no Militia who could be bought, but professional soldiers.

Llorc held a piece of fine parchment, scrolled and tied with expensive ribbon. The parchment was blank, it was merely a prop for his cover story for being in the Old City; a simple messenger boy delivering an important document. His real purpose was to gather information, to scout out the locations of the entrances to the Catacombs.

Llorc stood in line with the assorted traders, delivery boys and menials. Occasionally they had to stand aside as a chariot rumbled past, or some worthy was carried through in a palanquin . As his turn approached, Llorc took the scroll from the pouch and waved it at the guard, who simply nodded and indicated he could pass.

The streets were much wider on this side of the gate; not only wider, but cleaner. The place was busy, though Llorc noticed that the people were wearing much finer clothes, even those who were obviously servants. Everyone looked filled with purpose. There were no drunkards, lingerers or beggars here. The street curved up and away in front of him, leading to The Rock approach road. From enquiries he had made he knew that one of the entrances was on this road. Striding upwards, he soon found it, a wide double-gate of wrought iron set into the wall of The Rock itself. There was a hefty lock and chain barring the gate and beyond the bars Llorc could see little except a stone clad corridor that led off into the gloom. The lock may be got through given time, Llorc thought, but the entrance was in plain sight on a busy street. He decided to move on.

It took some time to find the second entrance, one that was

much more concealed and suited to his purpose. This was back down towards the centre of the Old City, in a burial area beside a small temple. The grounds were quiet and peaceful, most of the tomb markers new. At the rear of the area, older tombs stood around another barred gateway, this one set into the ground. On the other side of the gate stone steps led down into stygian blackness. Llorc cast a glance around, there was no one in sight. If the place was quiet at this time of day, how much more so at night? Having taken careful note of the lock and chain, Llorc returned to the busy streets and hastened back to the Ratteries.

Later that evening, dressed once more in his regular garb, which now included light leather body armour, Llorc was talking to a pair of rogues in The Bearpit when one of the street urchins ran up to him. Breathlessly, the youngster tried in vain to relay a message, red faced and pointing. It took some minutes for him to calm himself enough to blurt out. "They are attacking us!"

Llorc immediately rushed outside and sprinted towards the Ratteries. Within minutes he was working through the streets and alleyways, hearing shouts and the clash of arms ahead. Turning a corner, he found the way barred by a score of Militia set in line across the street. Locals jeered at them, some threw stones or other objects but the line held and none could pass. Llorc made a quick calculation, then span on his heel and returned the way he had come.

A short way back he jumped, grabbing the edge of a low

roof. Swinging himself up, he began picking his way across roof tops, leaping across the narrow gaps of alleyways. The dark bulk of the Den soon loomed ahead, lit with torchlight, its old walls echoing with cries and barked orders. The faces of many of the children peered from upper floor windows, some throwing stones at the intruders below. The large, heavy main door of the warehouse was surrounded by a press of Militia, two of them hacking at the door with axes. A tall, powerfully built figure in a black mail hauberk stood to the side, shouting. Flame red hair spilled from the horned helm atop his head, he sported a bristling moustache and his face was scarred and twisted. He held aloft a large axe, waving it to punctuate his barked orders.

With a snarl Llorc covered the last gap in a mighty leap then, drawing his sword, dropped from rooftop to awning to ground. Charging forward like a mad bull, he hit the group around the door like a hurricane. His first stroke bit into a Militia man's neck, the return swipe cut another deep in the back, then his thrust caught a third under the chin as the man turned to face the new threat. A gout of bright scarlet glistened in the torch glow as the man went down, choking on his own blood.

The rest of the group turned to face Llorc. Without pause he hurled himself into them. It was not as reckless a move as it seemed, in amongst the group Llorc had the advantage of a target rich environment. By contrast, his enemies got in each other's way and none could get a clear swing at him. The leather armour absorbed many cuts and slices, while Llorc's sword weaved an ever-moving web of steel; a thrust into a belly, a vicious upward cut that took off a hand at the wrist, followed by a flick across the eyes of another attacker. Within seconds he had disabled several of the men and at a command from the red headed warrior, the Milita fell back.

Llorc took advantage of the pause to shake the blood from his sword and wipe the sweat from his eyes. Another shout from Redhair and Llorc heard many footsteps approaching from behind. No matter, if he was to die, at least it would be in battle, fighting to his very last breath. A savage smile played upon his face and the blood pounded in his ears. A song of old heroes rang in his ears as he pointed his sword at Redhair and prepared for a death charge.

At that moment, the warehouse doors burst asunder and a flood of gang members, led by Galenna streamed out, wailing and stabbing as they came. Simultaneously, a large shout went up from the adjoining street as a large group of locals rushed and broke through the Militia line. The men around the door paused, not knowing which way to turn. To add insult to injury, more missiles began arcing over to land amongst the Militia; larger stones, pieces of wood, Llorc even caught glimpse of a chamber pot as it sailed through the air. Redhair barked orders, then flinched back as a crossbow bolt whistled past him from above to bury itself in the shoulder of the Militia man at his side.

"Withdraw!" he cried and the group began a retreat from the old warehouse, linking up with the group who had blocked the street. As they pushed past, Redhair glared furiously at

Llorc, who returned his stare with a sneering smile and mock bow. Some of the gang made to follow, but Stanler, striding out of the Den, called them back.

"Enough, let them run, lads. No point in further fighting, we've seen them off! In any case, the locals won't make their retreat easy"

Stanler strode up to Llorc and laughed. "Good timing lad, well met!".

Llorc grinned and wiped clean his blade. "Good timing? Bah, old man, I was just ready to finish them all off when you burst out, you spoiled my fight!"

Galenna strode up and kissed him full on the lips, eliciting another cheer from the gang. Stanler chuckled, then turned to some of the gang.

"Get extra eyes out, boys. I don't think they will be back tonight but we need to be warned if they do. Also get word to Draccus, I want him back here with his lads, quick. Trant?"

Trant limped out through the doorway, crossbow in hand. He, too, was grinning broadly.

"Yes, Chief?"

"I believe you have some barrels of rum tucked away in your stores?"

"I do, Chief. They were due to be sold to -"

"Never mind that, lad, wheel em out and break 'em open. Drinks for all!"

The gang and locals alike gave a cheer, slapping each other on the back and already swapping stories of the role they played in The Great Ratteries Siege.

"Lurk, Galenna," Stanler said quietly, " come inside, we need to talk."

The pair followed Stanler up to his quarters. Inside, he poured each a brandy and they swallowed the fiery liquid with relish. "Tonight was a close thing," Stanler said, re-filling their mugs. "We were lucky Llorc got back in time and all the locals pitched in. It's my fault. I've grown too comfortable, too complacent. Still, they underestimated us and paid the price. They won't be so careless next time."

"Who were they?" asked Galenna. "I mean most of them were Militia but the leader wasn't"

"That was Wulforr," Stanler replied. "Hired sword and general bastard-around-town."

"He's no Adelphian," noted Llorc. "Looks like a Njordir to me."

"Indeed, he is," confirmed Stanler. "It's not uncommon for rich folk to hire foreign bodyguards. Less chance of them having local ties and vested interests. Wulforr was last working for a gem merchant, from what I heard. It seems he has a new employer. Ah, Draccus, there you are."

They turned as the young man entered the room, his face pinched and mouth down turned as usual.

"Nice of you to join us," muttered Llorc, "now all the work is done."

Draccus drew a blood stained dagger and smirked. "Oh I got a couple on the way here."

"Alright, now listen." Stanler interjected sternly. "I know what this raid was about, that damned book. I'm still negotiating its sale but things are too warm here, so I'm going to move to a secret hideout and take the book with me. I want you three to accompany me there, just in case. We leave tonight." He called out the door. "Trant! Trant! I'll be away for a bit, you are in charge of clear up here. Keep everyone on alert!" Stanler turned back to the trio in the room. "I'll let it be known that me and book are no longer here, hopefully that will stop the Militia returning. Get ready, we leave before dawn."

The first rays of the autumn sun were spilling over the horizon, turning the ocean fiery orange. A skiff pulled through the gentle waves, its passengers shielding their eyes against the light. Stanler sat in the prow, Llorc and Draccus manned the oars while Galenna kept watch back towards the shore. Stanler directed them around a rocky outcrop and into a secluded cove, in which lay anchored a small boat of the type used by local fishermen. It had a furled sail and a single cabin. Once on board, Stanler stowed the gear he had brought with him and turned to the others.

"Right. I'll hide out here until the sale of the book is complete. Once it's gone I'm hoping Toutatis will lose interest in us. In the meantime, you three can run things. Take no chances, keep an eye over your shoulder and don't do anything to draw attention. Understand?"

Draccus and Galena nodded. Llorc admired the sunrise.

"Lurk! Understand?" Stanler insisted.

"Yes, I understand, Chief," Llorc mumbled.

CHAPTER 9

Wulforr ground his teeth together in ill-disguised anger as the short-arsed, prissy Senator turned on him again. Toutatis was still raging, flanked by his two giant bodyguards, Dim and Dumb as Wulforr thought of them, though he kept the thought to himself. The pair, twins, had been purchased by Toutatis after he saw them defeating all-comers in the Games. Not only were they huge, they were skilled fighters. The slight figure of Toutatis appeared almost comical between the hulking brutes but his wrath was no laughing matter.

"By Ophara's tits, Wulforr! Am I seriously to believe that a ragtag bunch of children and rancid slum dwellers saw off your force of trained men?" Toutatis hurled his goblet across the room. "You came highly recommended, Wulforr, it seems reports of your abilities have been somewhat exaggerated!"

"It wasn't like that...sir," Wulforr growled. "My men were attacked by a savage, one of those Clannacht swine. Also the street gang were well equipped with crossbows and the like.

"No burning, you fool, I need that book! But yes, very well longer would have meant no escape for any of us."

"Oh, I do apologise." Toutatis was suddenly calm and unctuous. Then he screamed, "I didn't realise you would fold when faced by a real man!"

Wulforr ground his teeth again. Nothing would give him greater pleasure than to cleave this fop from crown to teeth, twins or no. But he had been among civilized men for long enough to know how this would play out. He tried another tack. "Give me some real men to use! These Militia are fat old sacks, I've seen sheep with more fighting spirit! Give me a squad of City Guard!"

"We can't use the City Guard. Too many questions would be asked!"

"Then let me gather my own men. Men I have worked with before, professional mercenaries. They care not for questions as long as the coin is good. Then we will return and burn the scum out!"

"No burning, you fool, I need that book! But yes, very well, gather these men, Phileos will give you the required coin. In the meantime, I will try another approach. Every structure has a weak point, we just need to find that point in Stanler's gang. And when we do... we apply *pressure*."

Llorc glanced around once more, the street remained quiet and empty. The Old City gates had been shut but it had not been difficult to find the secluded garden from the previous job and climb the ivy clad wall. Carrying a sack and dressed only in high strapped sandals and a loincloth, a long dagger slung at his belt, Llorc drifted from shadow to shadow in the wide, empty streets until he reached the small temple. He glided like a ghost through the temple grounds to the barred gate. He was quite alone, the chirping of crickets the only sound. Taking the tools from his bag, began working on the lock. With a click that seemed very loud in the still night air, it gave way. Llorc slid the chain out and with a final look around, opened the gate and descended the stone steps.

He was soon in complete darkness so, crouching, he took out a flint and torch from the sack. A couple of strikes and he had the torch lit. In the amber glow he saw the steps continued down a little further, then levelled out into a corridor. The walls and floor of the corridor were stone and Llorc noticed a slight downward slope as he moved on. The corridor was wide enough for him to stretch his arms out side to side and he could just touch the ceiling if he stretched up. All was clean and dust free.

A few more paces on and he found an arched opening on his left, just before another barred gate blocked the way. He pushed the torch through the arch, the ruddy light revealing a small chamber containing nothing but a wooden bench, some tools, an oil lamp and a key hanging from a hook. Llorc took the key and moved to the barred gate. The key fit, turning easily in the lock. Pushing the gate open, Llorc passed through and pressed on into the Catacombs.

Another short flight of steps led him down into a chamber with a vaulted roof. With a start, Llorc caught sudden sight of two white faces across the room. He lifted the torch to illuminate the cold, stone faces of a pair of beautiful women, regarding him with blank eyes and serene expressions. The statues flanked an open archway that yawned darkly between them and were identical, apart from one head being slightly angled left and one angled right. Despite the human face, each had a large cat-like body, with eagle wings curled up and back, sat as though guarding the way. Something prickled at the back of Llorc's neck. Was it the faint sound of a whisper from the darkness ahead? Some draught no doubt.

He strode to the archway, thrusting the torch before him. A wider corridor stretched away, with regular, arched openings on each side. Moving into the corridor, Llorc peered into the nearest archway, finding a chamber with alcoves cut into the smooth rock walls. The alcoves were lined with jars, each with a small label around its neck. Llorc let out a disappointed sigh, there was no treasure here, merely the ashes of the dead. He decided to press on further, conscious of the fact that the torch was burning down.

A quick glance into other openings revealed nothing of interest. Most chambers contained urns, a few contained sarcophagi, whose lids, when pushed, grindingly aside exposed nothing more than dried bones. For some time Llorc wandered thus, exploring and finding nothing of value. He was about to turn back when he found another stairway leading down, short and narrow. The stonework here looked older than the rest of the tunnels. Could this lead to older, perhaps richer tombs?

Descending, Llorc moved along a short corridor, then sensed something different ahead, a cooling of the air. He came suddenly into a large cavern, the bounds of which lay beyond the circle of light. He walked left and right, lifting the torch high, discovering that the cavern was large and round. Along the wall to the right yawned another opening, similar to the one he had entered in by.

Turning back towards the centre of the cavern, he saw that the floor was bisected by a channel about twenty paces across, traversed by a single, narrow arch of stone. He moved closer, kneeling at the edge of the cut. Just below lay a still, black surface that seemed to be water, but was not flowing. Neither was it stagnant though, he had a curious impression of movement within the liquid. The impenetrable darkness drew him forward until, with a start, he realised that he was bent forward, his face inches from the surface. With a grunt he stood and shook his head to clear it.

He turned his attention instead to the bridge, moving to the near end of the span and lifting his torch. The far end lay in darkness. On impulse he drew his poniard and advanced slowly across the low arch, torch pushed forward. A shape took form in the gloom, a pale white face, much like that of the statues guarding the archway. Llorc sighed and lowered the torch, annoyed at having spooked himself with another statue. Then the face looked up and spoke. The voice was a dry whisper, the face immobile as the words floated across the air to him.

"Who disturbs the Guardian of the Deep?"

Llorc sprang back, knife whipping up in a defensive position.

"Who... what are you?" Llorc ventured.

The voice sighed a single word, the sound echoed by a soft rustling. *"Erisae!"*

Llorc raised the torch again and to his horror it revealed a pair of large wings spreading out from the shoulders of the figure. Bat-like they stretched into the darkness on each side of the thing, its body now revealed, black and leathery. The immobile face contorted into a terrible snarl as the creature raised its taloned hands and shot forward with unnatural speed. Llorc barely had time to lift his blade before the face was hissing and spitting into his own. A strike buffeted him and he was knocked back. The snarling creature allowed him no respite, raking his chest with its claws, wings lifting it off the ground to hover above the youth. Grunting a curse, Llorc stabbed out blindly with his dagger, gratified to feel the impact that travelled back along the blade. With another hiss the creature floated further up, then darted down again, claws sweeping out.

This time, Llorc was better prepared. His dagger blocked the creature's attack and he thrust the torch towards the bestial face. The leathery wings buffeted him but he held his ground and stabbed out again and again. He felt the dagger bite home and the creature let out a snarl. Sweeping the torch in a great arc before him, Llorc retreated until he was off the stone bridge. The thing dropped down onto the span and crouched glowering, its eyes fiery yellow in the gloom. Llorc noticed a cut on its breast, dripping dark ichor. The thing seemed undeterred, however, and gathered itself for another spring.

Llorc's torch was almost burnt down to the nub and he made a quick decision. He cast the flaming brand full in the thing's face and ran back into the corridor from which he entered. He was in total darkness now but, keeping one hand brushing the left hand wall, he moved swiftly forward. He heard a terrible hissing and beating of wings behind him, and felt sure he would feel the rend of talons any second but it never came, the thing seemed not to be pursuing.

Running back up the stairs he moved as quickly as he dared along the tomb corridor and was soon back in the chamber with the cat-like statues. He felt his way around the perimeter of the room and hurried up the steps to the first level, swiftly passing through the corridor gateway. Shutting it behind him, he paused in the small room to light the oil lamp. Finding the key, he locked the gate, then glanced down at himself. There were two deep scratches across his chest. In the heat of battle he had not even felt the wounds. Now they began to sting as blood ran down his torso. He sheathed his dagger and cursed, punching the wall in frustration.

Wounded, forced to run from combat, now his hand hurt and for what? Nothing, no treasure, no piles of riches, just dusty remains and some fiend from hell.

Holding the lamp aloft he made his way back to the

entranceway. Muttering under his breath he moved up the steps and back towards to the surface. In his anger he failed to notice the silence of the crickets. The first he knew of the men around him was a spear prodded towards his face. With a curse he looked up to see four City Guard positioned around the gateway, spears poised. Without thought, the young thief made a move towards his dagger but something crashed into his skull. The night was filled with dazzling lights, then all went dark.

The rattle and clang of iron brought Llorc back into the world. His head throbbed with a dull ache as he leapt up and moved towards the sound. He was brought up short by the chain that shackled his wrists and was set into the floor. Looking up, squinting in the torchlight, he saw he was in a cell, three walls of which were iron bars. The third wall was stone, with a small aperture set high up. A faint aroma of wood smoke drifted through it.

The cell door had just been shut and locked by an unkempt, corpulent figure in leather jerkin and kirtle who then sat at a small table in the far corner of the room and set to noisily demolishing a platter of food. He spared Llorc no glance. Llorc pulled at the chain in frustration.

"Hey! Hey you! Where am I?" he shouted. The man paid no heed and continued chewing on his food, wiping a large hand across his greasy face.

"I said where am I, dog?" Llorc pulled the chains so they rattled loudly. The heavyset door opposite swung open and a

City Guard poked his head around. "You're wasting your breath, boy, Achys is deaf. It's quite the advantage in this job, saves listening to whining bitches. Now pipe down or you'll get another crack on the head!"

Llorc hurled a curse as the guard slammed the door. There was nothing else to do, so he sat, head bowed and tried to will away the pain in his skull.

He awoke some time later, with sunlight shining through the aperture. Achys was no longer there and voices could be heard from the other side of the door. The scratches on his chest had stopped bleeding and his head was clearer, so the youth took some time to examine his surroundings. He tried but couldn't quite reach the aperture. The chain passed through shackles on his wrists which he tried to pull apart, but the metal dug into his flesh with no sign of bending or breaking. So, instead, he grasped the chain in both hands, sat down, put his feet to the wall, braced and tried to pull out the metal ring in the floor. Gritting his teeth, he straightened his legs and back, muscles standing out like cords on his thickset arms. So engrossed was he in this task that he failed to hear the door open behind him.

"Bet you wished you'd taken my advice now?" a voice ventured. Llorc turned and stood in one motion.

"Gaios! I'm glad to see you! Where am I?"

"You're in a gaol in the Lower Quarter," Gaios replied. "The sergeant here is an old colleague of mine. He sent me word when he saw who you were."

"How is it the soldiers were they waiting for me, how did they know I was there?"

"Bad luck and a simple mistake, lad. You left the Catacomb gate open when you went in. A passing patrol saw it and then noticed your lamplight."

Llorc cursed under his breath, how could he have made such a basic error? He rattled the chains at his wrists.

" So what happens now?"

"Best case?" Gaios rubbed his chin. "I call in some favours, there's a heavy fine to pay and we get you out of here today."

"And worst case?"

"You end your days broken and blind, digging in the King's mines."

"Hmm. I prefer the first option. What was that creature in the Catacombs?"

Gaios' gaze dropped to the deep scratches on Llorc's chest.

"A creature? So that's how you got those wounds?"

"Aye. I thought it a statue but it lived. It stood guard at a bridge that led deeper into the Catacombs."

"It must have been an Erisae. I told you there were monsters down there, lad. Most would call them myth but it seems there is truth behind many a myth. Old tales say they were placed there as guardians by the original builders of the Catacombs and that they are not alive as we think of it but are spirits imprisoned to do the bidding of those who trapped them."

"It seemed alive enough to me. I've not seen the like before, though we have myths of our own in the North. By Morrg my head pounds, could you at least get me some water?"

"Of course, then I will talk to - what the hell is that?"

There was a commotion from outside the room and the guard from the previous last night burst in.

"I'm sorry Gaios, I couldn't stop them!"

The guard was pushed aside by an corpulent figure in an extravagant toga. He waved a scroll in the air.

"My name is Phileos and I have orders that this prisoner is to be transferred immediately into custody of the Senate!"

Gaios protested loudly. "This is most irregular, this is a City Guard matter, not a Senate one. This man is a small-time thief, nothing more."

Phileos paused and turned, as if addressing a small child or idiot.

"This man is wanted on charges of murder and assault against the City Militia and their agents! In any case, sir, the concerns of the Senate are no concern of yours. Stand aside! Escort, in here, now!"

Two hulking figures squeezed through the doorway. Each wore a visored helm, only their lower faces visible. They towered above even Llorc, formidable figures of muscular development. They wore plain but high quality armour and carried short swords at their belts.

"Keys! Where are the keys?" Phileos demanded.

The giants parted as another figure appeared in the doorway. A savage grin split his scarred face as Wulforr brandished a large key ring with a flourish. He stepped into the room. "Well now, is the prisoner ready?"

With Gaios still protesting, the chain was unlocked and Llorc was dragged from the cell. He tensed in preparation to fight but the two large men held him fast in an iron grip. To

reinforce the point Phileos explained, with a lascivious smile.

"I have no orders to bring the prisoner in unharmed." He withdraw a dagger from his sleeve. As Llorc was held in place the blade was pressed against his cheek.

"An ear perhaps, or an eye removed... a shame, though, to spoil such good looks."

Llorc's eyes glittered in cold fury, his nostrils flared, but he ceased any struggle. Without further ado he was shoved outside and placed in the rear of a caged wagon. Gaios could only watch, helpless, as the wagon and accompanying escort set off up towards The Rock.

Llorc gripped the bars and glowered at the passing world. Wulforr nudged his horse close to the wagon.

"Caged, like all stinking Clannacht swine should be," he sneered.

"Remove these shackles and we'll see who's the swine and who's the man, you ugly bastard!" Llorc retorted.

Wulforr laughed and spurred his horse away. "Boy, by the time Toutatis has finished with you, you'll be lucky to have fingers enough to stroke your tiny prick, let alone wield a sword."

Llorc spat and settled back on his haunches. To one side,

only the rock wall was visible. To the other, the city was spread out below him, more of it coming into view the higher they climbed. The road twisted and wound its way up until, some minutes later, they reached the first gatehouse, built into the side of the crag. The party was waved through without pause and they soon arrived at the main entrance to The Citadel itself. The gate watch here were not City Guard but imposing figures dressed in black plate. Despite the heat, they wore full helm, topped with white plume.

"They are the King's Talons, boy." Wulforr was alongside the wagon again. "The finest Adelphis has to offer and the closest thing to a real warrior in these parts. Pretty, aren't they?" He laughed and moved off again.

Moving through the gate and along a broad thoroughfare, the party entered into The Citadel proper. Officials and messengers hurried hither and thither, a sedan chair passed carrying a lounging noblewoman who eyed Llorc hungrily.

Soon they passed through an archway and came to a halt in a courtyard, cooled by the shade of small trees. Llorc was removed from the wagon, dragged through a door and down a flight of steps, then was pushed roughly into a dank, airless chamber. The door slammed shut and he was left alone in the pitch black.

CHAPTER 10

They came for him a short time later. He had been dozing when the door was flung open and three figures rushed in. Before his eyes had time to adjust to the light flooding into the cell, they were on him, kicking and punching. His hands were still shackled, he could little more than curl in a ball and accept the beating. Almost as soon as it started, the assault stopped and Llorc was left again in complete darkness

Worse than the beating and darkness was the thirst. He had not drunk since before going into the Catacombs. Food he could manage without. On many a hunting trip he had endured on little more than nuts and berries but in this accursed heat he felt the lack of water keenly. His throat burned, his lips cracked, he wished for nothing but water. His wishes were answered when they came for him again.

This time he was held by the two large men as a laughing Wulforr pushed his head into a pail of water. It gave him the chance at least to gulp some liquid down but soon his lungs felt near to bursting and stars swam in his vision. Three times the process was repeated before he was left alone again, retching on the floor.

The third time the men returned, Llorc was ready. He crouched to the side of the door as he heard their approach. As the first twin entered, Llorc launched himself at the huge figure. Hands shackled, he unleashed a two handed blow to the man's face so strong it knocked even the large bodyguard to his knees. Llorc got no chance to follow up, as a huge fist smashed into his jaw from the second giant, now in the doorway. Llorc, expecting the blow, managed to ride it, which took some of the sting out but, nonetheless, he was flung back across the cell.

His attacker was on him instantly, grabbing Llorc in a bear hug and lifting him off his feet. Llorc responded by sharply whipping his head back, hoping to crack the man's nose. Against a normal size man it may have worked, against the huge bodyguard he succeeded only in catching the man's chin. With a grunt, the giant threw Llorc to the floor, knocking the wind out of him. The second bodyguard added a kick to the guts for good measure and before Llorc could recover a metal collar was placed around his neck and a chain attached to it. Llorc was pulled upright, snarling curses, as he rose and was dragged out of the cell.

The light stung his eyes and he raised his shackled hands to shield them. Prodded and pulled, he was taken back up the stairs and out into the courtyard. There, he was stood as two buckets of water were thrown over him by Wulforr. "To wash your stench away," he explained. Jaw throbbing, ribs aching, Llorc could do little but continuously swear under his breath in his own tongue.

Still, the cold water revived him somewhat, so he felt ready for anything as he was dragged inside the house and into a pleasant, airy chamber with open doors looking out onto an interior courtyard. Marble busts and small statues were placed around the edge of the room. A large sideboard stood against one wall, bedecked with platters of meats and fruits. At a table in the centre of the room sat a short, bearded man, eating fastidiously from a silver platter. He did not look up as Llorc was brought into the room. One of the twin giants took position behind the man, the other kept hold of the chain and thrust Llorc into a chair at the opposite end of the table. The man finished eating, patted his lips with a fine linen napkin and looked up at the ceiling.

"You see," the man declared, tossing the napkin over his shoulder, "strange as it may seem, we are in a position to help each other." He switched his gaze directly at Llorc. The bright green eyes bore into his own, but Llorc held and returned the man's stare. The man smiled and looked away. "But where are my manners? Food and drink for our guest, we are all friends here!"

Llorc glanced at the open doorway to the courtyard, calculating. The huge figure behind Toutatis caught the glimpse and shook his head, hand moving to sword hilt. In any event, the chain at his neck was pulled slightly to remind him of his bonds. A servant bearing a platter on a tray entered, went over to the sideboard and brought across a selection of foods as well as a goblet of wine, placing them before the youth. Llorc wolfed them down voraciously. Friend or foe, there was nothing to be gained by starving to death. With a satisfied belch, he wiped a hand across his mouth.

"Let's get to it, then," he nodded to the man. "Who are you and what do you want?"

"Direct and to the point, I like it! Very well. I am Senator Toutatis. You are Llorc. I believe you broke into my town house recently and stole some of my property?"

"There seems little point in denying it," Llorc replied. "In this city it seems that to be a thief is the only option open to an outlander such as I."

"Direct and honest too! Toutatis smiled. "My word, you certainly are new to Adelphis, aren't you. Very well Llorc, I shall respond in kind. The coin you took means little to me, I have more. The items in the small chest, however, they have great sentimental value and I crave their return. I know who has them. Where is Stanler?"

Llorc took another swig of the wine, it was like nectar! He shrugged. "I know of no Stanler."

Toutatis frowned. "Oh and you were doing so well. But listen, you are inexperienced in our ways, so I shall be patient. Tell me where Stanler is and not only will you go free, but there will be a purse of coin in it for you. We will even drop the charges of murder and assault on the Militia. They carry a death sentence, you know?"

"I murdered no one, I merely sought to defend children against those who would kill them. In my homeland that is not called murder, that is called honour."

"Honour? Oh dear." Toutatis sighed and pinched the bridge of his nose. "Let me tell you, young man, that here in the civilised world we have laws about such things. Laws to protect respectable citizens from robbery and theft. Laws against those who attack our brave Militia, or attempt to prevent them carrying out their civic duties."

Llorc snorted. "Your laws do nothing but protect your right to remain rich. You care not for the people of this city, only your own position and wealth. You have no honour, you have only empty words and lies."

He felt the chain at his neck tighten as the bodyguard behind the Senator stiffened at such impertinence. Toutatis remained impassive.

"I fear we are drifting from the topic. Let us return to practical matters. I seek only the return of my property. I know Stanler has it, so once again, tell me where he is and you go free. Think, boy, do you imagine Stanler cares a toss for you? He uses you for his own ends and would discard you as I did my napkin. Save yourself, Llorc, the choice is stark and simple!"

Llorc did not waver. "Sorry, I never heard of this Stanler."

A flicker of anger flashed across Toutatis' features and Llorc caught a glimpse of what lay beneath the suave, cultured surface. Nonetheless, he remained silent.

"I see. Let us talk of the Catacombs, then. What did you seek there? What did you learn from the book?"

Llorc's only response was to drain the wine goblet with a noisy swig. Toutatis motioned to the hulking figure behind Llorc and the collar chain was yanked, pulling him upright.

"Come, walk with me."

Toutatis arose and stepped through the opening into the courtyard. The silent giant pulled the chain and Llorc was forced to follow. Outside, Toutatis plucked a bloom from amongst the flowers and inhaled its perfume.

"Look around, barbarian. This is my official residence. You are in the heart of the Kingdom. I am a man of much influence, as such I make a good ally but a very bad enemy. Now, you are obviously a resourceful fellow; after all you took the book out from under Passang's nose."

In the far corner of the courtyard Llorc saw the Easterner he had fought during the robbery. The man turned and stared at him impassively. Toutatis walked over to the Easterner's side, Llorc being dragged along in tow. He could see a figure strapped upright by the wrists to a post behind Passang.

"Did you know, thief, that Passang's people have a very advanced knowledge of the body and all its intricate workings? They have systems of healing that put our sawbones to shame and of course, what can be healed can also be destroyed. Look!"

Llorc was dragged close to the post. He thought the man hanging there to be dead, his head was slumped forward, blood dripped onto the terracotta tiles. But the figure gave a groan and raised his head. Llorc had seen battle wounds aplenty but even he flinched at the condition of the unfortunate's face. One eye stared glassily in the red ruin, the other was a dark socket. Much of the skin had been removed, the exposed teeth shining whitely where the lips had been sliced away. The gory apparition made a moaning noise, blood running from the mouth. Glancing to the floor Llorc noticed, with a grimace, the man's tongue lying at his feet.

Passang sheathed the small, curved blade he had been using and wiped bloodstained hands on a cloth. Toutatis smiled thinly at Llorc's reaction.

"You see, thief, hurting people is easy. The real art lies in hurting people and keeping them alive. Passang is a master of the art, he has barely started on this wretch." He waved dismissively at the suspended figure.

"This is the servant who passed on the information that allowed you to rob me. This is how I reward those who would work against me. What do you say now?"

Llorc recovered some poise and hissed. "That rather than fist, I wish it were my dagger that had found your lackey's ribs."

Toutatis sighed. "I see there is no reasoning with a barbarian." He turned to the bodyguard holding the chain.

"Return him to the cell, let him think on a life with no eyes, nose or fingers, a life where women and children will scream at the sight of him and even his own kin will not recognise him."

Llorc made a sudden lurch forward, hands clawing for Toutatis throat but his guard was prepared for such a move. With a yank on the chain Llorc was pulled sharply away and dragged, cursing, back to the cell.

How long he was in the room he could not say. There was no daylight to mark the passage of time and only once was a bowl of slop and a mug of water slid through a shutter in the door. Llorc tried every wall and corner of the room and pushed and pulled every inch of the door, all to no avail. Eventually he sat, head bowed, the beginnings of a dark despair building in his mind.

He must have slept. A small noise brought him back to consciousness, the sound of the door being slowly opened. As quietly as he could he gathered his limbs beneath him, ready to strike. He had a vague notion of someone near him and was about to lash out when a voice whispered, "Ssshhh!"

Llorc froze and whispered back in cracked voice, "Who's there?"

The young voice replied "It's Vasil, I'm here to get you out. Come, quickly, Trant is outside with a wagon."

Llorc rose stiffly to his feet and reached out a hand. He placed it on the boy's shoulder and was led out of the room, up the stairs and out away from the house. Even the dim torchlight outside made his eyes smart, so he allowed the boy to lead him, now recognising the lad as his face was revealed in the yellow glow. The boy's grin flashed at him in the gloom.

"I sneaked in. Trant drove us up here in a wine-seller's wagon that we...borrowed. We hid until dark."

"But how did you know I was here?" Llorc croaked.

"Not now, " the boy replied. "We have to move quickly! Follow me!"

Sure enough, secreted in a side alley just outside the

residence sat Trant in a small wagon. He grinned at the sight of Llorc supported by the young lad, then helped him into the cart, where he covered Llorc with a large sheet.

"Keep still, keep quiet!" he whispered.

Llorc lay still and closed his eyes, the gentle rocking of the cart lulling him into a deep sleep. He awoke as they reached The Bearpit, where Meg had prepared an upstairs room for him. He ate and drank alone in the room, before falling once more into a deep slumber.

At first light next morning, he wandered downstairs to the main tavern. Thirst and hunger assuaged he took stock of his injuries. They were largely superficial, bruises and cuts, though his jaw stilled ached. Trant and Vasil had returned to the Den, there was no sign of Galenna or Draccus. He enquired after them to Meg, she was rinsing out pots as she answered him with a shrug.

"Not seen hide nor hair of either of them, nor Stanler come to that. There's been some strangers hanging round, though. I smell trouble, Llorc, something's brewing, you mark my words."

Minutes later, Meg's prophecy was proven true when one of the Den urchins rushed in.

"The men are back, they're attacking The Den!

Llorc immediately rushed out of the tavern, the lad running alongside him, breathlessly explaining what had happened. "They took us by surprise! They came in on boats at dawn and landed at the Old Docks! A big group of men, they headed straight for the Den!"

Llorc nodded to the boy then lengthened his stride, leaving the lad behind. Rushing through the Ratteries he heard distant cries ahead. Rather than take a direct route, he swung right and, cutting through back alleyways, approached the Den from the river side. Suddenly there came the tramp of feet and shouts of pain and anger from close by. He kept in the shadows of the side alley as a body of men burst around the corner ahead. These were not Militia but heavily armed and armoured warriors. From his vantage point, he counted at least thirty as they jogged past, the tall figure of Wulforr in their midst. Llorc's hand itched for his sword hilt but he was weaponless. He restrained himself with a silent curse, he thirsted for the Njordir's blood but to attack now would be suicide.

Instead, he let the band pass, then rushed to the Den. Bodies lay strewn around the entrance; two of them, he noted, armoured men stuck with crossbow quills. The heavy door was hanging off its hinges, just inside, in widening pools of blood, lay the bodies of some of the urchins. Llorc took the stairs three at a time up to the main room. The place had been turned over, all the furniture smashed, wall hangings torn down. At the far end of the room Trant sat slumped against the wall, hands desperately pressed to a great gash in his belly.

Llorc raced to his side, crouching next to him as Trant looked up, his face ashen, his eyes glazed.

"Trant! What happened?"

Trant grasped Llorc's arm with a blood-stained hand.

"Llorc... is that you? They came just after dawn... surprised us...not Militia, but fighters... said Stanler had been arrested... Draccus... Draccus..."

Trant's head slumped forward and his hand fell away, lifeless, from Llorc's arm. Llorc gently closed the young man's eyes and stood slowly, mind reeling.

A check around the warehouse revealed nothing but more corpses and devastation. Stanler's room had been thoroughly turned over, of his stash of gems and jewels only an empty chest remained. Llorc gathered his own meagre possessions then made his way back numbly to the front entrance. Locals were congregating, some crying as they held the small bodies to their chests. Llorc clenched his fists and raised them to the sky, roaring in anger, pain and frustration. *Draccus! Could it be that Stanler's right hand man had betrayed them all?*

He returned to The Bearpit, which was abuzz with the news that Stanler had indeed been taken and was now in the custody of the authorities. None knew how he had been found, or where, but Llorc was starting to piece together a story in his own mind, a story of betrayal and greed. For now, though, there was nothing he could do. One man could not search the entire city for a traitor, nor could he hope to spring Stanler from whatever cell he was being held in. So he called for strong drink from Meg. She took one look at his grim expression and cold, icy stare and poured.

For the next two days, Llorc stayed at The Bearpit. Between

drinking, he sent out what gang members could be gathered in order to gain as much information as possible. Galenna and Draccus remained absent, he noticed that Hespero was also missing, though it went unremarked by Meg. On the morning of the third day he received word from a wide eyed, panting runner - Stanler was to be hung in the City Market Square!

CHAPTER 11

Llorc grabbed a cloak and cowl and rushed north as fast as he could. As he crossed Pergares Bridge and got closer to the Market, the crowds thickened and he noticed groups of soldiers too, City Guard, not Militia. He reached the main square itself, forcing his way through the crowds whilst trying not to draw attention from the Guard. Ahead, he could see that a large scaffold had been erected, topped with three gallows.

The crowd seemed in good cheer, with much laughing and cat calls. Vendors wound their way through the throng, crying out their wares. Public hangings were a rare event but an event that was enjoyed by the local populous, it seemed. Llorc pushed as far forward as he could. A hissing and booing from the other side of the square alerted him to a wagon being driven through the crowd, accompanied by mounted Guards. Three figures sat in the back of the wagon, though he could not see them clearly from his vantage point.

The wagon drew up to the scaffold and the passengers, hands bound behind them, were hauled out of the wagons, each then stood by a gallows with a Guard behind them. Another group of Guard forced their way through the crowd to stand in line, swords drawn, at the foot of the scaffold. Llorc craned his neck to see the figures. The centre one was Stanler, faced bloodied and bruised. The figures on each side were unknown to him; a very scared looking youth and older man who sneered and spat at the baying crowd.

A drum beat began from somewhere as an official mounted the scaffold. Thrusting his jowled chin forward, the man unfurled a scroll and dramatically raised a hand for silence. The crowd hushed somewhat, apart from the occasional jest. In stentorian tones, the official announced the names of the three individuals and the crimes for which they had been sentenced. For Stanler, the crimes read were larceny, blackmail, robbery, extortion and smuggling. Each charge brought cheers from some and jeers from others. With a final flourish the official rolled up the scroll and announced, "The sentence for each... is death!"

The crowd cheered once more as each man was roughly manhandled into position. The drum increased its tempo as a hooded figure took to the scaffold. More cheers greeted his appearance. He waved his hands above his head and roared, eliciting laughter from some and squeals of fear from small children. He swiftly moved along the line, expertly placing a noose over each prisoner's head.

Stanler had his eyes closed, mumbling to himself, perhaps

in prayer. At the touch of the noose, his eyes opened and he scanned the crowd back and forth. Suddenly, they alighted on Llorc and the old man smiled sadly and gave a small nod. Llorc could only stand transfixed, fists clenched and teeth grinding as the executioner pulled the lever with a roar and the three bodies fell sharply to their deaths.

Llorc turned away, sickened by the sight and sound, sickened at those who took pleasure in such a spectacle. He pushed his way sharply out of the crowd, those who caught sight of his cowled face moving swiftly from his path.

In a daze, Llorc returned to The Bearpit. The news had preceded him and all in the room were quiet, staring silently into their drinks. Meg rubbed tear-filled eyes as she moved round the room, pouring drinks for all. Llorc sat stunned, alone at a table. From another corner of the room a voice cried out "To Stanler!" and the host stood as one, raising their cups and draining them in one pull. Many then cast the mugs to smash against the wall before sinking back into morose silence.

It was some hours later that Llorc came to. His head rested on the stained table, pounding unmercifully. With a groan, he lifted his gaze, something had caught his attention. The blurry room swam slowly back into focus, lit by flickering candles and lanterns. Then he realised what he had heard and why he had awoken.

"Oh, so you're back then, son? Happy travels?"

It was Meg's voice, followed by Hespero's reply. "Nothing special, but yes, I'm back now, did I miss anything? It's quiet in here."

Llorc pushed the pain to the back of his mind and tensed his wide shoulders, straining to hear more. He was largely concealed in the dark corner of the room and Hespero had obviously not noticed him. His first instinct was to rush over and beat the whereabouts of Draccus out of the youth but as he half stood he staggered and fell back heavily into his seat. He turned to the side and retched, which cleared his head somewhat. By the time he looked back up, Hespero had disappeared from view. Llorc staggered to the bar and gestured to Meg.

"Hespero, where'd he go?"

Meg turned from serving another drinker and replied.

"Don't know. He's only back for a minute, then he's off again."

Llorc made his way to the door and stepped into the warm night air. Glancing left, he saw Hespero just turning the corner at the end of the street. Taking a breath, Llorc immersed his head in the horse trough by the entrance, the cold water biting deep and reviving him. Shaking his head and wiping his face with the back of his hand, he set off in pursuit. Moving swiftly, he soon had Hespero in view once more as he walked across the square and into the Ratteries. Llorc hung back for a short while, then sprinted across the open space and began to follow the young man through the dim streets.

Llorc drew as close as he dared, easy work for one used to tracking deer in deep forests. Hespero obviously had no thought that he might be followed and walked as one without a care in the world. At length he arrived at a small house on the corner of one of the squalid streets. Going up a flight of stairs to a door, he knocked. There was a short delay, the door opened and Hespero slipped inside.

Llorc continued walking past the building to view it from the other side. The upstairs windows were shuttered but a dim glow could be seen through the cracks. Llorc sprang atop a water barrel, reached up to a neighbouring gutter and hauled himself up onto the neighbouring roof. From there he was able to climb onto the house roof and made his way to its edge, being careful to make no sound or disturb any tiles.

Once over the window, he gripped the gutter edge and lowered himself down. Swinging back, he then launched forward, feet first. The shutters gave way with a crash and Llorc burst into the room with a roar. Hespero and Draccus, faces pale in the dim lamplight, span around to face him.

Without pause, Llorc sprang across the room to grasp Draccus by the throat. The man gave a squeal of fear as he was rammed back into the wall. Hespero gave a shout and grabbed Llorc's arm but was sent reeling by a shove. Llorc's face was inches from Draccus, twisted in fury. He screamed at the terrified man.

"Why did you betray Stanler? Why did you betray Stanler?"

Draccus tore at Llorc's grip to no avail. His other hand reached for his dagger, at which Llorc turned and flung him across the room. Hespero had fled through the door, which swung wildly on its hinges. Draccus crashed into a table, stunned. He wrenched out his blade but Llorc grabbed him by his tunic front, lifted him up and backhanded him across the face. The knife clattered to the floor as Draccus was once again slammed into the wall. He slumped down to the floor, hands held palm up in front of him.

"No, no!" he pleaded. "It wasn't me! I swear it, it wasn't me!"

Llorc drew his sword and hissed, "Not you? You cur, then who was it!"

"It was me!" came a familiar voice from the doorway. Llorc wheeled at the sound to see Galenna framed in the entrance, Hespero just visible behind her.

"It was me." She stepped into the room. "I betrayed Stanler."

Galenna righted the table and sat at it. Hespero came into the room and moved across to Draccus' side in concern. Llorc stood as if in a trance, conflicting emotions playing across his face. He shook his head and pointed an accusing finger at Galenna.

"You?" he scowled. "It was you? And what was your price? How many pieces of gold did it take to buy you, Galenna? How many to betray us? What was your price, whore?"

Galenna stood sharply, pushing the table away, glaring at Llorc in fury.

"The price? I'll tell you what the price was! It was your life, you idiot!"

She strode from the room slamming the door behind her. Llorc remained frozen to the spot, dazed, trying to make sense of the situation.

"Llorc. Llorc! Put your sword away, sit down." Draccus

stood and slid over a chair. Llorc complied, accepting the mug of rum that Hespero thrust into his hand. Draccus retrieved his dagger and sat opposite Llorc, gingerly feeling the large swelling on his cheek.

"Let me tell you what happened. When you disappeared, no one knew where you had gone. Then we received word through your friend, Gaios, that you had been arrested and taken up into The Citadel by Toutatis. When Galenna and I told him what had happened, Stanler knew exactly what this was about; the book and the letters. So he came up with a plan. You were to be allowed to escape, in return for which, Stanler was to surrender himself and the book. Your life for his. Galenna was in charge of the negotiations and planning."

"My life for his? But why?"

Draccus sighed. "He was dying, Llorc he was very ill. He had but little time left. I think he preferred going out the way he did than to slowly waste away. He's back with his wife now."

Llorc remained stunned by the revelation. "The book, the letters... surely they were of worth?"

"Stanler always said *there will be other treasures*. The greatest treasure for him was us, his family. We shall honour his memory."

"But The Den, Trant and the others? His last words were your name, I thought he was blaming you."

"The raid on the Den was not part of the deal. Whether that was on Toutatis' order or Wulforr acting alone, we do not know. Either way, the agreement was for Stanler and the book only, nothing more. As for Trant's last words, I know not what he meant. Perhaps he had some message he wished relayed to me. Now we shall never know. What a grievous day, now we have nothing."

Llorc began at last to grasp the magnitude of the situation and lowered his head into his hands.

"You are right, Draccus, and it is all because of my foolishness."

CHAPTER 12

Queen Arpanas swore under her breath as she pricked her finger again with the needle. She threw down the embroidery in frustration and waved for her maid to take it away.

"I'll never get the hang of this blasted needlework! Why should I be expected to do it, Oresus?"

Oresus bowed as he stood opposite her in the tower chamber. It was the hottest part of the day and while the stone chamber was shady and cool, fierce autumn sunlight streamed in through the open casement. Glancing outside, he could see fishing boats crawling slowly to and fro across the glittering, azure sea.

"I'm afraid it is expected, Majesty, one of the skills to be acquired by ladies of station and breeding."

"Blast it, I'd rather be horse riding or out hunting with my brothers!"

Oresus smiled. The Queen was a dainty figure, her long straight black hair tied in a braid, her dark skin and caste marking a striking contrast to her Adelphian dress, dazzling white and trimmed with gold thread. But there was a fierceness in her glittering eyes that spoke of inner fire and she had a sharp intellect which had caught out many an unwary courtier.

"Do you really believe my being able to sew will make any of these people accept me as their true Queen? Be honest, Oresus, I'm a low-born foreigner in their eyes and will never be fit to rule."

"Never low born, Majesty. Is not your father the Raja of Darhmsala?"

"He is, indeed, though I'm sure the Adelphian high born regard us as little more than savages, despite our civilisation being at least as ancient as their own."

"Ours is indeed an ancient civilization, Majesty, though truth be told many of today's so-called high born are the scions of those who bought their way into the aristocracy. Rich merchants and the like, or worse. Trade is where the true wealth is these days, not in titles or bloodlines."

"Yet those bloodlines must remain pure, or at least appear to remain pure. And my colour will always mark me as an outlander to many."

Oresus could only shrug in agreement. The Queen gestured for him to sit and he chose the window bench, to best take advantage of the slight breeze.

"Yet they were all happy to attend your wedding. I recall, it was quite the occasion, Majesty."

The Queen laughed musically. "Indeed, it was. I'll wager it's the first time an oliephaunt has been seen in the city streets! And you conducted the ceremony with great aplomb, Oresus, it was a wonderful occasion. Nonetheless, I am the King's second wife and only Prince Leonte's step-mother, not his real mother. I fear the boy holds me in as little regard as many of the society elite." She sighed. "But enough of my self pity, what news?"

"Nothing good, I'm afraid, Majesty. It seems the book and papers are back in the possession of Toutatis. The man responsible for their theft was hung just two days ago."

"And you have no knowledge of the contents of these papers?"

"Only an outline. It seems Toutatis has been corresponding with one Dahkosh Khalsang, a sorcerer of the Order of Lheng."

"The Order of Lheng?" The Queen drew a sharp breath. "That is a name of ill omen. They hold sway in kingdom of Yarlung, which borders the lands of my Father. Their Priest-kings rule by fear and dark sorcery from a hidden mountain stronghold. In recent years they have sought to extend their influence, always by nefarious means. My own Uncle was assassinated by their hand, my father lives in constant threat of their machinations. What would one of their number seek in Adelphis?"

"We only know, Majesty, that this Khalsang has sent Toutatis some ancient grimoire as a gift and will, himself, be arriving in Adelphis soon. His purpose is unknown, though if Toutatis is involved, it will be nothing for our benefit!"

"Ah, yes indeed. Toutatis and yourself are still rivals?"

"Always, Majesty, since childhood. Though brothers, we have different mothers. Our father was a cruel and ruthless man, he encouraged our rivalry to the point of obsession. His passing did nothing to cool such obsession, in fact for Toutatis, it seems only to have increased."

"Your brother would see you ruined? To what end?"

"He would, Majesty. Partly from personal vendetta, partly because he has always despised the priesthood and partly through nothing more than pure lust for power. The Senate has been a growing force in the city, especially as the King ages - begging your pardon, Majesty."

"No pardon is required, Oresus. The King is much older than I and is certainly not in good health. You fear Toutatis seeks to influence the Prince?"

"Indeed, Majesty, he takes every opportunity to pour sugar into the boy's ear. The Prince no longer even attends the weekly rituals and avoids all my attempts to speak to him."

"Then it seems we can do little but wait, good Oresus, until the forces against us make their move. It is not a strategy I favour!"

Oresus nodded in agreement. "Nor I, Majesty. In the meantime I shall pray for guidance, mayhap the Gods will shine some light or grant us a weapon to be used."

There was a soft knock at the door and the Queen's bodyguard entered, a substantial, bearded man, bedecked in the turban, weapons and accoutrements of his native warrior Caste.

"What is it, Gurdas?" the Queen asked.

The warrior bowed. "Pardon, Divyani. His Majesty has requested your presence in the Throne Room."

The Queen sighed and rose, Oresus rising too and offering a low bow.

"Ah well," she smiled. "At least it gives me a break from this cursed embroidery!"

The wind whistled through the narrow streets and alleyways of Adelphis, rattling shutters in its wake. Torches flickered wildly under the assault and the few people abroad gathered their cloaks tightly about them and hurried about their business. Thunder rumbled far out to sea and lightning flickered on the horizon, briefly illuminating heavy waves and storm-tossed boats. The ships at dock clattered noisily in the swell.

Toutatis jumped as the shutter behind him was blown open with a crash, the sudden gust of wind scattering the papers on his desk. A servant rushed to batten the window, before bending to retrieve the papers. Toutatis waved the man away and resumed his conversation with Phileos.

"So, normality is restored. No repercussions from the street gang I take it?"

"None. The gang has scattered, sir, it seems, the destruction of their lair was as severe a blow as the execution of their leader."

"Ah yes, Wulforr did somewhat over reach his remit there. Nonetheless, it sends out a message. For far too long this vermin has been allowed to run unchecked, their cleansing has been long overdue. Once the area is cleared, the redevelopment plans can proceed."

"Why not just take in the whole of the Militia, or the City Guard, sir?"

"Because, especially after their last bumbling attempt, the Militia show a marked reluctance to get their hands dirty. Too many of them have ties to the area. However, I have some leverage against their Commander, he will become more pliable soon enough. What we also require is the support of the mob."

"You wish me to bring Malassos into play?"

"Indeed I do. It is time for my wife's nephew to exercise his talents. He achieved much at Court, he became quite the favourite of the old Queen."

"Since then he has been working behind the scenes in the Senate?"

"Indeed. Time now, I think, for a more direct approach. Instruct him to shift his focus to the streets and begin spreading word that the city needs a new, strong leader. One prepared to promote the interests of citizens above those of outlanders. One prepared to stand firm for Adelphian traditions, to be a standard-bearer for our values. To speak the truth about the threats to our way of life from the creeping tide of foreign influence and this insidious new cult that I hear is gaining followers in many places!"

"Ah, you speak of the Sharers, sir? Yes I believe a group of them are established within the Ratteries, from where they spread their poison."

"Ridiculous people! As though a slave or low born could have the same influence and rights as one such as I! It's a disgrace! Yes, instruct Malassos to begin immediately!"

Phileos bowed his head in acknowledgement and rose to leave. "I shall see to it right away, sir."

"Good. And send Passang in, if you can find him, I've not seen the skulker all day and would know the whereabouts of his Master."

"Wonder no more," proclaimed Passang, pushing past Phileos in the doorway. "My Master has arrived. I present the Dahkosh Khalsang of the Order of Lheng."

Phileos stepped back into the room and all eyes were on the darkened doorway as a gaunt, mask-like face slowly emerged from the gloom. Parchment like skin was drawn tight over a high forehead and pronounced cheekbones. Slightly oblique eyes blazed as if with some infernal fire, the thin lips, surprisingly red, spread in the approximation of a smile. The sorcerer emerged fully into the light, his long yellow robe brushing the floor, arms folded within the wide sleeves. He opened his arms, revealing sinewy hands with long, sharp fingernails and bowed in a slightly mocking fashion.

"I am Khalsang."

A thunderclap burst nearby and Toutatis flinched. Phileos muttered something under his breath and hastily exited the chamber. Passang stood motionless and impassive to one side, eyes downcast to the floor in the presence of his Master.

With an effort, Toutatis recovered his poise. "Welcome! Welcome indeed, good Khalsang. I apologise for the lack of reception, had I been advised of your imminent arrival I would have provided a suitable escort for you."

"I have no need of escorts, my ways of travel are my own." The sorcerer accepted the proffered chair.

"Ah, well, that's good. But you must be hungry after your long journey? Let me send for victuals."

Khalsang raised a hand. "None is required. Enough talk. You have recovered the book?"

"Yes, it is held in safety, here."

"And the those responsible have been punished?"

"Their leader was hung, the servant responsible... well, your man ministered to him, his treachery was repaid."

"Then we can begin our work. I shall need a private chamber, my servant will advise you as to the equipment I require. For now, I should like to retire. Tomorrow I shall see the city."

Toutatis rose and bowed slightly as the sorcerer stood. *Damn, he was starting to feel like a servant in his own household*! But he kept the thought to himself and merely replied "You may rest here for the night. My town house has been prepared for your use, we shall take you there on the morrow. Everything you require shall be supplied."

Without further word, his visitor swept from the room, followed by his smirking servant. Toutatis realised he was clenching the edge of his desk so hard his knuckles had turned white. With a sigh he poured himself another goblet

of wine and wondered once more if trafficking with sorcerers
was such a sound notion after all.

CHAPTER 13

Autumn deepened into winter, bringing with it heavy grey clouds and rain. The gloomy weather reflected the mood of the Ratteries and what remained of Stanler's gang. Galenna had disappeared, left Adelphis some said. The rest of the gang no longer used the Den and were, instead, scattered throughout the surrounding streets. Draccus tried to maintain collections but did not command the same respect as Stanler or Llorc and payments began to slide.

Rival gangs, sensing weakness and opportunity, started to muscle in. None moved too brazenly at first, preferring to wait and see how Llorc would react before making their play for power. Yet the barbarian seemed little inclined to do anything, despite Draccus' best effort to rouse the young man from his torpor.   Most days, Llorc could be found in The Bearpit, slumped over a table in the corner. He took a room upstairs, his daily routine consisting of little more than staggering up and down the stairs and drinking heavily. In the end, Draccus gave up and continued what work he could with the people he had available.

The rain had been falling in a steady drizzle all day. The early evening patrons at The Bearpit trudged in, mud spattered and damp. Cloaks were hung to steam by the cooking fire and a shaggy dog drew curses as it shook itself dry in the middle of the room. The crowd were mostly market traders in for an evening drink before returning home. A couple of rogues in the corner plotted an elaborate blackmail scheme that would likely never be brought to fruition. Meg cleaned behind the bar while Hespero stirred the large stew pot over the fire and ladled out portions to the customers. Meg called over her son and nodded towards the figure of Llorc, sat, as usual, at a corner table staring morosely into his stew.

"Take him over another ale and talk to him, for Ioanthe's sake. He is starting to take root and he's putting off the other customers."

"I'll try," replied Hespero, "but he does nothing more than grunt and drink."

He carried a jack over to the table and sat beside Llorc, who barely glanced up, instead reaching straight for the ale and taking a long draught.

"How goes it, Llorc? Draccus was in earlier, he asked if you were about. I told him you were sleeping off a hangover but I expect he will be back in later tonight."

There was no response from the slumped figure. Hespero sighed and returned to the bar, prompting a scowling Meg to throw down her cleaning rag and stride over to the youth. Hands on hips, she stood over him.

"Now then, as you are so fond of telling us, you're from the Wolf Clan, right?" Meg waved a finger. "The protectors of your people? And yet here you are, the big, bad wolf, skulking in his den, stinking drunk!"

Llorc barely seemed to acknowledge her presence.

"And, in the meantime, what is happening to the Clan? Yes, Llorc, for these people are your Clan now! The young ones, the men and women here, they look to you as a leader, their pack leader. And how do you respond? You stew in your own filth! Think of them, think of your clan! For Zantus' sake, prove yourself a leader!"

There was still no response and Meg threw up her hands in disgust and returned to the bar. As she got there, the door curtain was suddenly flung aside and four ominous figures strode into the steamy room. Two were slight, wiry men in nondescript garb. Meg recognised them as having been in the tavern before, just recently. One of them nudged the third figure and nodded towards Llorc.

The third man was huge, with the build of a wrestler. His teeth flashed white beneath a large moustache as he grinned, the hoop earring in his left ear glinting in the lamplight. He threw back his cloak with a flourish to reveal a bulky torso and great, hairy arms. Coarse black hair spilled out over the top of his singlet, his close shaven scalp was covered in lumps and bumps. He took a couple of strides forward and spoke to the whole company, though his gaze never left Llorc.

"Well well, isn't this a cosy little pigsty. Stinks like one too."

The dog growled, the regulars cast their eyes down into their ale, the rogues glanced at each other and stopped talking, hands slowly moving to dagger hilts. Meg motioned to Hespero, whispering urgently.

"See if you can find Draccus. If not, get whoever you can back here as quick as you can. Go out the back way."

Hespero nodded and moved through the curtain at the rear of the bar. The large man had taken position in the centre of the room, his two wiry companions hanging back. Meg looked to the door where the fourth man leant against the wall in apparent disinterest. He was cloaked and wore a wide hat, a thin waxed moustache and neatly trimmed beard the only things visible beneath its flared brim. An ornate rapier hung at his side and he wore finely tooled leathern boots.

Shit, she muttered to herself, placing her hand softly on the heavy cleaver concealed under the bar, *Salazar del Vallego!* A known hired blade, though it was unusual to see him in this part of the city. The large man was talking again.

"I am Yurrtaz the Mighty, none has bested me! I had heard there may be some men here who could offer me a good challenge but I see nothing but dotards and drunks!"

The patrons huddled even further down into their seats, none met the man's gaze. Llorc remained oblivious. Emboldened by lack of challenge, the hired muscle strode over to Llorc's table. He placed his large palms on the table and leant forward to get into Llorc's line of vision. Still drawing no reaction, he spoke directly to the young man.

"So this is the big, bad barbarian everyone's talking about. You look like a girl, with your pretty long hair and fancy tunic, I'll wager you wouldn't last two minutes against me."

Llorc's eyes remained downcast, he seemed to neither hear or see the man stood in front of him. Yurrtaz dipped a finger into the bowl of cold stew and licked it.

"Well this tastes like swill but then swill is the only thing fit for Northern pigs."

Disgusted at the continued lack of reaction, the large man spat into the food, then suddenly swept Llorc's tankard aside, the ale flying across the floor. There was a clatter as the mug hit and spun on the floor, then an absolute silence. Even the wind outside seemed to have abated. It felt like the world was holding its breath. With glacial slowness, Llorc looked up, bloodshot eyes staring glassily through the unruly hair that hung over his face. The room tensed...then Llorc cast his eyes down again. Yurrtaz roared with laughter.

"This is your champion? The slayer of Beorthe? This is no man! I've seen whipped curs with more spine. Look, even this flea-ridden hound shows more spirit."

He pointed to the still damp, growling dog in the corner of the room, its lips drawn back over yellowed teeth.

Seeing how things were progressing, del Vallego glided smoothly over to the bar. He spoke softly, but firmly, to Meg.

"This hovel now belongs to my employer. You may continue to run the place, but all earnings will be handed over. If you cooperate, you can continue to live here and will be paid a small salary. If this arrangement is not satisfactory, you can leave tonight."

Meg said nothing, but her grip on the cleaver tightened and her eyes blazed with fury. Llorc rose unsteadily to his feet.

"Leave her alone," he spoke, in a slurred whisper.

"Hark, the little doggy is whining!" laughed Yurrtaz. He pushed the table aside and slapped Llorc hard across the face. "Silence doggy, your master will tell you when to speak!"

Llorc reeled at the force of the blow, staying upright but making no move in response. Yurrtaz, like all bullies, thrived on success. He grabbed Llorc's tunic and balled his hand into a fist, shaking the youth, then shoving him back into the wall. In doing so he snapped the chord of Llorc's necklace and with a clatter the wolf teeth fell to the floor. Llorc, slumped against the wall, saw the scattered teeth in the dirty straw. The sight shifted something in his brain, he rose slowly to his feet, his eyes fierce with murderous rage. Yurrtaz had turned to face the room, sweeping an arm out in front of him.

"Well? Any other curs want to bark?" He spat into the straw, cursed, then froze as a sound reached his ears. It was a low growl, primal, animal. It stirred the hairs on the back of his neck, as if awakening some deep ancestral memory. He turned as the sound grew louder to see Llorc stood before him, teeth bared in a grim smile, a gleam of pure madness in his eyes. The growl became louder still then, with a loud cry, Llorc sprang forward with amazing speed.

The large man brought his hands up as if to grapple, but Llorc was in a state of primal fury, with no thought to the conventions of civilised bouts. Before he knew it, the wrestler was borne back by the charge and Llorc's teeth were at his throat. With a savage wrench of his head, Llorc tore away a chunk of bloody flesh from Yurrtaz's neck. Arms flailing, letting out a high-pitched scream of fear, the man fell heavily to the floor. Llorc spat the gobbet to the ground and snarled.

"You call me dog? No, not dog, but wolf!" Blood ran down his chin and chest as he tilted his head back and let loose a spine chilling howl. Yurrtaz scrabbled backwards, one hand desperately trying to halt the jet of blood that pulsed from his ruined throat. Crimson it flowed, through the fat fingers to mingle with the spilled ale and wine on the straw covered floor. The man let out a short sob then slowly sank back, legs twitching, feet drumming a tattoo on the ground as his eyes rolled back in death.

The room was frozen into a shocked silence. Even the hired blade, del Vallego, was stunned by the turn of events but he was the first to recover. With a hiss, his sword left its sheath.

"Barbarian scum! I'll skewer your heart for that!" He advanced, blade extended before him. Llorc made no move but stretched his mighty arms out wide and laughed.

"Come, little man, I'll taste your blood too!"

There was a sudden commotion as the door curtain was again flung aside and Draccus entered, followed by Hespero and a handful of gang members. The two wiry men were out through a window before anyone could blink. Del Vallego made a swift calculation, then slowly sheathed his sword. Raising his palms, he moved slowly toward the door. The newcomers tensed, Draccus' hand resting on his own sword hilt, but Meg called out.

"Let him pass. He won't be back." Then she addressed the swordsman. "Tell your boss thanks for the offer but things round here will be staying as they are."

The group parted and del Vallego slunk through, pausing only to straighten his hat. With a final flourish of his cloak he vanished into the drizzle.

The room let out a collective sigh, save for Llorc who swayed slightly on his feet. He seemed as though a man awoken from some strange dream.

"By Zantus, lad," Meg moved to his side. "I've seen some things in my time but nothing approaching that! Hespero, bring ale for Llorc!"

But Llorc grabbed her arm, his eyes having lost their former bloodshot madness.

"No. The time for ale is passed. The time for grieving and regret is done. Wrongs have been visited upon us. Now comes the reckoning!"

CHAPTER 14

Llorc resumed the gang operation with a vengeance. He came down hard on any who wavered in their payments and several rival gang members were seen off or fled when they heard of his return. He began to recruit new members from the denizens of the Ratteries and surrounding areas and, with Draccus' help, started putting new strategies into place. Little did they know, though, that a new enemy was moving against them, one far more powerful than the criminal gangs.

Malassos strode confidently into the Old Market and surveyed the surroundings with disdain. Unlike many Adelphians, he had blonde hair, perfumed and set into tight curls as was the fashion amongst young gentry. His clothes, however, were plain, a dark cloak, woollen leggings and boots. Apart from his hair, soft, pale face and haughty expression, he may have been taken for an artisan or merchant of some kind. He whispered a few words to the bully at his side, then motioned to the small group of men behind him. All were garbed in similar plain, dark cloaks, faces sinister, most sporting scars and broken noses. At one end of the market square stood the preacher Guryon, proclaiming the way of The Prophet, surrounded by his small group of robed devotees. Malassos headed directly for them, while the rest of his entourage spread out into the crowd. He took position ten paces in front of the preacher and began his harangue.

"You there! Why do you decry our good Adelphian gods? Keep your foreign nonsense to yourselves!"

One of his men cheered from the back of the crowd, another shouted in agreement.

"Friend," responded Guryon, spreading his hands, "the words of The Prophet are for all! We are all brothers!"

"You don't look like my brother, more like my grandfather!" Malassos retorted, his lackeys and some of the crowd laughing at his wit.

"We don't want your outland gods!" shouted another voice from the back.

"Adelphis for Adelphians!" cried another.

The preacher raised his palms in appeal.

"We seek only peace, brothers and sisters!"

"Here's a piece of shit!" a voice called, followed by a flung handful of horse dung which narrowly missed the preacher.

"You know they sacrifice babies!" shouted another voice. "Kill the filthy scum!"

The crowd became more agitated, voices were raised and people started pushing back and forth. Someone was punched in the face and tempers flared. The acolytes around Guryon looked worried as several of the crowd turned towards them, spitting and hurling insults and curses. A few stones flew overhead, crashing into the wall behind the preacher. Someone began a low chant which spread through the crowd and grew.

"Sharers out! Sharers out!"

The acolytes drew close together, Guryon in their midst. The crowd moved forward, jostling and pushing. More stones were being thrown now, two of the acolytes were hit and began to bleed.

"Be not afraid, brethren," Guryon spoke calmly. "The Lord will protect his servants!"

At that there were more missiles, then a sudden surge as the crowd came forward like a wave. Three of Malassos' thugs were in the front now, each drawing short staves from beneath their cloaks. They began to beat the nearest acolytes, at which the crowd bayed as if for blood.

There was a sudden roar, followed by a hush, when Llorc and a number of the gang appeared and pushed their way through the crowd.

"Back, get back you swine! Leave these people be!" he shouted as he strode through.

A space cleared around him, the thugs now hesitant. They glanced at Malassos who had moved back from proceedings. He took the opportunity to study the young barbarian, now dressed in a vivid red cloak over black, leather armour, gleaming white wolfs' teeth in contrast at his breast . A heavy sword and dagger hung from a broad belt, his chiselled face framed by tied back black hair. The grey eyes swept across the crowd, lingering a little on each thug, then finally coming to rest on Malassos. With a slight smirk Malassos gave a whistle, the signal for his bullies to withdraw. Within seconds the group had gone, the market quickly settling back to its usual routine.

The preacher grasped Llorc's hand.

"My thanks, brother, I knew the Lord would save us!"

"I know nothing of your Lord," Llorc rumbled. "Only that outsiders were here to cause trouble."

"Whatever your motive, you have our thanks. The Lord will watch over you, be sure of that."

"Take my advice, preacher. Temper your sermons for a while, keep a low profile. These are troubled times. I may not always be around to protect you."

"I shall bear your words in mind, young man." Then the man moved close and grasped Llorc's arm in a firm but friendly grip.

"We share your loss, brother. Stanler was a good man at heart. We shall pray for him."

Llorc nodded and grunted in return, before moving on to continue his daily rounds.

"Well, Uncle, I can confirm that the Northerner is back in circulation." Malassos waved away the goblet offered by a servant.

"We were in the Old Market, about to beat the tar out of the Sharers when he intervened. I have instructed the Militia to post eviction notices throughout the Ratteries tomorrow but I fear that as long as the barbarian is in place the scum will stand firm. Even our bribes and threats go unheeded! "

Malassos signalled to the serving girl to instead bring over a platter of cooked meats. Toutatis, reclining on the couch opposite, nodded thoughtfully.

"The delinquent certainly needs dealing with. I should have disposed of him when he was in my custody, regardless of what promises I made. Still, there is no point crying over spilt wine. Ah, Wulforr, there you are."

The tall warrior slunk into the room and leant against the wall by the door.

"You called for me?" he grunted.

"Yes. The Northerner is back and causing problems again. I'd like you to deal with him once and for all."

Wulforr shrugged with indifference and nodded to Malassos.

"I thought your nephew was taking care of things now. Did he quail at the sight of the big, bad barbarian?"

Malassos flushed and half stood, his platter dropping with a clatter to the tiled floor.

"Why, you impertinent swine! I have no fear of that Northern savage! I'll have you know I've trained with the finest sword-masters in the Kingdom! Were he here now, I would skewer his verminous hide!"

Wulforr merely grinned and folded his thick arms across his chest. Before he could respond, Toutatis interjected.

"Silence, the two of you! Wulforr, do not try my patience lest you incur my displeasure! You know full well that Malassos' talents lie in other areas, else I would not need you and your sell-swords! Now, can you take care of this cursed stripling, or should I ask some other muscle head to do the job?"

The Njordir grit his teeth. "Aye, I can take care of him. A strong group of men, in and out quick, we will corner the rat in his lair. I'll begin preparations at once."

Without a backward glance, Wulforr spun on his heels and left the room. Malassos sat back down and waved his hand in a gesture of disgust.

"I don't know how you put up with these filthy outlanders, Uncle. I can smell him from here! Do they never bathe?"

"They are simply tools, nephew, nothing more. You must learn how to wield such tools if you are to understand and hold power."

"You think he can storm the Ratteries and kill the outlander? The place is a stinking maze, surely the Northerner could hide in there for weeks?"

"You fail to comprehend how these barbarians think, nephew. They have a childish notion of honour. I will see to it that word of the attack reaches the rabble. Hearing that, Llorc will not hide, he will seek Wulforr out for personal combat. In any event, the death of the barbarian is not the main purpose in letting Wulforr's hounds off the leash."

"It is not? But surely you wish him dead, Uncle?"

"Indeed I do and if Wulforr succeeds, then so much the better. But my primary goal is to ferment trouble and unrest in the area. That, in turn, will strengthen my case for using the Militia or even the City Guard to restore order. Who can object if our forces are merely enforcing the law? The eviction notices have been prepared?"

"They have, Uncle, though Captain Hermeros was somewhat reluctant when I instructed him."

"Hermeros! That decrepit sot has been commanding the Militia for far too long, we shall replace him soon. Should he exhibit any further hesitancy, just remind him who holds certain letters sent from a married Captain to a young serving wench!"

Malassos nodded, taking another sip of wine. "And the sorcerer? Is he a tool also?"

"I'll confess he makes my skin crawl but he is someone I would rather have as ally than enemy. In any case, I suspect even the greatest sorcerer is not immune to an unexpected dagger in the back..."

Malassos grinned evilly. "Just give me the signal, Uncle. I will be ready."

A weak, watery sun rose over the Old Market, illuminating a group of slowly trudging Militia, led by an unenthusiastic Captain Hermeros. A portly figure, atop a skittish bay horse, he frequently mopped his face and neck with a kerchief, despite the early morning chill. By the time the group reached The Bearpit, Meg was stood in the street, hands on hips.

"Morning, Meg," the Captain slowed to a halt and nodded.

"Morning Cap'n'. Might I enquire as to your business here today?"

The Militia shifted nervously, aware of the many eyes watching them from windows and rooftops.

"Orders of the Court. We have to post these notices of eviction. We don't want any trouble!"

Meg thought for a moment then shrugged.

"Very well, Cap'n. In you go. But groups of three at a time only! Folks here are nervous of armed men and I can't guarantee your safety if you go in mob handed."

The Captain nodded in agreement and Meg stood aside to let the men pass. Within minutes, small groups of apprehensive Militia were moving swiftly through the neighbourhood, nailing notices to various doors, then fleeing back to where the Captain waited, sipping from his flask. Notices posted, the group melted back over the bridge, leaving the locals to gather round the bills.

Few in the area could read but those that could relayed that the notices proclaimed each property had to be vacated by the end of the month. Following that, the full force of the law would be brought into play. Few denizens even realised that ownership of the buildings they lived in had changed. None could know that a cartel of powerful men had been slowly and secretly buying up almost every property in the Ratteries and the Old Docks. By the end of the day the neighbourhood was alive with rumour and gossip.

That evening Llorc was eating at The Bearpit when a familiar figure appeared in the doorway.

"Gaios!" the youth exclaimed. "What brings you here? Sit, will you have some ale, some food?"

"Just ale, Llorc. You have recovered from recent experiences, I take it?" The old soldier pulled up a bench and sat, elbows resting on the stained tabletop as Llorc poured ale for him.

"Aye, I have. And my gratitude for your aid and intervention."

"Think nothing of it, lad. It's just a shame that nothing could be done to save your friend. A man who gives his own life to save that of a comrade exhibits the highest qualities. Here's to Stanler."

Both men raised their mugs and drank. Gaios wiped his lips and leaned forward.

"But that is the past; I come to warn you of the future. I have received word that your old friend Wulforr has recruited more men for his mercenary band. He has them stationed up at the old North Barracks. Word is there is a price on your head that Wulforr plans to collect, that he is planning another assault on the Ratteries."

"And Adelphis would allow this group to operate within its walls?"

"Normally no, such a force would be a cause of concern but Toutatis has played a clever and long game. His men agitate in the market places against foreign influence. His allies in the Senate speak of the lawlessness rife in areas such as the Ratteries and of the *low-born immigrant scum* who live there.

In short, he has the Senate almost begging him to clean up this mess."

"To what end? What matters it to him how we live here?"

"Property, lad. The Old Docks are prime, waterfront property. There is talk of constructing new docks, of attracting more trade into the city, of building waterfront palaces for the rich and elite."

"Let me guess, it is Toutatis buying up the area?"

"Oh, he is not so open as that, but, aye it will be him, through other people. He is an ambitious man and quite ruthless. He will stop at nothing."

"And the book? He seemed most concerned over it."

"I know not, lad, I'm not one for letters. But he has some cursed sorcerer staying with him. Who knows what dark plans such a one may have."

Llorc cursed in his own tongue and took another swig.

"So this force, they mean to attack us?"

"Aye, lad, they do. Within the week I hear."

"Then we shall sell our lives dearly!"

Gaios shook his head. "Lad, have you learned nothing from me? Sell your own life by all means but what do you think that would achieve for the people who live here? The families, the children? You would serve only to inflame the situation. Think, boy, think! This is not about open battle!"

Llorc sat back and pondered."I understand. This calls for a different approach. We must think of this more like a hunt. You don't attack a whole pack, you break individuals away from the group. After all, we will be fighting in a maze, with some preparation we can channel and split Wulforr's forces."

"Now you are thinking, lad. But what numbers can you raise? Will you have enough arms to meet the challenge?"

"I don't know how many will answer the call now Stanler is not here. But there may be others who can help." Llorc stood and called out to Meg.

"Meg, can you get a message to Kagas?"

CHAPTER 15

King Thelios II grimaced as icy claws of pain gripped his insides once again. With an effort of will he returned his attention to the droning Senator in front of him.

"So you see, Majesty, we respectfully request that the current tax rate be adjusted in order to maintain a healthy profit margin for our indigenous traders, as opposed to giving a distinct advantage to outlanders who travel here to trade from other lands. The Senate feels that -"

"Yes, yes, that is fine, you have Royal assent." The King waved his hand as the Senator bowed and scuttled off. He shifted in his throne and whispered to his grey haired advisor. "How many more, Myonaris? I would rest."

"Just one more, Majesty," the aged, stooped retainer replied. "Senator Toutatis has requested an audience, he has a foreign dignitary visiting, I believe."

"Very well, send him, send him in." The King made an effort to appear regal. He pulled himself upright in his throne, adjusted the gold circlet on his balding pate, then rested his elbows on each side of the chair, thin arms held across his body, hands covering the pot belly. His face, aged at the best of times, was now lined with pain. He was, he knew, a far cry from the warrior kings of his forefathers' day but nonetheless he had ruled fairly and was well respected for the most part.

Now, sallow skin hanging from his bones, Thelios' only desire was to have enough time to prepare his young son, Prince Leonte, for the rigours of rule. To date, that had not been going well. He had thought that marrying again might have given the boy some stability but, if anything, it had the reverse effect. The marriage had also alienated much of the Adelphian aristocracy who, in line with tradition, wished him to wed one of their own daughters rather than a foreign Princess.

He glanced over at his young son, who sat fidgeting on a small throne set just to the side of the Royal Couple. Thankfully, the boy took more after his mother in looks, being somewhat plump and fair of complexion, where the King was dark. Blond curls fell over and around a soft, pale face and the boy's bottom lip seemed permanently thrust out in a display of petulant obstinacy.

"Are you well, Husband?" The Queen leant over in her throne and placed a cool hand on his forearm.

"Thank you, my dear, I will be fine." He smiled at his young Queen and wondered again at how kind she could be to such an old ruin as himself. His reveries were interrupted by the loud cry of the Door Herald.

"Senator Toutatis and the Dahkosh Khalsang of the Order of Lheng!"

The ever immaculate Toutatis swept into the audience chamber, bowing as he approached the dais on which the Royal Family were seated.

"Your Majesties, may I present the Dahkosh Khalsang."

Toutatis stepped aside with a flourish as a gaunt, saffron-robed figure glided forward and gave a slight bow to both King and Queen. The King was put in mind of a vulture. Nonetheless he graciously nodded in return and replied.

"Greetings and welcome to our fair city. How may we be of assistance?"

Khalsang replied in a tomb-dry voice. "We seek only access to the lower Catacombs of your city, as part of our ongoing research into ancient histories, Majesty."

"Well, I can see no problem in granting this access. What say you, Myonaris?"

"I have no objection, Majesty, though our esteemed visitor should be made aware that there are rumours and legends of dangers that lurk within the Catacombs."

Khalsang gave a thin smile. "Gratitude for your concerns but an Adept of Lheng has no fear of the dark."

"Oh, well, that is settled then. Good," replied the King. "And how are things in, er..."

"Yarlung, Majesty." Toutatis interjected with another bow. "All is well there, I believe. It is a place of much learning and development, unlike the more backward kingdoms that surround it." With this, he threw a mocking glance at the

Queen, whose hands tightly gripped the arms of her throne.

"Yes, well, I'm sure it is a lovely place. Now, unless there is any other business?" The King made to stand but a voice from the main doorway halted him in mid rise.

"Pardon, Your Majesty, might I speak to you in private on this matter?" It was Oresus, slightly flushed and breathless. He had only just heard of Toutatis' audience and had rushed here from the Temple.

"In private? Why, surely Oresus has nothing to say that cannot be said openly?" Toutatis sneered. "Speak your piece, priest!"

"I thought it was the King who commanded here, not Toutatis?" observed the Queen, at which Myonaris attempted to stifle a smile.

"Pardon, Your Majesty, I forget my place as a mere Senator." Toutatis bowed with a venomous glance at the young Queen.

"Nonetheless, speak openly, Oresus," pronounced the King. "We are all friends here."

Oresus sighed and strode forward to the dais, barely glancing at the sorcerer.

"Majesty, we know not what dangers lurk in the Catacombs, nor what other things may be buried there. Since learning of this...man's wishes, I have been carrying out research in our scrolls of lore. Some speak of a dark portal to Hell hidden deep within the Catacombs. In fact, some accounts claim the Catacombs were built in order to guard this gateway, in order that none may open it in the future."

Toutatis' mocking laughter floated across the audience chamber.

"Stories to frighten children. Good Khalsang seeks only to study certain ancient carvings believed to lie below. This talk of gateways is nonsense, Majesty."

The King seemed undecided, then Prince Leonte spoke.

"I should like to see the Catacombs, father. Are there really monsters down there?"

Toutatis seized the opportunity. "See them you shall, young Prince! We can send yourself and a group of Talons to ensure that no harm befalls anyone."

"Majesty," Oresus spoke again, with barely restrained anger. "Is it really advisable to allow a foreign... sorcerer," he fairly spat the word, "access to whatever might lay beneath our city?"

"You object to foreigners?" Toutatis glanced meaningfully at the Queen. "How interesting."

"It is not my people out inciting trouble in the streets against foreigners, Senator, so spare us your selective outrage!" Oresus responded, voice raising.

The King stood, another spasm of pain passing across his face.

"Enough!" he cried. "It is decided! Khalsang may visit the Catacombs in company of a group of Talons, at a time to be arranged. Leontes, you may accompany them. Now, we shall retire."

All in the room bowed as the King slowly left the room, accompanied by the Queen and the Prince. Oresus turned to face his brother.

"You fool, you know not with what you deal!" With a last withering glance at Khalsang, he span on his heel and exited the chamber.

A light sea fog rolled down the River Geryos as it flowed through the heart of Adelphis. The pale dawn sun brought a rosy glow to Pergares Bridge as it lifted above the horizon. A small boy sat at one end of the bridge, idly throwing stones into the water, when a noise caused him to quickly look up, then slide from the stone wall and dart off into street behind him. It was the tramp of feet, the jingle of harness and an occasional barked command, the sound of a war band on the move.

Through the fog a body of men slowly became visible. At their head strode Wulforr, bull-horn helm atop flaming red hair, chain mail hauberk glistening with condensation, scarred face set in grim purpose. In his hands he carried a large war axe. Behind him marched a group of more than three score hard-bitten warriors, the early morning rays glinting off their many different styles of arms and armour. Reaching the southern shore, Wulforr held up a hand and the band halted. The tall Njordir glanced around, sniffed the air, then hawked and spat into the river. With a wave of his hand, he motioned the band onward.

The group moved through the Old Market, strangely empty and quiet even for this time of morning. The streets remained totally empty as they marched into the square before the Ratteries, then halted in a loose formation. Some felt the glare of unseen eyes from side alleys and windows but no locals dared show their face. Wulforr had the instincts of an old warrior, though; something was twitching between his shoulder blades. While some of the band relaxed at the apparent ease of their forthcoming job, Wulforr tightened the grip on his two-handed axe and glanced around warily. His suspicions were confirmed when he waved the band on and they strode into the main street leading into the Ratteries.

Some yards ahead a barrier had been built across the street, a barricade of barrels, a wagon and some furniture. Atop it sat Llorc, swigging from a wineskin, seemingly without a concern in the world. He glanced up as the war band approached. Tossing the wineskin aside, he stood atop the barricade, his red cloak the only splash of colour in the drab surroundings, to look down upon the approaching group.

"Well now, if it isn't Toutatis' little red headed lap dog. Come to murder some more children have you? Care to face a man in open battle, or will you be running away like the spineless cur you are?"

Wulforr lifted his hand to halt the group. He planted the head of the axe on the ground and rested both hands on the end of the haft. Puffing out his chest he gave a curt nod to Llorc.

"And you are it, are you? The great defender? The mighty warrior who is going to take us all on by himself?"

Llorc sighed and shook his head. "No, not all by myself, Njordir. Unlike you, I have friends."

Llorc gave a whistle and heads appeared over the edges of the surrounding buildings. Garishly dressed, grins flashing white in sun-darkened skin, Kagas and some twenty of his pirates, many armed with short bows, looked down upon the mercenary band.

"Ho, Llorc," Kagas shouted down from his vantage point. "Are these the lasses you were talking about? Not the prettiest bunch, are they? Will they want to dance, d'ye think, or will they go running off back to mummy's teat?"

Wulforr snarled. "So, you have some pirate dogs! So what, you are still alone on that barricade!"

The Njordir was proven wrong again, as another score of heads popped over the barricade, local residents and gang members, armed with a hodge podge of weapons. A shout came up from the rear of the band and Wulforr turned to see children and adults swiftly pulling out old carts and barrels across the street behind them.

Only the side alleys now offered a way out but Wulforr was a veteran, he knew the best way out of an ambush was often to go straight forward. He lifted his war axe and gave a roar. Without waiting to see if anyone was following, the red haired warrior ran full pelt at the barricade in front of him.

Most of his band followed, though some turned to face any threat from the rear. At this, the pirates atop the roofs began loosing arrows down onto the mercenaries. Some of them grouped together and raised shields for protection but a number went down as feathered arrows sprouted from shoulders and necks. Those not going forward or back made a break for the alleyways at the sides and that was where Draccus and his rogues were waiting. Slings and rocks rained down on the men caught in narrow passageways, before the gang members darted in, stabbing with short words and knives. In the restricted space, the mercenaries were unable to deploy their usual tactics or weapons, and within minutes most were bleeding or dead. Those who attempted to stand and fight found no solid foes to hit, just a quick hit and run from lightly armoured, mobile attackers. And all the while, missiles rained down from above.

Wulforr made the barrier and gave a great leap to land atop it. A local feebly thrust a spear at him, which he contemptuously brushed aside then split the man's skull with an overhead swing of his axe. Other members of the band were close behind and, with a heave, they pushed part of the makeshift barricade aside.

As the band charged forward Llorc leapt down behind the barricade and drew his broadsword. He glanced at the nervous faces to the left and right and flashed them a grin. The men smiled back and gripped weapons tighter, then the first wave of attackers were on them. Two figures leapt up and over directly in front of Llorc. He aimed a slash at one's legs but the man twisted and leapt down behind Llorc. The other thrust out with a short spear from atop the barricade. Llorc dodged his head to one side, the spear point flashing over his shoulder. He grabbed the shaft with his free hand and yanked hard, pulling the man forward from his perch. Immediately he had to turn to face the first attacker, a short, wiry figure whose eyes blazed through the slits of his Adelphian helm.

The man stabbed at Llorc's belly with a short sword, simultaneously sweeping a large circular shield up in defence. Llorc batted the stab aside, then staggered back as the man struck him full on with the shield. Snarling a curse, Llorc swung at the man's face peering at him over the shield edge. The man deflected the blow, then glanced to his left. The glance saved Llorc's life, he immediately moved in the opposite direction, away from the second attacker who had discarded his spear for a curved sword. The sweeping cut hissed past and Llorc immediately returned a back-handed swing that caught the man in the ribs and crumpled him on the spot.

The first attacker saw his chance and moved in, stabbing again, shield held high. Llorc was able to keep the short sword at bay with his longer reach, but cursed in frustration as he was unable to find a way past the large shield. The man's eyes appeared to be mocking him over the rim of the shield, prompting Llorc to move in with a roar and begin raining down blow after blow. The man calmly absorbed the strikes, which had no more effect than denting the painted surface of the shield. He then suddenly thrust out again, the blade slicing into Llorc's leather armour, but not quite deep enough to draw blood. Llorc swore once more and the man laughed.

Calming his natural impulse to make an enraged charge straight into his enemy, Llorc instead had a sudden thought. He swung up as if to make an overhead cut and the man lifted his shield slightly in response. The barbarian immediately dropped to the ground, sword lashing out as he did so to cut the man deeply across the ankle. The man gave a shout and staggered. Llorc gave him no respite, grabbing the edge of the shield with his left hand, he pulled it aside and unleashed a terrible downward blow into the man's neck.

As his enemy fell lifeless to the floor, Llorc glanced around. Despite numbers, the locals were having a hard time holding the line against the more heavily armoured and experienced attackers. However, Kagas' archers were tilting the balance with their deadly aim.

Llorc careered into two mercenaries who had beaten one of the gang to his knees. As they prepared for a killing blow, Llorc's sword caught one across the back of the neck, then returned to stab deep into the side of the other. With a grunt of pain the man fell, to be finished off by the knives of the locals. Llorc glanced around again. Wulforr was but yards away, surrounded by four locals, each darting in and out with short swords. The Njordir's eyes blazed as he gave a defiant laugh and swung the terrible axe with deadly effect. Two of the men fell back, one grasping the bloody stump of an arm, the other clutching the ruin of a face.

With a downward swing, Wulforr chopped deep into the shoulder of the third attacker, a gout of blood spouting forth, vivid and bright in the morning light. The fourth man, thinking he had an opening, rushed in but he underestimated the speed of the war axe. It swung back with surprising speed and force, taking the man's head from his shoulders as though it were no more than wheat before the scythe. Wulforr, blood spattered and with the madness of battle in his eyes, howled and shook his bloody axe at Llorc.

"Come, Clannacht scum! Come and taste death!"

Llorc wasted no time on insult or boast. Something stirred deep in his blood, the ancestral feud between Clannacht and Njordir awakening a primal urge to kill in the young barbarian. Screaming his clan's war cry, Llorc hurled himself towards the grim figure. Halfway there, he had to convert his charge into a drop as the bloody axe swung in a powerful arc towards his chest. He hoped to get in close enough for a stab but the Njordir once again reacted with blinding speed, bringing the great axe down into a chop. Llorc rolled aside at the last minute, the blade biting into and tearing a great rent in his cloak. He thrust up and out as he sprang to his feet, a wild strike but it forced Wulforr back for a second and bought Llorc some time.

Llorc immediately went onto the attack, weaving a figure eight pattern of constant movement with his broadsword, swinging in tight arcs that Wulforr could barely deflect. The war axe was not a defensive weapon and needed time and space to wield. Just as he had settled into the pattern, Llorc broke it, spinning out of the figure eight in an unexpected direction. The blow caught Wulforr on the arm, but did not bite through the mail. The Njordir snarled and immediately thrust out with the head of the axe, catching Llorc in the chest and pushing him back. Given space, the great axe began its deadly swing again but this time Llorc had the measure of the weapon's range and fighting arc.

He ducked low and deep, under the swing of the axe, feeling it almost skim across his back, then straightened up inside the arc of its movement, thrusting his sword forward with all the power of his hips. The tip of the sword caught Wulforr under the heart and ripped through his mail as though it were paper. Llorc pushed forward, the blade passing through Wulforr to embed in the wooden door behind him, bringing him face to face with the Njordir. Wulforr's last act was to curse and split blood in Llorc's face, then his body went limp and the great axe fell from nerveless fingers.

Llorc took a second to recover, wiping the sweat and blood from his face. Glancing around he could see that the line was still holding, as more and more mercenaries fell victims to missile attacks. Some of the pirates had dropped down into the street and joined the hand to hand fray The war band had been broken up into several small groups, each of which was getting slowly worn down by the defenders. Soon only a small knot remained, forming a shield wall at the entrance to one of the alleyways. With no way out, they had little choice but to sell their lives dearly. The defenders gathered for one final attack, but Llorc jumped back up atop the barricade and waving his bloodied sword, shouted.

"Hold! Hold!" All combatants stopped and turned towards him. He jumped down into the street and walked towards the small band who nervously held shields upright and weapons at the ready. Llorc pointed his crimson blade at them.

"Cast down your weapons and go free, or fight and die.

Choose now!"

The group glanced amongst themselves then, as one, dropped their swords and spears into the dirt. The defenders moved in, as if for the kill.

"Back, back! Let them pass!" Llorc waved his sword, indicating the way. The crowd reluctantly moved aside as the mercenaries ambled out, eyes downcast. Of the three score who had marched in at dawn, only a dozen remained. Llorc barred their path before they could flee, fixing each in turn with a stern gaze.

"Tell Toutatis that we in the Ratteries are not his to order around. Our homes are not his to buy and sell. Come to us with swords and we will give you blood and pain. We are not to be cowed, beaten or bought, nor can we be scared and driven out. Tell him this!" The last was in a great shout.

The defenders roared their approval, waving bloodied weapons in the air. The remains of the war band swiftly moved out of the area, and none hindered their passing.

CHAPTER 16

Toutatis burst into his town house in a uncharacteristic flurry of agitation. Malassos had requested an audience in order to appraise him of recent developments and, from the rumours circulating, the news would not be good. The sorcerer and his manservant stood, inscrutable as ever, in the reception chamber. Malassos rose as Toutatis entered and nervously spoke.

"All goes well, Uncle. Our agents have been active in the market squares, we have public speakers on major street corners and the eviction notices have been posted in the Old Docks. Feelings are running high against the Queen and other foreign influences. Given the right circumstances it would be easy to mobilise the mob, I believe."

Toutatis nodded impatiently. "Yes, yes, I know all this, Malassos. But what of the Ratteries?"

Malassos scowled. "Ah, that news is not so good. I have received word from the survivors of Wulforr's force. It seems they were beaten back by numbers and sheer determination. The whole population turned out, assisted by pirate scum and led by that thrice-dammed barbarian. Even Wulforr fell before him! It would take an army to clear out that rat's nest."

"An army indeed," muttered Toutatis. "Still, we have good reason now to mobilise the Militia, though they fall somewhat short of being an army. The City Guard would prove far more capable but I have not yet the authority to command them."

The Sorcerer, who until now had stood quietly in the corner, glided forward.

"If I may offer a suggestion? Where swords fail, sorcery may triumph."

Toutatis glanced at the gaunt face. "You have something in mind, Khalsang?"

"Indeed, something that will serve dual purpose. It will assist with your own schemes and also demonstrate to you something of the capabilities of my order."

"What do you require? Name it, it shall be provided!"

"Few items are needed. An open space adjacent to the target area, a brazier, some ritual powders which I carry with me. And one other thing." The sorcerer paused and gave a ghoulish grin.

"What, man, what?" asked Toutatis.

"Simply a life, preferably one that is young and pure."

"You mean a sacrifice?" Even Toutatis was slightly aghast.

Khalsang merely bowed his head slightly in affirmation. Toutatis thought briefly, then made a decision. What was the life of some guttersnipe when weighed against the riches and prestige to be gained from redeveloping the Ratteries?

"Very well," he swallowed hard and nodded. "It shall be so." Kagas reached up to clap a hand on Llorc's shoulder.

"Well done, lad. You did Stanler proud"

The young man nodded and grasped the pirates forearm in appreciation.

"Gratitude, Kagas, we couldn't have done it without your crew."

"Ah, some of the crew, I brought as many as I could. The rest remain on guard and at work on the ship. We mean to put out to sea as soon as I get back, every day spent beached increases our risk of getting caught."

"Then you must away with all speed. Our work here is done."

"What will you do next, lad? You've won a victory today, but this could be a long and costly war. Those you fight have considerable resources and if they fall back on the law, you cannot fight the whole city."

"In truth, I know not," the youth sighed. "I don't know what Stanler had planned in the long term. You're right, we cannot fight the whole city, but I know no other path than to take up arms. I can't imagine any would speak up for us in the Senate. Money speaks louder than the voices of the poor here it seems."

"Not just here, lad, almost everywhere. But listen, if you want to kill the snake you need to strike off its head. You understand me?"

"I do, and you may be right. But if Toutatis is gone, does another step up to take his place? Maybe the only solution is for the people to move out but where to I do not know."

Kagas rubbed his bearded chin. "A puzzle indeed but one I'm

sure you will solve. You know you can rely on our help if needs be. But for now I must depart."

"Well I wish you fair wind and good hunting! There's always a safe harbour for you here, even if you do smell of fish!"

Kagas roared with laughter and clapped Llorc on the shoulder once more. Whistling up his crew, he gave a final wave and disappeared off towards the Old Docks.

Draccus appeared at Llorc's side, his leather armour torn and bloodied. Llorc pointed at the tear.

"You are wounded?"

"Just as scratch," Draccus replied. "I'll survive." He grinned and waved a hand at the scene around. "Well we gave them a bloody nose, didn't we. And with little cost. We have twelve dead and a score wounded. But the people's hearts are aflame, Llorc. You have shown them that they can fight and prevail!"

"I hope so, Draccus but I worry that I may have given them false hope. The next attack will likely not be so easily repulsed. But enough worry, the future is another day. For now, let us celebrate our victory and drink to our dead!"

The Royal Family, accompanied by personal servants and bodyguards, climbed the marble steps to The Temple. The King leant heavily on Myonaris, his face once more etched with pain. The Temple was the highest point in the city, situated on a small rise at the very apex of The Rock. The sun was dipping just below the horizon, its last rays flashing off the golden dome set atop The Temple's large white columns. The soft chime of bells and a faint smell of incense floated out from the interior on the evening breeze.

Once a week, the Royal Family attended a private ceremony to give thanks and seek aid from the Gods. As they entered the lamp-lit interior, Oresus stood ready before the altar, hands out, palms up, face tilted in supplication. To the right of the altar a blue flame burned steadily from a fissure in the rock floor. Behind it, through an opening in the wall, stone steps wound down into the darkness. This led to the Cavern of the Flame, the most holy part of The Temple. It was here that the High Priest communed directly with the Gods. Rumours spoke of further steps and passageways going from this chamber deep into The Rock; some claimed there to be an even deeper chamber wherein lay the slumbering body of Zantus himself.

Following the sacrifice and service, Oresus spoke softly to the Queen as the group took refreshment in an ante-chamber.

"His Majesty remains in pain?"

"He does, Oresus, more so each day. The draughts from the physic seem to have less and less effect. I fear the end is near."

Oresus sighed. "That is sad. I worry who or what may try and fill the gap left by the King's passing."

"Surely the crown shall pass to the Prince?"

"Normally, yes. But as he has not attained age, he cannot yet rule. It would be yourself who takes the throne as Queen Regent. In theory, the Senate can propose one of their own members as Regent but they never have done so in all our history."

"But with Toutatis in the ascendant..."

"Precisely, Majesty. Who knows how he may influence the Senate. We would be wise to fear the worst. Also this accursed sorcerer has me on edge. The greed and ambition of Toutatis I can understand and counter but who knows what infernal plans this seer has in mind?"

"He has not yet visited the Catacombs?"

"Not yet, Majesty. He claims he must wait for the right time, for some astrological alignment that is important to him. It stirs unrest within me, for why should the stars have any bearing on such a visit? It speaks to me of ritual but ritual for what, I do not know."

"Can you not counter any foul sorceries?"

"I have some skills, Majesty, but without knowing the specific nature of the ritual, or its purpose, I would be like a blind man struggling in the dark. If only we had managed to get possession of that blasted book, it may have given us some clue as to the villain's intentions!"

"The book was stolen once before. Might it not be stolen again?"

Oresus raised his bushy eyebrows and tilted his head to one side. "An interesting thought, Majesty but to sanction a Guard raid on a Senator's house would be akin to lighting a fire beneath us in the present political climate. Such a task would be best suited to a thief and, unfortunately, they are not the type of person I normally consort with."

The Queen gave a short laugh. "Dear Oresus, you need not be so coy with me. I know full well of your recent dealings. You have been discrete to be sure but there is little that happens in The Rock that I have not heard about. And was not the very thief in question recently held at Toutatis' own house?"

Oresus gave a broad smile and his shoulders rocked as he chuckled. "Majesty, you are constant source of surprise and delight to me. I must take care to be more covert in my dealings in the future lest all my secrets be laid bare to you! Indeed, the very youth who stole the book was held at Toutatis' house. I believe his freedom was exchanged for the book and the life of the master thief."

"Might we not speak to this thief? One so daring may be persuaded to help us. Could you arrange a meeting?"

"I could, but Majesty it is not seemly that a Royal personage such as yourself should associate with such a rogue. A low-born outlander at that!"

"We would be one outlander to another, good Oresus. Besides, I would see something of the man in order to judge his character. Added to which, the more links in the chain of communication, the more chance of our secret being discovered. No, I will speak to him in person to him at some discrete location. Please arrange it."

The enclosed coach rolled slowly through the Old Market, accompanied by six mercenary outriders. No light shone from within and any onlooker would have seen only two pale faces inside, Khalsang and Toutatis. Passang sat next to the coach driver, eyes warily scanning the surrounding streets and buildings. At this late hour, none were there to see the coach pull up outside a derelict building on the fringe of the

Ratteries. As the coach rolled to a halt, three armed figures emerged from the shadows, one opening the door for the passengers to alight. The man spoke quietly to Toutatis.

"All is in order, sir. We have secured the building, you will not be disturbed here."

"And the child and brazier?"

"Both up on the roof as you specified, sir"

"Good. Keep your men downstairs, guard all entrances to the building. We are not to be disturbed!"

The mercenary nodded and signalled to the rest of his men to take their positions. Toutatis, Khalsang and his servant moved swiftly up to the flat roof. From here, they looked down over the Ratteries, spread dark and still under the cloudy, night sky. In the centre of the roof was an unlit brazier and small lectern. In the corner, a young boy lay bound and gagged, eyes wide with fear. Khalsang reached into his bag and, removing the book, placed it open on the lectern. He turned to Toutatis.

"Stand here, next to the lectern. Whatever occurs, do not step outside of the circle."

Toutatis nodded and swallowed nervously. However, he could not deny the small thrill that ran through him at the prospect of seeing real sorcery in operation. Khalsang took out a phial and, unstoppering it, began pouring red powder out in a large circle, chanting in a low voice as he did so. Before the circle was complete he motioned for Passang to bring the child within the circle and to light the brazier. Once both were done, the circle was closed.

The sorcerer now produced a curved knife from inside his robes and, consulting the book, began making passes with it in the air, all the while continuing the chant, his face infernal in the sulphurous glow. Passang dragged the boy close to the brazier as the chant increased in pitch and intensity. A wind blew up, fanning the flames of the brazier, lifting sparks up and into the night air. The sparks did not fly away but seemed to congregate in a spot just outside of the circle. They began to assume a vaguely humanoid shape.

As the chanting reached fever pitch, Passang lifted the boy and, swiftly and without mercy, slit his throat in such a way that the unfortunate's blood flowed directly onto the brazier. The flames took on a darker hue and flickered with unnatural life. Toutatis shivered and pulled his cloak around him. More sparks rose and were added to the figure, which assumed a more and more solid outline. It soon resolved into the figure of a burning man, dark holes where eyes should be. It lifted flaming arms and a whispery voice issued from it.

"Command me!"

Khalsang pointed out over the Ratteries.

"There! Go! Burn!"

The figure twisted, flickered, then shot into the air like a comet, with a sound of crackling flames. Up and out it flew, in a curved trajectory that took it into the heart of the maze of streets and old buildings. The men on the roof watched as it landed on another flat roof, which immediately began to smoulder, then flame. They watched the distant figure flit from building to building like a firefly, leaving a deposit of flame wherever it touched. Soon the distant crackle of flames reached their ears, the smell of burning touched their nostrils, and still the flaming figure moved from building to building.

"Come, Toutatis, we are done here. We may now leave the circle." Khalsang turned toward the stairs.

"Will the creature not need more guidance?"

"None will be necessary. It is an Elemental, limited of intelligence, but fixed in purpose. It seeks only to burn, to express its primal nature. The spell to bring it here will not last long, it will soon return to its own plane. But in the meantime it will have achieved our purpose. Let us see how swords fare against flame!"

With that the trio left the roof and were soon travelling back to the Old City.

Llorc awoke with the smell of burning in the air and cries of "Fire!" ringing through the building. He had decided to stay over in the Ratteries while things were so unsettled. With a curse, he grabbed his sword, slid into his boots and ran out into the narrow street. An orange glow filled the sky, smoke came billowing out of the windows of the old warehouse opposite. People were running back and forth, some carrying buckets.

The fire seemed to be spreading like a living thing and within minutes a large section of the Ratteries was an inferno. The wooden shacks and huts caught quickly and the flames passed easily across the narrow alleyways. Once the alarm had been sounded, the crowd grabbed buckets or whatever they could and began chains carrying water from the river to the blaze but they fought a losing battle. With a crash and roar a whole warehouse wall collapsed, burying several people beneath it and the crowd moved back onto the Old Docks. Llorc stood amongst them, impotent rage building as he watched the devastation spread. Then something caught his eye, a man shaped fiery figure that leaped and capered in the flames, moving from building to building.

"Look! Up there!" He pointed and heads turned towards the strange figure.

"What in Zantus' name is that?" croaked a young man. His companion wasted no time in conjecture but loaded, then lifted his crossbow to his shoulder. Taking a second to steady himself he aimed, then released the bolt, which flew in a flat trajectory to hit the figure in the leg. The crowd let out a cheer, which was quickly dulled by the realisation that the bolt seemed to have passed clear through and thing had not fallen. Instead, it turned a fiery face towards the crowd, as if seeking out the source of this intrusion into its activities.

At once the thing sprang and flew towards them, scattering the crowd as it landed on the dockside. Only Llorc remained, sword hissing as it left its scabbard. The creature appeared to be a living flame, man shaped, small orange and red tongues of fire constantly flickering over its surface. It turned empty eyes on Llorc and advanced. The barbarian could feel the heat of its approach and struck out with a savage cut towards the thing's outstretched hand. To his horror the blade passed completely through the arm as though there was nothing there. Before he could recover from this surprise, the thing grabbed Llorc's wrist in a burning grip that sent a wave of agony through his body. The smell of burning hair and flesh filled the air and Llorc leapt back in pain, switching his sword to the left hand.

As he did so another crossbow bolt hurtled through the air, this one hitting the flame creature in the chest. This time the bolt stuck, the thing seemed to have more mass at its centre. Heartened by this knowledge, Llorc struck for the thing's centre mass. The blade pierced the thing's body and Llorc felt more resistance the deeper the blade pierced. Did the thing have a heart? It seemed not, the blow perhaps slowed the creature slightly but had no other effect.

It advanced again, arms creating a fiery trail as they reached and grabbed for him. This time he twisted away and was able to avoid contact but in doing so could not bring his sword into play. He realised he was backing up along the wharf and space was running out. As he glanced around for an avenue of escape a sudden thought sprang into his mind.

"Nets!" he shouted to the crowd, who hung back hesitantly. "The nets! Throw the nets!"

Some of the crowd reacted immediately. Draped over part of the wharf were old fishing nets, long disused. Heavy with dampness they were, it took two men to lift each one. As Llorc danced out of reach of the fiery hands, the nets were flung over the creature. It turned to meet this new threat but its movements were now hampered by their weight. The old rope began to steam but, damp as they were, the nets did not yet burst into flame. In the meantime, others in the crowd had grabbed poles and sticks. Swiftly they advanced on the creature, pushing and prodding it back until it reached the edge of the wharf until, with a final push, the thing was pitched into the dark, still water. There was a mighty hiss and huge cloud of steam. Some later claimed they heard a shrill, high pitched scream as the thing flickered and faded. Soon there were only the empty nets floating on the surface.

Llorc grimaced and examined his wrist. Large blisters in the form of a hand grip were raised on his skin, his forearm throbbed like hell. Gritting his teeth, he sheathed his sword and dipped his hand in a water bucket. Then he turned his attention back to the conflagration.

Little could be done but to pull back and keep people safe. The only relief came later that night with a downpour of heavy rain, which at least halted the advance of the flames. All through the night, people worked to move family and meagre possessions and more than one perished while seeking a loved one or some personal item amidst the flames.

When dawn came, it was barely visible through the haze of smoke that filled the sky and drifted slowly across the river. No help had come from any other quarter; the rest of the city, it seemed, had been content to let the Ratteries burn. Daylight revealed the full extent of the damage. Llorc and Draccus walked the streets along with the community leaders, every smoke-stained faced etched with anger and grief. Anger at the ruined shells of buildings that had been homes, grief at the number of adult and child bodies that lay in rows on the dockside, covered in makeshift shrouds.

"Kagas was right." Llorc wiped his smoked filled eyes with the back of his hand. "This is a war. And one we are hard pressed to win."

Draccus drank deeply form a water flask and passed it to Llorc. "What was that thing? They say it was flame in man shape?"

Llorc took a swig and replied. "I know not, but it was certainly not of this world. The work of Toutatis' pet wizard, I'll wager. Word has come in of a child's body and sorcerous markings found on a nearby roof. The bastard, what sort of man can do such a thing, Draccus, if man he be and not devil-spawned?"

"Oh, he is a man alright." Draccus took back the flask. "Stanler told me something of what he had found while researching that damned book. This sorcerer is of the Order of Lheng, they are a priesthood that rule a country called Yarlung, in the East. It seems these sorcerers are chosen at a young age, barely more than babies. It is believed that when they die they are reborn anew into another body, in order to continue their work. The chosen new born are taken into the monasteries and prepared for a life of sorcerous priesthood. They know nothing of earthly pleasures, no wine, no women, no song their whole life is devoted to the dark arts. At fifteen summers they undergo some test where only the strongest and most skilled survive. There is no escape from the Order but death."

Llorc shook his head. That men should submit to such a regime was beyond him. "Your civilisation never ceases to surprise me, Draccus."

"Not mine, Llorc, but I take your point. In any case, this man is a dangerous foe, what are we to do?"

"What Kagas advised," grunted Llorc. "Cut off the head of the snake."

CHAPTER 17

The atmosphere in The Bearpit was muted. The smell of smoke still hung in the air, most present had it embedded in their clothes. The day after the fire, Meg had rallied together the traders and set up a soup kitchen in the Old Market. Lines of bedraggled, red-eyed refugees from the Ratteries soon formed, grateful, at least, to get a hot meal. Most of the children were taken in by local families. As ever, the worst of situations brought out the best in people. Those who had perished in the flames were laid to rest in the burial ground on the other side of the square. Guryon spoke words over the departed and his followers helped comfort the bereaved and injured.

Llorc was sat plotting with Draccus and some of the gang when a small red-haired girl ran in to tell of riders and a carriage and a wagon that had pulled up outside. Before Llorc had a chance to reach the door to see for himself, Gaios was framed in the doorway. He nodded to Llorc and motioned him to follow outside, where he strode to a wagon and pulled back the cover.

"Blankets, some clothes, some provisions. It's not much but we hope it will help."

Llorc was taken off guard. "But what...where did this come from?"

"I cannot say but it is offered without expectation of recompense. A gift to those in need, from one who wishes to help. Ask no more but accept and distribute."

Llorc called for Meg, explaining the situation to her. Meg nodded, beamed at Gaios, then immediately set to work with her team of helpers.

"Will you stay and have ale?" Llorc asked.

"Nay lad, but I would ask that you come with me. There is a person who would like to meet you. The person who organised these gifts."

The bemused Llorc nodded and soon found himself seated in the plush carriage which carried him across town and through the Old City. It was when they began to climb the winding road up The Rock that he became perturbed.

"Fear not," laughed Gaios, "we shall not be calling on Toutatis. Oh, I will need your sword though."

Llorc bristled. "The last time I went out without my sword, I found myself in a cell. Still, it was you who tried to get me out, so..."

The youth unbuckled his sword belt and handed it over to the old soldier. In time the carriage passed through a number of gateways and shortly drew to a halt in a large stable yard.

The pair disembarked and Llorc was quickly led by a Talon through a door in the wall and into a small, enclosed garden. The inside walls were lined with beds full of fragrant yellow flowers and at the centre was a tinkling fountain, by which sat an elegantly carved wooden bench. The surrounding walls were high, the garden overlooked only by some shuttered windows in the ivy-clad tower that loomed over it. At the foot of the tower was a heavy, closed door.

He was inside The Citadel, Llorc guessed, perhaps even in the Palace itself. The door behind him was shut and the Talon stood in front of it, eyes never leaving Llorc. Gaios had not come through the door with him, so having nothing else to do, Llorc sat on the bench and, for the first time in days, began to relax. His bandaged forearm still throbbed but sheltered from the wind here, the sun was warm on his face. He stretched his limbs out and enjoyed the peace, so much so that he began to drift into sleep.

He was pulled from his revery by the sound of the tower door being opened and a slight, feminine cough. He looked up to see a fair haired young lady, dressed in a fine white toga, walking towards him. She carried a silver tray on which was a pitcher of wine and a jewelled goblet. Placing the tray beside him, the woman moved back into the doorway.

As Llorc poured himself a goblet of wine, another figure loomed through the doorway, a large, fearsome looking man with a beard and turban, a heavy scimitar hanging at his waist. The man moved aside and, crossing his arms over his broad chest, leant against the wall. Like the Talon, his eyes never left

Llorc. Following this came a petite, black haired woman with light brown skin. She was dressed in a plain but expensive dress and wore a finely crafted silver circlet upon her head. Without pause she strode up to Llorc as if to sit beside him. Llorc guessed who this may be but had no notion whether to sit, stand or bow. The Queen, sensing his discomfort, smiled.

"No need to stand, young man. Just let me sit here, I would talk with you awhile."

Llorc nodded, bowed his head, then moved aside to make space for the Queen.

"I will come straight to the point as I hear you are a direct man. You once stole a certain book belonging to Toutatis, correct?"

"I er, well, you see..." Llorc for once was lost for words.

"Fear not, I seek not to punish you for this action, merely to ascertain the truth."

"Yes, milady, I stole the book. Though it was later returned in exchange for my freedom. And the life of my friend."

"Indeed, I had heard this. We feel this book may represent a threat to us. We would feel much safer if this book were in the hands of our own priesthood and not that of a foreign sorcerer, whose mind and plans we know not. Do we make ourselves clear, young man?"

"You wish me to steal the book again? But why me? Surely you command an army?" Llorc gestured to the Talon. "Why not send a squad of these in?"

"Because to send Talons into the house of a Senator for no good reason would be to invite trouble and unrest. Already many hearts are turned against us, this would only add fuel to the fire that certain people seek to spread. As for why you, well, you have already demonstrated that you are capable of the task and have the necessary skill and courage to accomplish it. In addition, I hear you have certain qualities, that you show compassion for others, a rare commodity in this city."

"I merely seek to protect those who need protection against those who would bring them harm, but I am no saint, to be sure!"

The Queen laughed. "Your honesty does you credit, young man and sometimes the best wine may be served in a chipped cup. I trust the aid that was sent will assist? If we can, we shall send more."

"Thanks. milady, it will indeed help. The people of the Ratteries will be most grateful to you."

"No, they must never know, it shall be our secret. If it was known that the outland Queen had aided the low born of the Ratteries, well... who knows what would happen?"

Now it was Llorc's turn to laugh. "A wealthy person who seeks no public credit for a charitable act? Your humility does *you* credit."

Llorc raised the goblet in a toast.

"I give my word I shall do my best to deliver the book into your hands, milady."

The Queen nodded and her face became set in a serious frown. "Indeed. It need not be explained that this meeting never happened and should you be captured, no assistance can be offered."

"I understand."

"Very well, it is decided. Gaios will be your point of contact." She called back to the waiting maid. "Calinope, you may take away these things." Then she turned once more to Llorc. "Good luck, young man, may your Gods be with you."

Llorc bowed stiffly. "Thank you, milady."

The Queen nodded and turned to walk away. Before she did she glanced back over her shoulder and with small smile and a twinkle in her eye said, "Oh, you should call me Your Majesty, not milady."

Then she was gone, along with the turbaned bodyguard. As the maid collected the tray and goblet, the Talon rapped on the outer door. Gaios opened it and stepped through, motioning Llorc back into the carriage and soon they were winding back down The Rock towards the Old City.

At the appointed hour, Passang moved slowly into the upper chamber of the town house, carrying a small tray of fruit and a jug of water. Khalsang sat cross legged, immobile on a mat, eyes closed, face impassive, fingers curled into an esoteric hand seal. Passang gently placed the tray on the low table, then softly the chimed the small gong sat atop it three times. As the last of the sonorous notes died away, the sorcerer's eyes opened and he gave a great inhale, as of a man coming up from the deeps of the ocean for air.

Khalsang took a minute to re-orient himself then reached for the tray. His order demanded very strict dietary requirements but it was important to keep the body nourished, so it may serve as a vessel for the soul.

"What news, Master?" Passang bowed.

"The elemental did its work, though it seemed to perish in some way. No matter, it served its purpose."

"And the inhabitants of the slum? The barbarian?"

"It is most peculiar." For the briefest second the sorcerer appeared perplexed. It was not an emotion Passang had seen his Master display before; the experience was unnerving. Khalsang continued.

"I attempted to view events there through the ethereal plane, yet could not. It is as though there is a fog or barrier surrounding the area. I was able to make out only indistinct shapes and features. This is most irritating. I am not aware of any other adepts in the city, yet can think of no other source for such a barrier."

"The priest, Master? Oresus and his brethren?"

Khalsang's lip curled back in disdain. "Burners of incense and intoners of empty prayers. No, this is something else. I shall make a further attempt tonight."

Khalsang took his food and drink as Passang relayed news and events from the day. "Master, Toutatis has pressed me again on the Catacombs visit. He seems most eager for us to conclude our business and be gone."

The sorcerer spat out a grape pip. "The fool. The time is still not right and I will not risk failure at this late stage. The ancient writings are most specific about celestial alignments. Without the expenditure of considerable power, the gateway will only open at certain junctures - and these come but once in hundreds of years. It was by using the power of such alignments that the Old Ones were imprisoned by the Ancients. They had the secret of tapping the knowledge of those beings, a secret lost until now."

"And there exists no other gateway, Master?"

"There are rumours and legends. One is said to lie deep beneath the Great Pyramid of Sahkmet. Tales tell of others in hidden places in the forgotten corners of the world. The Adelphian gate is the only other known location. For at one time this was a haunt of great and powerful sorcerers, long before these accursed priests and traders colonised the area. If only they knew what lay beneath their feet!"

The sorcerer sighed heavily and Passang flinched slightly.

"I crave pardon for my ignorance, Master. Let me clear away these things."

The manservant busied himself with the tray and Khalsang rose to his feet, stretching like a gaunt, angular cat. His joints popped as he worked through the body positions taught to his order.

"One more thing, Master." Passang paused at the door before exiting. "Toutatis has requested further instruction in using the grimoire. I think he sees it merely as a tool to consolidate his power."

"Let him think that. Tell him I will give him further instruction tomorrow. Once the gateway is opened and we establish contact with the Old Ones, what Toutatis wants or doesn't want will be irrelevant. We will establish a new order here in Adelphis and none shall stop us!"

Llorc tightened and rechecked the straps on his dark clothing. Sword slung across his back, he also carried a dagger at each hip and a sack tucked into his leather jerkin in which to place the book. Despite previous advice to the contrary, he was determined to carry his sword this time. It at least gave him the option of cutting his way out of trouble. Finally satisfied, he slipped downstairs from his room at The Bearpit and into the waiting carriage, which set off at brisk pace through the dark streets.

Just before reaching the Old Gate, the carriage drew to a halt and three figures boarded. All were masked, though the outline of Gaios was obvious to Llorc. A few whispered words were exchanged, Gaios explaining that the trio would hang back outside the property to deal with any pursuit, while one of them would take charge of the book from Llorc and deliver it straight to Oresus.

The carriage was swiftly waved through by the Guards at the Old Gate and not far past the Old City wall, the carriage halted once more, a few streets from Toutatis' town house. Like ghosts the four figures melted into the shadows and glided noiselessly to their destination. Within sight of the courtyard wall, Llorc halted and checked himself once more.

"Give me until the moon touches that spire," Llorc pointed up. "That should be enough time."

"Good luck, lad," Gaios muttered, "and remember, this is all about the book. Leave personal feeling aside!"

Llorc's eyes flashed in the moonlight but he nodded and padded quietly away into the narrow alleyway at the rear of the property. With a leap and a stretch he caught a handhold on the lip of the wall and pulled himself up and over, dropping softly into the courtyard. The house was dark and quiet. The night air was still, only the faint bark of a distant dog disturbed the air. From the shadows, Llorc checked each window in turn for signs of light. Seeing none he moved in half crouch towards the rear door. Grasping the handle he slowly pushed down and in but the door would not budge. He withdrew a small oilskin pouch from his jerkin and, kneeling, applied one of the tools therein to the gap between door and frame. Within seconds, he had the latch lifted and the door, this time, opened to his touch.

Moving inside, the youth gently shut the door behind him and allowed his eyes to adjust to the interior gloom. The layout of the house was well known to him but the exact whereabouts of the book was not. Llorc made a careful inventory of the downstairs rooms, avoiding those doors he heard snoring behind, presumably staff quarters. Satisfied, he set a foot carefully on the stairs and began to ascend.

Thinking it was best to start in the most obvious place, Llorc moved past the bare plinth, directly to the large chamber at the end of the upstairs passageway. All remained dark and still, his tread making no more noise than a cat. Drawing a dagger with one hand, he gently pushed the door open with his other. There was a faint glow in the room, the source a small flame from a palm oil light. It cast flickering shadows around the room and illumined the gaunt face of Khalsang! The youth involuntarily started, then paused and stopped himself. The sorcerer's eyes were closed, he sat cross-legged on a dark mat. There seemed to be no sign of life, in the dark the youth could not even make out any rise and fall of the chest.

Llorc struggled with the dilemma. The book was the aim of the mission but a single slash could end the life of this fiend! Llorc gritted his teeth and cursed his indecision. His delay proved costly. The sorcerer's eyes snapped open, curiously aglow in the faint, orange light. That burning gaze snapped Llorc out of his mental torpor. With a bound he was across the room but Khalsang had reflexes honed by years of intense training. He flung his hands up and uttered a single syllable, a word that rang in Llorc's ears and hung in the air.

To his fury, Llorc found himself unable to move. Though he strained every muscle and sinew, he felt as though heavy chains lay over his limbs. Llorc's lips were drawn back in a snarl as the sorcerer arose, tendons stood out on his arm as he strove in vain to drive the dagger forward into his enemy's chest.

Khalsang approached close, as though examining some exhibit in a museum, or a captive animal in a zoo.

"Interesting! There am I wandering the ethereal plane for sign of you and here you are, in the flesh. How serendipitous!"

Llorc was unable even to respond, the only movement he was capable of was to roll his eyes. He watched helpless as the sorcerer inspected him.

"Most puzzling. You are obviously a powerful physical specimen, yet there is no trace of sorcery about you. How is it you remained hidden from me?"

Llorc found he was able to make a strangled reply, though the effort broke beads of sweat out on his forehead.

"Not... hiding... want...you...dead..."

Khalsang shrugged and took a step back.

"What you want is irrelevant. You are nothing but a savage, out of place amongst your civilised betters."

"Civilised...child...killer...I... spit on... your... civilisation."

Khalsang sneered. "How tiresome. So you despise civilisation, barbarian, but here you are in its beating heart. You desire its wine, its riches, its women. You come here to find power, fortune, fame, things no more substantial than the smoke that filled your slum but two nights ago."

At mention of this, Llorc strained once more, blood pounding in his temples, teeth grinding.

"Yet it may surprise you, barbarian, to know that I share your disgust for this pigsty." Khalsang waved his hand in a vague gesture. "Though for reasons your dull mind could scarcely comprehend."

There was a rap at the door and Passang entered. "I heard voices, Master, I... ah!"

The servant seemed to derive satisfaction from seeing the barbarian paralysed as he was.

"I was concerned, barbarian," Khalsang continued, "that you had some special interest in our affairs, or some sorcerous ability. But now I see you are nothing more than a dumb brute with a sword. Passang, deal with this animal, will you?"

What passed for a smile flickered across Passang's features, he drew the small curved knife from his belt.

"Not in here, take him downstairs. Muffle his screams with a cloth. I shall relax the spell so he may walk."

Khalsang made a pass with his hands and Llorc found he had some movement returned to his legs. He tensed as if to spring but found his movement cut short at the hips. Instead, he staggered, into the waiting arms of Passang, who grabbed him roughly by the shoulder and pushed him out of the door and along the passageway.

Llorc redoubled his efforts as they trod down the stairs, but to little effect. Did he imagine, though, the spell to feel a little weaker the further they moved away from the sorcerer?

The noise had awoken some of the household staff, who came out to discover the cause of the disturbance. Passang motioned them to open the kitchen and light the lamps, clearing the kitchen table and pushing Llorc back against it.

"I've not forgotten my ribs, barbarian," he hissed. "I will make this very slow and very, very painful!" Then, to the servants. "Fetch a rag for his mouth and rope to bind him. This may take some time."

Llorc struggled anew, kicking out with his legs but the Easterner easily avoided the clumsy movement. Before he knew it, Llorc's hands were twisted behind his back and tied, a cloth stuffed in his mouth. A deep growl born of anger and frustration hummed in his throat as Passang lifted the knife, holding the blade close to Llorc's left eye as if to show him the instrument of his torture

Of a sudden there was a crash, the sound of a door splintering. It was followed by three masked figures bursting into the room, short swords drawn. The house staff scattered like hens, as Passang turned in surprise.

Llorc, regaining some mobility, took the opportunity to butt the Easterner squarely in the face. The Easterner shot back, blood pouring from his nose, crashing into a shelf, plates and dishes falling with a smash to the floor. Even so, he was quick to recover, the curved knife shooting out in a vicious arc, forcing Llorc back into the table. One of the masked figures grabbed Llorc and dragged him, still snarling, eyes fixed with murderous intent on Passang, out of the room.

There were shouts from other parts of the house, followed by drumming footsteps and the light of a torch as figures pursued the trio and Llorc into the courtyard. One of the trio stood firm with drawn sword, to buy the others time to escape. Llorc's bonds were cut and feeling began slowly returning to his limbs, with some help he was able to clamber up and over the wall. He paused at the top to look back.

The colleague with the sword held three of the house staff at bay but one fellow was braver than the others. He lunged forward to grapple the intruder. His reward was a crack on the head with the sword hilt but as he fell he took the intruder's mask with him. The face of Gaios was revealed clear in the light of the torch held aloft by one of the servants. With a curse, Gaios turned and ran, leaping up so that Llorc could grasp his hand and help pull him over the wall. Without pause, the four ran full pelt through the streets, all thoughts of stealth gone, until they reached the safety of the coach. Within minutes, they were rolling back through the Old Gate towards The Bearpit.

A couple of stiff drinks later and Llorc had fully recovered his faculties. He cursed in his own tongue and banged the cup down on the table.

"Apologies, Gaios. I hesitated like a boy on his first hunt. I should have killed the sorcerous dog without delay."

"No matter, lad." Gaios drained his mug. "With no sight of the book, Khalsang' death would have been a good enough prize. But we have bigger problems now."

He smiled as Meg swayed over to place another full mug before him on the stained tabletop, then returned his gaze to Llorc.

"Firstly, I was seen and perhaps recognized. A former City Guard assisting in the theft of a Senator's house is heavy ammunition for Toutatis. Second, we may have incurred the further wrath of his cursed warlock."

"What next, then?"

"More trouble, boy, that's what. I think it may be best for me to lay low in the Ratteries for a few days, if that can be arranged?"

"Aye, it may. We still have places, despite the damage caused by the fire fiend. My people will hide you well. We will keep everyone mobilised too, in case of further incursions.

"And then?"

"I will get word to the Queen. We can't expect direct intervention but she may be able to turn wheels behind the scenes. And promise me one thing, lad?"

"What's that?"

"That if you are ever in blade distance of that devil in human form again, you strike without delay!"

Llorc grunted in assent. "By Morrg, I swear it!"

CHAPTER 18

Bells tolled across the city in the late afternoon gloom. From the smallest chapel to the main Temple atop The Rock, they rang a mournful peal. All knew what it meant; the King was dead. He had passed away peacefully in his sleep early that morning. Word spread quickly throughout the Palace, from there through The Citadel, then flowing down like a river, to the city below. A large beacon had been lit atop the The Rock and preparations were already under way for a state funeral.

Toutatis stood stiff and proud, a small smile playing around his lips, as Phileos fussed with his robes and regalia. He had already called an emergency meeting of the Senate because of last night's events at his town house. The King's passing brought another reason to meet and could not have suited Toutatis better in terms of timing. *At last, the old King has proved useful!* Satisfied with his appearance, Toutatis waved his servant away and stepped out to his chariot for the short ride to the Senate building. He knew most of the members would already be in place, his supporters already no doubt spreading discontent amongst them. Toutatis always liked to arrive slightly late, so all heads turned as he entered. *If all goes well tonight, they may soon be bowing to me*, he reflected.

The atmosphere in the chamber was highly charged, a combination of grief at the King's passing mixed with outrage at the incursion to Toutatis' property. Some feelings were genuine but many were contrived. With a slight pause to draw breath and puff out his chest, Toutatis entered the large, circular room. As he anticipated, the murmur of voices from the surrounding benches quieted and all eyes turned to face him. Seizing the moment, without pause, he strode to the centre of the floor. Nodding to the assembled, he addressed the Foreman.

"May I speak, good Knassos?"

"Indeed, you may," replied the venerable Foreman, long in Toutatis' pay.

"Fellows," Toutatis began, feet astride, one hand clasped to his toga at the chest.

"Colleagues! Brothers! Adelphians!" The last was in raised voice and a murmur of approval ran through the assembly.

"First, let me express the grief of the Senate at the sad news we received today. King Thelios was a giant of a man, a most wise and loved ruler."

Once again, the ripple of assent.

"I understand that preparations are already under way for

the funeral. We will, of course, give every support to the young Prince at this time."

"But what about the Queen?" A supporter of Toutatis shouted out the prearranged question.

"The Queen?" Toutatis scowled and strove to affect an expression of outrage.

"This foreign Queen? This Queen who flouts our fine Adelphian customs? This Queen who would fill our court with outlanders and their strange ways?"

A low murmuring went around the room, many shaking their heads in disapproval.

"This Queen who spits on our traditions, who consorts with known villains, whose City Guard ransack and rob a Senator's house, attacking his staff and guests? I ask you, is this a Queen fit to rule?"

Toutatis flung a hand up in the air to emphasis the point, his supporters amongst the assembly now baying and jeering. Toutatis raised his voice above the din, making a cutting motion with his hand as each point was made.

"No, I say! No, we will not be dictated to! This city is our own, our homes are our own, our traditions are our own! Adelphis for Adelphians!"

He repeated the chant and it was taken up enthusiastically by the Toutatis faction, then spread to many others. There were those, though, who kept silent and turned away quietly in disgust. Toutatis raised a hand to silence the room.

"Be calm, my friends. Now is not the time for politics. Now is the time for mourning. Let us bury our dear King and pay him due respect. Further, I propose, Foreman, an open vote on electing a Regent to rule until such times as Prince Leonte attains age."

"Seconded!" a voice immediately shouted.

"Show hands," proclaimed the Foreman. "All in favour!"

Almost all hands in the chamber were thrust upward. The Foreman did not need to call for nays. He banged his staff on the marbled floor.

"Motion carried! We reconvene post-funeral to vote on whether the Queen is to rule or whether a Senate Regent is to be voted in to rule until the Prince comes of age."

Toutatis allowed himself a wry grin of triumph as his supporters gathered round him to clap him on the back.

While preparations were being made for a State funeral in the Old City, the denizens of the Ratteries were busy in their own way. Following meetings with community leaders and gang members, the decision had been made to resist any coming evictions. Fire-ruined buildings were torn down and the rubble and blackened timbers used to create barricades across the main streets. Overseen by Llorc and with the assistance of Gaios, more barriers were made that would effectively funnel attackers into specific streets and alleyways. Rocks, flasks of oil and other missiles were placed in readiness on surrounding roofs. Those ruins not demolished were converted into strongholds. The call went out far and wide, to kith and kin near and far to come and aid in the defence of the area.

Calls also went out to rival gangs across the city. Following a back and forth of messengers, a meeting of all the major gang leaders was organised, set on neutral ground - the back room of a large brothel in the southernmost quarter of the city. The brothel was operated by one Callianessa and catered to the whims of many members of Adelphian high society. As such, she had enough riches and influence to remain above the machinations of the city gangs.

Llorc, Draccus and Gaios arrived at the building just before noon on the allotted day. From the outside, it was rather plain and unprepossessing, it could have been some civic building or a library, perhaps. The three men mounted the steps and were shown in though a heavy, ornate door with a small shuttered window in it. The staid impression quickly disappeared as the interior was revealed; richly decorated with ornate hangings, a large fountain, finely-woven rugs and numerous statuettes, urns and busts. Soft music floated through the air, which also carried the heady scent of opiates and incense. Scantily dressed courtesans lounged on couches; a black panther, restrained with a silver chain, gave a low growl and bared its fangs.

In one corner of the room, still as a statue, stood a large man, arms crossed over chest. His scarred, dark face and broken nose gave him the appearance of an old soldier, or at least of a man familiar with violence.

Callianessa herself, accompanied by a half naked, fan-waving, muscular youth, glided over like some stately warship to greet them. She offered a heavily bejewelled hand for each of them to kiss. Her outward appearance bespoke sophistication and wealth, though Llorc recognised something steely in her gaze. He had the impression this was not a woman to cross.

"Greetings! Welcome, one and all!" She gestured towards a door at the back of the room. "Your colleagues have arrived, please come through. Wine and food are in place. Following your meeting please feel free to avail yourselves of our facilities. You are most welcome here!"

Llorc thought that her mouth said one thing but her eyes said something else He had not missed the fleeting expression of disdain as the madam had first taken in their appearance and clothing.

"One more thing, house rules. All weapons to be left at the door."

Callianessa clapped her hands and the large man in the corner strode over purposefully.

"Please hand all weapons over to Centius. You can retrieve them upon leaving."

Llorc and Draccus unbuckled their belts but, as Gaios went to do so, Draccus murmured to him.

"You'd best wait here, Gaios. A former City Guard may not be so welcome around the table. But I would be grateful if you would stand watch and be alert for any treachery."

Gaios nodded and repaired to a nearby couch, drawing a scowl from Centius. His two companions passed over their weapons, then followed Callianessa through the door, along a short corridor and into a rectangular chamber. A long table dominated the room, about which sat a motley assortment of a dozen roguish faces. Atop the table were several pitchers and mugs, alongside platters of food. The low murmur of conversation stopped as the two men entered the room and took their places. All eyes moved to the figure at the head of the table.

"Deinokrates," whispered Draccus to Llorc as they sat. "Head of the oldest crime family in Adelphis."

The man in question did not raise his eyes and with a few deft movements of his fork dissected the lightly-roasted game bird on the platter in front of him. He took a small mouthful, chewed, swallowed, then looked up at the newcomers. Llorc thought he looked more like a patrician than a crime lord; expensive clothing, closely trimmed silver hair, a clean shaven, thin face, with finely chiseled features set in a permanent stern expression. Flanking him, standing against the wall behind, were two figures, one of which Llorc dimly remembered as Salazar de Vallego from the fight at The Bearpit. The swordsman returned Llorc's stare with undisguised contempt.

"So," Deinokrates fixed Llorc with a cold gaze, "this is the young man we have been hearing so much about."

Llorc nodded slowly in return. Draccus whispered, "Let me do the talking."

He stood and gave a short bow. "Greetings, Deinokrates, and to all here gathered. Gratitude for agreeing to this meeting."

"You know everyone here, I'm sure." Deinokrates gestured

around the table. "So let us get straight to the point. What do you want?"

Draccus rested his palms on the table and leant forward to address the group.

"As you know Stanler was taken from us and hung by the authorities."

A ripple of disquiet moved around the table. Professional rivalries aside, none relished the prospect of execution by the authorities.

"Since that time, we in the Ratteries have been under sustained attack; from the Militia, from mercenaries and, most recently, from foul sorcery."

At this last, there was another ripple of unease. Thieves of all classes tended to be superstitious by nature. Draccus continued.

"We believe these attacks to be orchestrated by Senator Toutatis. He desires the Ratteries cleared in order to complete his plan of rebuilding the area, a rebuilding that will bring him great wealth and control."

"And from us you would ask what?" Deinokrates sat back in his chair.

"We believe there will be another attack shortly. We have seen off all incursions so far, but we know that Toutatis will not give up. What we seek is aid from our colleagues, bodies and swords to help defend our area and our homes. If we can repel Toutatis again, it buys us some time to consider other possibilities to solve this problem."

A wiry figure with dark, wrinkled face and gaudy head

scarf leaned forward.

"And why should we help, boy? What's in it for us?"

"A fair question, Brahim, and I will give you two reasons. First, we will of course pay what we can in recompense, perhaps a share of profits from future operations. But second, consider this. Do you think Toutatis will be satisfied with just the Ratteries? Do you not imagine there are other areas which have caught his eye, areas in which you all operate? Think on this too. We know Toutatis is politically ambitious. If he gains power over the Senate who knows what measure he will pass in order to curtail our activities? I tell you, comrades, a strike at the Ratteries is a strike at us all!"

There was more murmuring around the room and Draccus sat down. The hubbub continued until Deinokrates raised his hand. As the muttering died away the crime boss leant back in his chair, pressed his palms together and addressed the room.

"You have spoken well, Draccus. And all of us here were sorrowed to hear of Stanler's untimely demise. He was always a fair and honourable man, so I shall be fair with you now. Call on me when needed and I promise fifty armed and armoured men. In return, I ask for a one fifth share of your future income."

Draccus seemed slightly surprised at this offer. He stood once more. "Gratitude, Deinokrates. Your offer is most generous and the terms acceptable."

Deinokrates suddenly sat up straight and slapped the arm of his chair.

"Settled, then! Send word through the usual channels and

within a short time, I will have the men there. But send for them only when needed, I will not have my men standing idly by! Others here will, I am sure, follow my lead in aiding you. We will discuss the details between ourselves."

Deinokrates stood, the rest of the assembly standing with him. He moved round to Draccus and Llorc, eyeing the latter carefully. He grasped Draccus by the shoulders.

"Fear not, Draccus, I will do the right thing by you, you have my word on it!"

Draccus gave a relieved nod and expressed his thanks once more. The two men returned to the entrance chamber to find Gaios happily chatting to the small throng of courtesans who had gathered around him. Draccus gave a cough and Gaios looked up, reddening somewhat. Llorc grinned.

"Ready to go, old soldier, or would you prefer perhaps to linger awhile?"

Gaios stood up and straightened his cloak. "No, I'm ready. Thank you ladies, it was very nice to meet you." He gave a formal bow and the women giggled and scattered.

Buckling up their belts as they descended the outside steps, the trio were soon back in their carriage.

"Well," Gaios asked, "how did it go?"

"Better than expected." Draccus replied. "Deinokrates agreed to help and set very reasonable terms. Perhaps he was fonder of Stanler than I thought."

Gaios grunted. "I doubt sentiment has anything to do with any decision Deinokrates makes. He'd cut his own grandmother's throat if the purse was heavy enough. Still, you've done well, lad."

Llorc sat in silence, keeping his thoughts to himself. He had felt nothing but contempt radiate from Deinokrates and, with the natural wariness of the predator, had no inclination to trust the man or his word. To Llorc's thinking there seemed only one way out of this situation and that was, as Kagas had advised, to cut the head off the snake. Llorc decided at that moment that he had to kill Toutatis.

Back at the brothel, Malassos emerged from the curtained alcove at the opposite end of the meeting room. He strode over to Deinokrates.

"You heard all?" the crime lord asked him.

"Indeed. I shall report back to Toutatis that all is as planned. With none to aid them, The Ratteries will be cleared by our forces in short order."

"Good. Forget not to remind Toutatis who will be given control of the new gambling houses in the new development."

"I shall remind him. Fear not, Toutatis is a man of his word. Are you not concerned, if I may be so bold, that you gave your own word to Draccus?"

Deinokrates affixed Malassos with a sneer.

"I promised only to do the right thing which, in this case, I shall. In any event I am dealing with an outland savage and a degenerate, neither is worthy of my word. Let them perish with the rest of the scum."

CHAPTER 19

Black flags fluttered from every flagpole and official building as the pale, winter sun rose over Adelphis. Despite the early hour, City Guard lined the Old City streets, along with many citizens. After a private dawn service at The Temple, the funeral cortège wound it's slow and steady way down from The Rock and into the streets below. Led and followed by an escort of Talons, resplendent in full polished armour and nodding black plumes, the King's bier, bedecked with flowers and drawn by two black horses, rolled through the streets. Citizen and Guard alike bowed their heads as the cortège passed. The Queen and Prince, along with other Royal Family members, followed the bier in an open carriage, the Queen veiled as was the tradition in her own land.

The procession made a circuitous route of the Old City before finally coming to a halt at the entrance to the

Catacombs that was set into The Rock. This area of the ancient subterranean network contained exclusive crypts for Royalty and the leading aristocratic families. As Talons made an honour guard and a small Temple choir sang a dirge, the King's coffin was borne through the iron gate, down the sloping passageway and into the Royal crypt, accompanied by immediate family and the High Priest. Following a short ceremony, the party came back to the surface and into their carriages, preparing to return to The Rock.

It was then that the trouble started. As the cortège headed back through the Old City streets, a shout rang out from the gathered crowd.

"Show your face! Show your face!"

It was quickly taken up by others. Malassos had positioned his people at strategic places on the return route, some shouting, others agitating the crowd. The baying grew louder and insults to the Queen increased as the cortège rolled on.

"Outland bitch! Respect our ways!"

"Adelphis for Aldephians! Foreigners out!"

At one junction, a natural bottleneck, a cart had been drawn across a narrow street, forcing the Royal party to come to a halt. Immediately an angry crowd swarmed around the carriage. City Guard and Talons sprang into action, forcing the mob back, using spear butts where necessary. This cleared the crowd but inflamed the situation.

"Protect our own, not foreign scum!"

The first missile sailed overhead, a small rock, bouncing off the side of the Royal carriage. The Queen moved to shield the young Prince, the Talons forming a tight defensive cordon around the family. Her personal bodyguard was back at the Palace, advisers thought it best he not be seen today. Fortunately for the Queen, the cart was quickly shoved aside and the cortège was now able to move off, picking up pace in response to the danger. Soon the party was winding back up the twisting road to the Citadel, leaving behind a volatile situation.

Having stirred up the fury of the mob, Malassos and his gang now directed it. Sweeping out of the Old City the crowd descended on the market area. The stalls and stores of many foreign traders were ransacked, men and women beaten. It took the City Guard more than an hour to restore order.

News of the troubles reached The Bearpit. Though none of it extended across the river, it served only to increase the growing sense of unease felt by all. Almost everyone went armed, Llorc and Draccus had increased the number of watchers throughout the neighbourhood and already a number of spies had been caught and run off or killed. The pair took a walk around the area to check on defences and readiness before returning to the tavern. Both were quiet and lost in thought as they supped ale. Draccus spoke first.

"It will be soon, I think. I've had word that the Militia has been mobilised in numbers. I also heard Toutatis has used the unrest to try and get control of the City Guard too, though there has been some resistance to that."

"Aye," replied Llorc. "Gaios told me there is no love lost between City Guard and Senate. But even so, a strong force of

Militia backed up with what remaining sell-swords that cur Toutatis commands will sorely press our defences, maybe even overrun us."

"And that's without his pet sorcerer. Who knows what deviltry he may yet throw at us. But with the aid of Deinokrates we will yet prevail."

" You have confidence in that old goat?" Llorc spat into the straw.

"He gave his word did he not?"

Llorc merely shrugged and took another swig of ale. His path was clear to him now. Tonight he would kill Toutatis and perhaps his sorcerer too. It was the only way to save the Ratteries. Tossing a coin onto the table top he patted Draccus on the shoulder.

"I'm going out for a time. Back later."

Pausing only to retrieve some items from his room, the barbarian set out into the darkening twilight.

Toutatis strode impatiently around the chamber. He muttered once again to Passang.

"We strike tonight, I tell you! The Militia are gathered, the mercenaries are ready and this time I will lead them myself!"

"You would lead troops?" Passang seemed vaguely amused by the notion.

"Damn you, yes, I'll have you know I studied military tactics at the Academy! Also, I would have your Master with me. His sorceries may be required again!"

"I speak not for my Master. He is currently in

contemplation and is not to be disturbed," the impassive manservant replied as he stood, arms crossed, in the centre of the room.

"Contemplation be dammed! We must strike while the blade is sharp! Clearing the Ratteries sends a message as to who is in control of the city. It further aids in distancing me from other...events...that are planned for tonight. I'll not wait on some conjuror's meditations!"

Passang remained unmoved but Toutatis jumped in fright as a voice whispered in his ear.

"No need to wait on my account, Senator." Khalsang had noiselessly entered the chamber and stood directly behind Toutatis.

"What, I, uh..." Toutatis recoiled as if from a cobra. Ever the politician, he quickly recovered himself. "I merely meant that I appreciate your input in our joint venture and would always seek your council, valued Khalsang."

The gaunt figure gave a thin smile. "That is reassuring to hear. However I shall not accompany you on this evening's mission, for I have my own. I leave shortly for the Catacombs."

Toutatis goggled like a fish out of water. "The Catacombs? Does this mean then-"

"Yes, the stars are in alignment on this very night. The time is here, we descend tonight."

"And the Prince?"

"The Prince is attending, as he wished and as his father agreed. Malassos will be bringing him to meet us." Toutatis reeled slightly as he felt events slipping from his control.

"But the assault on the vermin?"

"Not my concern, these are matters of politics, not lore. However, you have been most forthcoming in accommodating my needs, so I have prepared something for you. Passang, fetch the book."

The servant left and returned with the grimoire, wrapped in its black silk cloth. He placed the book on the table and Khalsang opened it with a long nail.

"Here," he pointed with a bony finger. "You recall the chants I taught you, here and here."

Toutatis glanced at the page and nodded.

"At the edge of the Ratteries is a burial ground. Take the book there, intone the chants, hold aloft this amulet." The sorcerer produced a small amulet from his robes. "At the culmination of the chant, you must bathe the amulet in blood, then shout out these calls here."

"I understand. What will this do?"

"It will raise the dead for a certain distance around you. Be sure to be within earshot of the burial grounds."

"Raise the dead? Why, that is miraculous!"

"No," Khalsang spoke as if to a small, unintelligent child. "It does not raise so much as reanimate. For a short time the bodies will be filled with vital force. During that time they will react to simple commands. They will fight whatever you point them at, they will have no fear, nor no will of their own."

Toutatis was struggling with the concept, though a grin of pure malice played across his features.

"Deepest gratitude, Khalsang. This is a mighty weapon

Indeed!"

"A mere trifle, nothing more, I trust it will be of use. Now, Passang, we have a rendezvous with the Prince."

"I will leave with you, my carriage can drop you near the Catacombs." Toutatis buckled the belt holding a short sword at his waist, donned the cloak offered by his servant and strode purposefully out to the waiting carriage. The twin bodyguards were already sat atop. With a flourish and lightness of step the Senator bounded aboard.

"Onward! Let us ride to victory!"

Llorc ducked into the shadows as the City Guard passed. Following the earlier disturbances the streets were empty of all but the Guard, patrolling in large groups. The detritus of the riots still littered the streets in places, all windows were shuttered. None saw nor disturbed the youth as he climbed the Old City wall and was soon again approaching Toutatis' town house. He was cowled, black leather jerkin under a dark blue cloak, sword and long poniard at his belt. His heart was filled with a simmering, murderous rage, tempered by a new found caution and strategic awareness.

As he crouched close by, the gate of the town house opened and Toutatis' carriage exited. From the faint light of the lantern within, Llorc caught sight of the vulture like profile of the sorcerer and the pale face of Toutatis. With a grim smile he followed. The horses moved at a slow trot, an easy speed to keep up with for one used to jogging through forest and over hill. After a short time the sound of voices rose ahead above the clatter of hooves and the carriage drew to a halt outside a large building close by the south face of The Rock. A group of armoured men were gathered there, heads turning at the approach of the carriage. Conversation halted as Khalsang disembarked, a few of the men making gestures as if to ward of the evil eye. Ignoring the mercenaries completely Khalsang, with Passang at his side, strode off into the night.

Toutatis leaned out of the window and spoke to the group. Llorc could not hear the words from his vantage point and to move closer was to invite discovery. Before he could decide anything, a number of the group climbed up on board the carriage and it set of again, the remainder of the men following at a trot.

Llorc cursed. Toutatis was no longer a viable target, he would have to cut his way through more than twenty men to reach him. The sorcerer seemed the easier kill, with only his servant to protect him. The youth made a quick decision and padded off into the darkness on Khalsang's trail.

To his surprise, he saw the Easterners heading towards the Catacomb entrance set in the Rock wall, just a street or two away. Llorc closed the gap quickly and quietly but was nowhere near striking distance by the time the gate was reached. Besides which, there was a group already waiting there, lit in the crimson glow of the torches they held. Talons, four of them, plus the short figure of a young boy stood beside the man who had led the thugs in the Old Market square. Llorc faded into the shadows and drew as close to the group as he dared, straining his ears to hear.

Khalsang strode forth confidently, addressing the boy.

"Greetings, Majesty, I trust you are ready to visit the Catacombs below?"

"Ready indeed," replied the Prince, " I do hope it will be exciting!"

The ghost of a smile flitted across Khalsang's bony face. "I think I can promise a night you shall not forget, Majesty. Shall we?"

The Prince nodded and waved a hand at the barred entrance. One of the Talons stepped forward to unlock the iron gates and, one by one, the party stepped forward, the torchlight gradually receding as they moved into the tunnel. Llorc did not hesitate. The Talons were a problem, but with the element of surprise and the darkness in his favour, Llorc was confident of reaching and killing the sorcerer without having to fight his way through them. After that? Well, he would accept whatever fate had in store for him. Moving like a great cat the barbarian drew his sword and trod quietly down into the passageway.

CHAPTER 20

Queen Arpanas laid back and sighed as her personal maid, Calinope, laid a cool cloth across her eyes then left the chamber. The throbbing in her temples was immediately eased. It had been an awful day. Such an early start, so many things to arrange, then the interment of her husband followed by that awful ride back through the mob-ridden streets. Thank heaven for the loyal Talons and the stout City Guard. Tomorrow foreign dignitaries would begin to arrive, the next two weeks would be taken up in formal mourning and receiving visitors who wished to pay their respects.

Added to her woes was the news that Toutatis was to force a vote in the Senate, making her own position somewhat unclear and fragile. She began thinking it may be best simply to return home to her father. Yet that would leave the young Prince exposed completely to Toutatis' poison. No, she would stay, she owed that at least to her husband.

The Prince had not spoken to her all day. He seemed little upset at the passing of his father and had immediately retired to his chambers on returning to the Palace. At present she had no notion of where he was or what he was doing, Malassos had spirited the boy away. Only the last minute intervention of Myonaris meant that four Talons now accompanied the lad, wherever he was.

The Queen reached out a hand for the bell to summon the maid. As she did so a strange sound reached her ears, a scraping from outside the window. It was quickly followed by a light thud on the balcony. Curiosity roused, she removed the cloth from her eyes and sat up. Her vision, still slightly blurred, took in the sight of a figure gliding into the room through the balcony door. Dressed head to foot in dark clothing, a cowl covering the face, the long curved knife in his right hand made plain the intruder's intent.

The threat spurred the Queen to action. The closest thing to hand was a water jug on the low table next to her couch, which she grabbed and hurled with all her force at the menacing figure. The intruder ducked, the jug smashing into pieces against the wall. From behind him, another thud signalled the arrival of another dark figure dropping onto the balcony.

The Queen screamed out "Gurdas!" and then the attacker was on her. Dagger raised, he rushed in to strike but the Queen was not defenceless. The custom in her own country was for women, even Princesses, to learn the moves of attack and defence disguised in her peoples' traditional dances.

Bringing both hands up, she managed to deflect the first knife thrust with the heavy bangles she wore on each wrist. The assassin cursed and slapped her heavily across the face with his left hand, the blow sending the Queen reeling back across the couch. Dazed, she could only look up in horror as her assailant advanced again, dagger poised. The second figure was already in the room, and a third appeared on the balcony.

"Die, slut!" growled the masked man. The Queen reached desperately for the small blade concealed at her ankle, knowing she could not draw it in time, nor would it be enough against the three knives arraigned against her.

Of a sudden, the door to the chamber exploded inward and the burly figure of Gurdas burst into the room. Assessing the situation in an instant, he had tulwar drawn and was striking at the second assassin before anyone had a chance to move. The thrust caught the man high in the shoulder and he sprang back with an oath. The first attacker had a moment of indecision over which figure to strike at. The Queen took the opportunity his hesitation brought to draw the short blade and, lunging forward, plunge it into the assassin's thigh.

The man gave a bark of pain and grabbed the Queens wrist in an iron grip. Bending her wrist back he raised his own dagger for a savage thrust. The Queen closed her eyes and prepared to die. The blow never came. Opening her eyes, she saw the point of Gurdas' sword burst through the man's chest in a shower of red drops.

The third attacker saw his chance. Swiftly closing the gap he struck at Gurdas with his knife. The bodyguard managed to turn slightly, but the blade bit deeply into his upper shoulder. With a curse, he turned to face the new attacker, grip loosening on his tulwar as the blood streamed down his arm. The assassin struck again, a high slice at Gurdas' face, forcing the bodyguard back and closer to the Queen.

"Keep behind me, Divyani!" he cried in their own tongue. The Queen struggled to her feet and tried to comply. Now began a game of cat and mouse, as the assassin moved and Gurdas matched the move to keep himself between the attacker and his target. The blood flowed freely from Gurdas' wound and it was clear he could not last much longer. The assassin's eyes glowed with satisfaction as the large man's eyes fluttered and his head drooped, the point of his sword falling to the floor.

The attacker saw his chance, faked a movement to his right, then sprang forward and left, knife flashing in a murderous arc. But Gurdas had tricked his opponent. Kicking up with his foot, he flicked the point of the tulwar up and out, catching the assassin just above the hip. The masked figure spun in mid-move, as though knowing what was coming next, but he was too late. The upward swing of the tulwar reached its apex and was turned into a terrific back hand swipe that took the assassins head clean from his shoulders. The headless body stumbled for a couple of steps then fell, with a lifeless thud, staining the richly woven rug beneath with gore.

The Queen uttered a most unladylike oath and spat on the body before her, then moved swiftly to support Gurdas as he swayed, face twisted in pain.

"It is nothing, Divyani, please do not concern yourself. Calinope, your maid, she attempted to draw me away from my post with some tale. I believed her at first and followed but something did not ring true, so I returned"

"It is as well you did, Gurdas. Now, sit here on the couch, I will fetch aid. Guards! Guards!" she cried, the sound of running feet soon echoing along the corridor outside the room.

There was no attempt at surprise or concealment. The large body of Militia loomed out of the evening twilight and tramped heavily across Pergares Bridge. In their midst, Toutatis sat in his carriage, atop which sat the giant twins and around which marched the reconstituted group of mercenaries. The young watchers at the south bank scurried away quickly at the sight of the force and the first barrier was pulled across the south end of the bridge and set alight. The barrier was designed to slow down rather than stop and it achieved its goal. The Militia men took some minutes to pull the barricade aside with their spears and toss the burning timbers and rags into the river below. From the streets ahead they could hear many shouts and the clanging of bells.

Bridge cleared, the group swept on through the Old Market and towards the Ratteries. The streets were deserted, all windows barred. Occasionally a small face could be spotted peering over the edge of a rooftop, or from round a corner, before darting away. There were even a few missiles that came winging in from overhead but these were easily deflected with raised shields. The group halted in the plaza overlooked by the shuttered and deserted Bearpit. A whistle blew and the Militia men moved into a square formation, shields raised, all eyes outward. At the centre of the formation Toutatis exited his carriage and looked around.

"There!" he pointed to the burial grounds. "Take positions!" he ordered Captain Hermeros, sat astride his horse beside the carriage.

"But sir," the Captain replied. "We can see the scum ahead." He pointed with his sword to the barricade across the street ahead, behind which pale faces could be seen, with expressions of grim determination.

"One charge," he continued, "and we will sweep the rabble before us!"

"Hold your formation, Captain. I have something special planned for these vermin. Your men can sweep in and clean up after. For now, I need a space to work, just there!"

Toutatis gestured to a spot next to the low wall surrounding the burial ground. The Captain shrugged and ordered his men to move. The group slowly shuffled across to the cemetery. The twins leapt down from the carriage and took up position behind Toutatis. A lectern and the book were produced from the coach, along with the figure of a small, trussed child. Some of the mercenaries held torches aloft, casting Toutatis face in an crimson glow.

Draccus had received word from several of the runners at once. He ordered the alarms rung, and word spread quickly throughout the streets, people flooding out from the buildings in order to man positions. Gaios was already at the first barricade when Draccus reached it. Some fifty paces away they could see the Militia force positioned in the square.

"How many?" Draccus asked as he crouched next to Gaios.

"I'd say about seventy Militia and maybe thirty mercenaries. A strong force, to be sure. You think we can hold?"

"For a short while. Word has been sent to Deinokrates, let us hope his men come with all haste."

"I've sent word to some old comrades in the City Guard. Whether they are able to come and help I do not know." Gaios grinned. "Old dogs but they have plenty of bite left in 'em and they have no love for Toutatis and his rabble."

Draccus returned the grin. "Then let us buy a little time in order that our friends may arrive while we are still alive!" The grin faded. "I wish Llorc were here though, I know not his whereabouts."

"That is a worry, it's not like him to miss a fight. Let's hope no ill has befallen him."

"Indeed. What are they doing now?"

Both men peered over the barrier. The Militia seemed to be changing formation. Draccus called to a young, red haired girl up on the rooftop.

"Ambera, what can you see from up there?"

The girl shaded her eyes from the torch glare and squinted. "The men are standing in a big square. There's a man on a horse and a smart looking man in the middle with two big men stood behind him. He looks like he is singing!"

"Singing? Are you sure?"

"Yes, Draccus. Well, he is waving his arms around about, too, and - oh!"

"What?"

"He has a little boy, he... Draccus, he just cut the little boy's throat!"

At this, a roar of anger rang out from along the barricade and several stood, as if readying to charge over the barrier and across to the Militia.

"Stay, calm yourselves!" Gaios' steely voice rang out. "This may be a ruse to draw us out into the open. In any case, we are too late to save the child. Let his death strengthen our resolve and let our fury drive our sword arms!"

The crowd growled in assent, many hurling curses towards the distant Militia.

"Draccus," the girl's voice floated down from the rooftop. "There is something strange happening. The soldiers are moving away to one side... there's things coming up from out the ground! I don't know what they are, Draccus, but there's things coming up from the ground!"

As the crowd watched, the Militia at the front of the square moved aside, exposing the group within. Toutatis stood to the fore, mercenaries behind him. The ground to the other side of the short wall was rippling as though it were water. Vague shapes could be seen emerging from the dark earth, pulling themselves up and out of the cloying soil. First a handful, then more and more, til three score figures stood swaying unsteadily in the red glow. At this distance they could see

Toutatis raise a hand and point, his cry echoing across to them, a single word of command.

"Kill!"

At the shout the figures began crossing the wall and shambling across the square towards the barricade. Draccus raised himself above the barrier to get a better view.

"What in Bel's name are they?"

As the things grew closer it soon became apparent what they were. Eyeless sockets, rotted features, bony hands held claw like in front. Most were dressed in rotted rags, or stained shrouds. Some were little more than skeletons. Many were the size of young children, features both rotted and burnt.

"The dead!" gasped the man next to Draccus. "They are the dead!"

CHAPTER 21

Llorc slipped quietly between the wrought iron gates and into the passage beyond. It was wider than his outstretched arms, lined with white stone, and had a slight downward slope. Just ahead, disappearing out of sight around a turn, he could see the flickering torches of the sorcerer's party. Head thrust forward, sword in hand, Llorc stalked on. The tunnel curved slowly to the right, then straightened and levelled out. At intervals along each wall were archways surmounted by elaborate carvings, family crests from what he could make out in the diminishing glow. Beyond each archway lay impenetrable darkness, leading to vaults Llorc guessed. These tombs seemed more well appointed than those he had explored before and his palms itched at the thought of what riches may lay within. However he forced himself to continue in pursuit of his quarry, in any case the glow of light had almost disappeared ahead.

At the far end of the straight corridor he could see the faint light descending some steps at a narrow archway. He hurried to the top of the stairs and took a swift, darting glance down. The stairway was curved in a spiral, the stone here appearing somewhat rougher than the vault area. The real entrance to the ancient Catacombs, then?

Taking care not to hit his sword blade on the wall, Llorc descended. He paused as he heard the low whisper of voices ahead, then moved on as the torchlight receded once more. Around the next turn, the stairway ended in a passageway leading off into the dark. The stonework here again was rougher than upstairs and there was a distinct smell of damp in the air. In a crouch Llorc stalked forward, following the dim glare of torchlight.

After a short while the glow halted and Llorc stopped, kneeling against the wall, sword at the ready. He had not been heard, as he at first thought, it seemed the party had come to a stop for some other reason. The sound of a hissing voice floated through the darkness, followed by a sonorous cry in some foreign tongue, then a burst of light and sound. All became quiet and still and, after a short while the torchlight faded once more.

Llorc continued, the passageway opening out into a wider room, through which flowed a narrow stream. A single span stone bridge crossed it, from what Llorc could tell this was the same chamber he had found himself in on his earlier excursion. The gateway to the underworld then? But what of the guardian? As he crossed the bridge he made out the vague shape of a twisted form on the floor, claws raised, face contorted, quite dead it seemed.

Beyond, the passageway sloped down, steeper now and Llorc could see or sometimes sense openings on each side, at irregular intervals. More than once he fancied he heard the faint pad of a footstep, or the swish of something against stone whisper out from the openings. He paid no heed, but continued on, eyes fixed on the glow ahead, his only link with the outside world. As time passed he began to feel he was descending into the very bowels of the Earth itself. The air was becoming thicker, the weight of rock above him almost a tangible force pressing down on his shoulders. There were twist and turns in the passage way and further steps to descend, becoming narrower each time. At one point he had the impression of disturbing carvings and bas-relief on the walls, thankfully he could not make out details in the near total darkness.

Time lost all meaning and Llorc was almost in a trance when he realised the party ahead had once again come to a halt. He edged forward in a low crouch and was soon peering from the narrow passageway into a large chamber.

The four Talons each held torches aloft as Malassos lit a large brazier near the centre of the room. The chamber was roughly carved out of the living rock, around fifty paces across with a domed roof. Around the lower edge of the wall ran a carved frieze, though Llorc could make out little of it aside from vague figures with human outlines and other, more disturbing shapes.

In the centre of a chamber, three steps led up to a black stone dais on which stood two circular pillars. They stood around ten paces apart, each quite narrow, little more than the circumference of a person's arms and roughly the height of two men. The pillars looked green in the ruddy glow of the torchlight, thought the colour seemed to shift as Llorc gazed on them, now more red, now blue. Atop each pillar sat a dark globe, the size of a man's head. Although they appeared to be made of some type of crystal, the globes did not reflect the torch glow but rather appeared to absorb the light into their pitch black depths.

Khalsang stood before the dais, face stretched in a rictus grin. Malassos stood to one side, close to the brazier, his hand on the Prince's shoulder. The four Talons took up position close by the Prince, glancing uncertainly at each other. Passang placed the large bag he was carrying on the floor next to the sorcerer. Llorc caught a quick glimpse that passed between Khalsang and his manservant.

"Splendid," intoned Khalsang. "Now we can begin." He moved to the bag and began removing items, a bowl, a curved knife and a stoppered vial which he placed on the floor. Lastly he took a large scroll from the bag and, unrolling it, began a monotonous chant in a sibilant tone. The language was no tongue that Llorc had heard before and he had the disquieting notion that it was not one developed by, or for, the human voice.

The Talons looked increasingly uncomfortable. One turned to Malassos.

"Sir, with respect, we were asked to accompany the Prince here on sightseeing. There was no mention of a ritual."

Malassos imperceptibly tightened his grip on the boy's shoulder. "You will keep your place and hold your tongue, soldier. The King himself, Zantus rest his soul, sanctioned this venture, would you go against his wishes?"

The soldier shuffled his feet awkwardly and coughed.

"Well no sir, it's just that the Queen-"

"The Queen?" Malassos sneered. "Her words hold no sway here. Keep your peace or leave, it's all the same to me."

The Talon glanced at his companions and resumed his position. Khalsang, meanwhile, continued the low chant. Llorc scowled in frustration, with the four Talons in the way it would be hard to reach the sorcerer for a killing blow. As all eyes were on Khalsang he decided to risk moving to a better vantage point. With the stealth of a timber wolf he crept into the chamber and began a slow circuit, holding close to the rough, stone wall, eyes never leaving the gaunt, yellow robed figure.

"By Bel, you are right," hissed Draccus. "The dead rise against us!"

The faces of all behind the barricade were pale with horror as the ghastly figures stumbled towards them. The ruddy torchlight gave the whole scene a hellish glow as the blank-eyed dead drew closer, step by faltering step. Swords were gripped tightly and missiles were readied, then a faltering voice cried out from the defenders.

"Phylia! It's my Phylia, don't shoot!"

Before anyone could move, one of the defenders leapt over the barrier and ran towards a small, stumbling figure. Tears streamed down his face as the man dropped his weapon and stretched out his arms towards the blank faced child.

"No!" Gaios shouted. "Stay back! It is no longer your child!"

But the man paid no heed, falling to his knees he clasped the revenant in his arms, sobbing. The figures nearest to the man halted and began turning towards him, the rest continuing their relentless stalk towards the barricade. The little girl, carried up in her father's arms, made no other reaction other than to turn her head and bite him savagely in the neck. The man let out a high pitched scream as his daughter bit again and half a dozen living corpses fell upon him, tearing his body apart in front of the horrified onlookers. His screams continued shrill and agony-laden, until a watcher from the roof raised a crossbow and brought the man's suffering to a merciful end.

The stunned onlookers could only watch, mouths agape as the figures drew closer.

"Fire, you fools! Shoot them!" shouted Gaios. Some did from the rooftops but the nerve of those behind the barrier was seriously tested. More than one dropped a sword and ran screaming as the ghoulish figures began clambering over the barricade. Others gritted teeth and began the grisly work of hacking at the walking corpses, trying not to meet the blank stares of former neighbours, friends and family.

The defenders stabbed and slashed at the wave of

mortified flesh but the corpses proved resilient. It seemed nothing less than a crippling blow or beheading would stop them and in meantime they wreaked a bloody harvest. Claw-like hands and yellowed teeth sought soft flesh. Those corpses that fell continued to bite and scratch from the ground, pulling defenders down into the bloody mud. The second wave of dead hit and Gaios, casting a glance around, made a decision.

"Pull back! Back to the second barricade!" He unleashed a vicious back cut at a mottled, shrivelled arm that clawed towards him, taking it off at the elbow before pushing those colleagues around him away from the barrier. Draccus shouted up to the rooftops.

"Don't wait, fire as soon as we are clear!" He cut down a putrid figure in rags beside him, before grabbing and clasping the hand of a comrade next to him who had two of the corpse things swarming over him. He chopped deep into the back of one corpse, then beheaded the second before pulling his comrade out and away. Too late, the man's torso had been opened by the vile creatures, glistening innards trailing in a bloody stream as Draccus dragged the man clear.

The defenders ran, Gaios holding back in order to buy them some time. At once he became the focus for six of the shambling dead but the group on the rooftops now came into their own. They poured a hail of arrow and crossbow bolts into the creatures below. Few were taken out of action by the volley, but they were at least slowed. Other defenders threw down flasks of oil, followed by a flaming brand or arrow and some of the living cadavers became engulfed in fire.

The brief cheer of victory from above was cut short by the sound of tramping feet from the advancing Militia, now grouped in a tight phalanx. At the edge of the formation, crossbowmen took position and began shooting at the rooftop defenders, forcing them back from the edges.

The phalanx gained pace and soon, with a crash, smashed into the first barricade. Those archers above who dared to take a shot were feathered by bolts and fell heavily to the street below. Within minutes the barricade had been all but destroyed and swept aside. The Militia were in the Ratteries.

In their midst strode Toutatis. Leaving the book and amulet behind, he entered the Ratteries like a conquering hero. This was the closest he had ever been to battle and the sights, sounds and smells filled him with excitement. Ahead, he could see the undead lurching towards the next line of defence. Around him lay the corpses of the vermin he had come to exterminate. The twins stood at each shoulder, each with a large shield, to protect the Senator from missile fire. But now even those on the rooftops were falling back, lest they be cut off from their fellows as the Militia advanced.

Gaios scrambled over the second barrier and dropped panting next to Draccus.

"By Karnos, I've never seen the likes of this before! That damned sorcerer, is it not enough we have to fight living men, he throws corpses at us too!"

"Aye," replied Draccus. "What do you suggest we do?"

Gaios grinned. "We fight, lad. And some of us die. I would say retreat, but where to? Much further and we will have the river at our backs. Nowhere to run!"

"True enough. Fight it is, then!"

At that moment, the wave of revenants hit the second barrier. This time the defenders were somewhat better prepared. Those with long spears began picking off the corpses as they reached the top of the barricade and the rooftop fighters kept up a steady barrage from above. Numbers began to tell though and more and more corpse-creatures dropped down behind the barrier. They had no fear, felt no pain and seemed filled only with the desire to kill. And beyond, all could hear the steady tramp of feet as the Militia force drew closer.

Slowly, inexorably, the defenders were pushed back from the second barricade, finally breaking to retreat and gather in a group further along the street. Captain Hermeros, now dismounted,directed his troops, forming a line four deep that slowly approached the barrier. Ahead of them, more corpses clambered over or simply tore through the barricade and, as if sensing the end was near, gathered themselves in a seething mass, pausing as if relishing the horror of the situation.

Draccus, bloodied from a deep cut in the scalp, shook his blade and roared defiance. Gaios, still breathing hard, leant on his sword and bowed his head as if in prayer. To left and right, defenders hefted weapons uneasily, stood silently waiting the attack, or swigged from wine flasks and shouted curses at the shambling crowd before them.

Covered by the twins, Toutatis came through to the head of

the Militia group to stand beside Captain Hermeros. Two of the soldiers cleared aside the remains of the barrier so that he might witness his final triumph. All was quiet for a moment, only the cry of a small child behind the defender's line broke the stillness. Then Toutatis pointed to the ragged line beyond his corpse army and screamed.

"Kill them all!"

At once, the rotting, ragged figures began their slow lurch forward for the final kill. They were almost within striking distance of the defenders when a sonorous, three-toned chant floated up and over the street. From a side alley came Guryon surrounded by his flock. Each was singing the soft but persistent chant and Guryon held aloft a wooden icon. The effect on the walking corpses was dramatic, at once they faltered and came to a halt, grey faces turning towards the sound.

"On! On!" screamed Toutatis, to no avail. He had failed to understand that sorcery involved more than chanting words written on a page, that force and direction of will was as important as ritual and words; that the amulet he had discarded as a useless trinket encapsulated something of the force of will of Khalsang, who had prepared the resurrection spell earlier. Without that will and in the face of opposition, the power of the ritual faded. Before Toutatis' horrified eyes his corpse legion sagged, then dropped into the mud, becoming, once again, nothing more than inert flesh and bone. Work done, Guryon and his flock retreated once more to the alleyway.

Captain Hermeros swore under his breath and muttered to himself "Sorcery be dammed!" Then, to his men he roared "Onward! Charge! We will carry the day yet!"

His cry broke the spell, the Militia raised a shout and charge ahead towards the defenders. Toutatis, caught in the group, was jostled and shoved forward, soon finding himself uncomfortably close to the fighting. The Twins were still beside him but he was now separated from his mercenary group. With the press of bodies, retreat was not possible but, spying a quiet alleyway opening, he gestured to the Twins.

"There, down there. Follow me!"

The trio slid away from the main street battle and into the relative calm of the side alleys. The Twins maintained a watch all around and above as Toutatis led them deeper into the twists and turns, thinking of nothing else but escaping that terrible place of swords and shouts and mud and blood.

The Militia charge hit the defence line with a clash of steel and flesh. The defenders fought as men possessed but were slowly pushed back by the sheer weight of numbers. Militia crossbowmen not only covered the rooftops but some had themselves clambered up to the roofs, where they either fought or fired down on the defenders at the rear. Behind the main fight the mercenaries, less concerned about formation or fighting, began to fan out in small groups seeking plunder, kicking in doors, ransacking and looting whatever they could find.

Meanwhile the main street was filled with small groups

stabbing, slashing and grappling in the mud. There was no grand strategy at play here, no glorious trumpets or waving flags, merely a desperate struggle for survival as the Militia men began slowly to push their foes back step by bloody step.

CHAPTER 22

Llorc came to a halt and crouched deep in the shadows of the underground chamber, resting a hand on his sword hilt, its point in the dust. For some time now, Khalsang had been intoning. Llorc could make out few actual words, most of the chant seemed to be noises, hisses, guttural cries. All eyes were drawn to the strange pillars, for as the chant progressed a glow appeared between them. It began as a soft violet light but as the chant grew in fervour, the glow grew in intensity and pulsed with weird colours which hurt the eye.

Khalsang, his face barely human in the eerie radiance, ceased his chant and raised both arms.

"I-ya! I-ya! I-ya!" he cried, then again, then once more. The atmosphere in the chamber subtly changed. Llorc felt the hairs on his arms bristle and his muscles involuntarily tighten as if in anticipation of action. There was a dull ache at the back of his skull, a feeling of a vast, unseen presence. Something was coming.

The Talons obviously felt similar. The officer once again stepped forward as if to speak. Before he could utter a word, Khalsang wheeled and fixed the four soldiers with his gaze, flinging out a hand towards them. He curled his talon like fingers into a fist and, with a gesture, commanded the group, "Come!"

The Talons' faces fell slack, torches fell to the dust and, as a man, they trod slowly forward. Khalsang led them up the steps, to stand atop the dais in front of the shimmering field that flickered between the pillars.

"Kneel!" He swept his fist down towards the ground and each of the men knelt, faces still devoid of expression. There was a whimper from the Prince as Malassos' grip dug into his shoulder. Khalsang once again flung his arms aloft.

"I-ya! I-ya! I-ya!"

Llorc thought he must be hearing things. On the very edges of perception he fancied he could hear a strange fluting, a distant sound as of blown pipes. Yet the notes and scales they played sounded like no melody he had ever heard before. The fluting grew louder, discordant, dissonant, maddening in its tone and repetition. Llorc was forced to place his hands over his ears, dropping his sword. Even Khalsang and Passang seemed affected, both also blocking out the sound. The Prince was now sobbing, Malassos flinching, though not releasing his hold on the boy.

Louder and louder, swirling, soaring high, then crashing low, the obscene fluting reached a fever pitch... and suddenly stopped. There was not just silence, there was the total absence of sound. Yet all felt the presence of something beyond the shimmering veil. The coruscated curtain bulged in the middle and a disquieting outline began pushing through it, in some obscene mockery of birth.

Llorc thought it was a face but his brain struggled to make sense of the features upon it. Toad, spider, eyes, screaming human mouths, all seemed part of the alien features, yet as he made out one seemingly solid characteristic, it changed and melded into something else. With a force of will, he tore his gaze from the abominable face and cast his eyes downward. Seeing his sword lying there, forgotten, he grasped it once more, the familiar action doing something to steady his nerves.

Khalsang and Passang both had eyes averted; they knew none could look upon the Old Ones and remain sane. Malassos, not privy to such knowledge, was unable to tear his terribly fascinated gaze from what happened next. From around the mockery of a face tentacles emerged, glistening, pulsating. Three encircled the necks of the Talons, lifting them to their feet and pulling them gently towards the curtain of light. The touch seemed to dispel Khalsang's enchantment, for each man touched suddenly regained his senses. Better that they had not, for each found themselves staring full into that inhuman face, before being pulled, screaming, through the shimmering veil and into whatever hell lay beyond.

The fourth tentacle did not grab the remaining Talon but instead snaked around him. With a terrible grinding crunch, the tip of it bored into the base of the man's skull. The Talon stood, lurching like a marionette. His bulging eyes were completely black, his mouth opened wider than should be possible, in an distorted grimace. There seeped forth a voice, a sound from a being not used to speaking with human vocal chords, a travesty of natural speech. It sounded incredibly old, heavy with the weight of aeons.

Llorc, on hearing it, felt he was nothing more than an insignificant speck before something huge and beyond his comprehension. Eyes still downcast, his brain struggled to find something mundane to grasp, some oasis of normality in this waking nightmare. His grip on the sword hilt tightened, nails digging into his own flesh deep enough to draw blood.

"I shall withdraw," the voice was saying. "I am aware how your kind finds my visage... unsettling."

Llorc risked a glance up. That awful face had moved back behind the glow, just the tentacle remained attached, leech-like, to the unfortunate Talon. Khalsang made a low bow then addressed the soldier.

"Gratitude, most Ancient One. We bow before your magnificence."

"Why do you summon me? What do you seek?"

"Knowledge, Great One, I would know the secrets of existence!"

What might have been laughter issued from the extended jaws of the Talon, though it grated the nerves of all those in the chamber.

"Existence is futile. We exist only to feed. Feed me."

" Of course, Great One. Here, an untouched, pure soul."

There was a hiss of pleasure from the Talon and his head

lolled from side to side.

"Bring it to me!"

"Malassos!" snapped Khalsang. But Malassos was beyond hearing. His hand still gripped, knuckles white, the Prince's shoulder, though the Prince squirmed and shouted in his grasp, hands thrown over his own eyes. Malassos' eyes bulged, tears streamed down his cheeks, his mouth frothed, he gibbered insanely.

"The god! I've seen the face of the god! He saw me! The god looked at me!"

Khalsang turned and motioned to Passang, who drew his sword and strode across the chamber. With a single sweep, he cut off Malassos' head, the body falling with a thud to the dirt. Taking advantage of the grip being released, the Prince at once made a bolt. In the unearthly glow, though, he had lost sight of the entrance and ran blindly towards the wall. Passang was but a step behind him, when a large form hurtled out of the shadows and careered into him, knocking the Easterner off his feet.

"Dog!" cried Llorc. "Die now, die in the dirt!"

He lunged at the fallen figure, aiming to skewer him on the spot. But Passang was fast, he twisted aside and in one smooth move sprang back to his feet. With a short bark of laughter he launched his own attack at the young barbarian. The Prince cowered back against the wall and tried in vain to follow the course of the fight. Both blades flicked back and forth like snakes, the chamber silent apart from the shuffle of feet and the hiss of steel sliding on steel.

Llorc had begun with a ferocious assault, aware that he was facing an opponent of far greater skill than he ever had before. The Easterner weathered the first frenzied blows, then launched a dizzying series of movements, whirling and sweeping his wide sword in hypnotic arcs. Never still, he flowed from posture to posture, striking out with fist and foot as well as blade. Llorc allowed himself to be moved back by the onslaught, weathering the storm. Where he saw an opening he launched a thrust of his own, towards a seemingly exposed head or arm but Passang always managed to twist away, or deflect the blow.

Llorc gritted his teeth and redoubled his efforts, then came another opening. With a shout he stabbed forward, realising too late he had been tricked. Passang pivoted around the lunge and punched Llorc in the face with his free hand. Llorc was knocked back by the blow. Lip split but with the instincts of the wolf, he immediately dropped low to avoid the follow up slash that would have removed head from shoulders. As he did so, in one fluid movement he drew his poniard with his left hand and stabbed it down into the Easterner's foot.

With a cry of pain, Passang fell back and the two crouched in the lurid glow, eyes blazing; Llorc with blood pouring from his mouth, Passang gingerly testing his injured foot. Khalsang, meanwhile had made a lunge for the Prince and was now dragging him, screaming, towards the possessed Talon. Llorc spat blood towards Passang's face and followed up with a blinding whir of steel. The Easterner was forced back, each desperate block throwing up sparks as the blades clashed. He was forced to take a step onto his bad foot and his face creased in pain, awareness dropping for a split second. It was all the time Llorc needed. With a mighty sweep he chopped into Passang's sword arm, blade crunching deep into the bone. The heavy curved sword clattered to the floor as Llorc stepped in and buried his poniard deep in the Easterner's chest. With a soft sigh Passang slid slowly to the ground, life's blood oozing away into the dust.

Panting for breath, Llorc turned, eyes flaring, towards the sorcerer. Khalsang held the Prince, curved knife to his throat, at the foot of the dais.

"Curse you, barbarian! You have killed my servant but you are too late to save the Prince! The God shall feed on his soul!"

"Swine!" Llorc spat, "I'll have your head!" He sprang forward but Khalsang pointed the dagger and uttered a single syllable. Llorc found his movement brought to an abrupt halt, held in that invisible iron grip he had felt before. However, this time he was filled not with indecision but with murderous rage.

Khalsang had turned his back on the barbarian and was dragging the struggling Prince up the steps towards the grinning husk of the Talon. Trusting fully to his sorcerous powers he did not see Llorc, sinews straining with the effort, take step by laboured step behind him. Blood streamed down Llorc's chest, the veins stood out on his temples, his teeth were bared in a vulpine snarl as he stalked his yellow-robed prey. With each step, the power of the spell seemed to recede a little until, with an oath, Llorc broke free of the enchantment.

Khalsang was preparing to push the Prince towards the grasping tentacles that undulated through the shimmering curtain when a hand gripped his shoulder. He was spun around and received a buffeting blow to the face. Knocked sideways, the sorcerer fell down the steps to the foot of the dais. Llorc did not pause. Casting sword aside, he leapt upon the sorcerer and rained blow after blow upon him. Stunned and bloody, Khalsang could do nothing against the primal onslaught. Llorc hooked a fist into the sorcerer's robe, dragged him to his feet, then back up the dais. The Talon stood unmoving, watching with tilted head and inhuman black eyes.

"I once heard, cur, that your kind forego all pleasures of the flesh, is that true?"

"Yes, yes," the confused sorcerer replied through bleeding lips.

"Then if your god desires a virgin soul, let him have yours!"

With a roar, Llorc lifted the figure above him and hurled him headlong into the expectant tentacles. Pulsing and shimmering, the tentacles wrapped around the sorcerer, then drew him swiftly back through the shimmering veil. There was a high pitched scream that faded, then nothing.

Llorc wiped a bloody hand across his eyes and retrieved his sword. The Prince lay wide-eyed at the base of the dais. Llorc caught his gaze and nodded, then whirled as the Prince raised as warning hand to point behind him. The Talon had closed in, arms outstretched, mouth yawning. What his intention was Llorc had no idea but, in reflex, he struck out, lopping off first one arm, then the other. The body convulsed and shivered before being pulled back at high speed through the curtain. There was a moment's pause then several tentacles exploded forth, reaching out for Llorc and the Prince.

"Run, lad, run!" cried Llorc before hacking left and right at the wavering pseudopods. As quick as he slashed and cut one member, foul ichor spraying forth, another tentacle rose in front of him; one snaking round his leg, another his right arm. Soon, he was reduced to stabbing with his poniard as the strangely cold flesh closed around him. A further tentacle sprang forth from the shimmering barrier and wound around his torso. It squeezed mercilessly and Llorc felt himself lifted into the air. In desperation, arms pinned, he bit into the foul substance, feeling it writhe obscenely between his teeth. It made no difference, the air was being forced out of his lungs.

Vision blackening, Llorc began to see stars. Worst of all, he saw the glimmering veil drawing closer as he was pulled towards it. A war cry burst from his lips and he gave one final burst of effort for freedom but the grip was unbreakable. As he blacked out, Llorc thought he heard a chanting fill the chamber, then all went dark.

CHAPTER 23

Draccus cleared some space with a swing of his sword and glanced around. The Militia were swarming down the street now and fighting up on the rooftops too. Gaios still fought at his side, mowing down any who dared come near, but the old soldier was obviously flagging, his breath coming in great, rasping gasps.

"Where the hell is Deinokrates?" the young man shouted aloud, though none had an answer for him. Suddenly there came a call from behind the fighting line, it was Hespero.

"Draccus! Draccus! Get them back to the docks! There's aid!"

"Archers!" Draccus shouted to those few still above. "Cover us! Withdraw! Back to the docks!"

Missile fire redoubled as the defenders withdrew. Draccus met Gaios gaze as he fell back, the veteran had not moved.

"No!" cried Draccus, sensing what the man planned.

Gaios nodded sadly, then smiled and let forth a huge war cry. The last Draccus saw of the old soldier was him charging headlong into the Militia line, hewing left and right like a madman, before he himself was swept back in the tide of retreating defenders.

Gaios and the rooftop archers bought enough time for the defenders to regroup at the Old Docks. This was the last position, there was no retreat from here. Hespero clapped Draccus on the shoulder and pointed out over the water .

"There are boats coming up the river."

"How many? Is it Deinokrates?"

"Only two and no, it's not him, it's Galenna."

"Galenna? But how?"

"I've been keeping in touch with her through the pigeons. She went back to her home village but has returned to help. She has brought kinfolk with her."

Draccus rushed to the quayside as the two boats drew up and moored. First to jump onto the quay was Galenna and the two embraced warmly.

"Heard you might need some help. I've not many but they are all itching to fight!"

Draccus laughed for the first time that grim day.

"By Bel, it's good to see you Gal! And all swords are welcome!"

Around twenty men armed with sword and spears followed behind, bearded faces split with grins.

"Let's split some city folk heads, shall we lads?" one cried and with a shout they moved up to the line of defence, locals clapping them on the shoulders in greeting.

Despite the reinforcements things still looked desperate for the defenders. There came a natural pause in the fighting, during which each side reorganised their lines. The struggle was all but over on the rooftops, the powerful crossbows of the Militia had done their work. Soon no defenders were left alive up above and the remaining survivors formed a line on the dockside to await the final attack.

The Militia numbers had been swelled by an extra unit just arrived, they now outnumbered the defenders by three to one. The mercenaries, done with plundering and ransacking, sauntered back to the fray. Of Toutatis, there was nothing to be seen but the Captain had his orders. With a nod to his officers he motioned his forces forward into position, ready to attack.

The arrival of Galenna and her friends stiffened the defender's resolve but all present no had no doubt as to the outcome of the battle. Hemmed in against the river by a wall of spears and shields, all they could do was sell their lives dearly. The Captain steadied his troops and was about to give the order to fire to his crossbowmen, when a horn sounded from streets behind. It blared out again, and was followed by the galloping of hooves as a Talon raced headlong through the streets.

"Cease! Cease your fighting!" he shouted as he pulled his steed up alongside Captain Hermeros.

"What is the meaning of this?" bristled the Captain,

"This is a Militia operation! You have no place here!"

The Talon sneered and handed the Captain a scroll. "It's by order of the Queen!"

The Captain flushed and fidgeted in his armour. Any remaining doubt as to his next action was removed by the steady tramp of armoured feet as a squad of thirty Talons, accompanied by a group of City Guard, marched in formation down towards the docks. In their midst, a palanquin was being carried, accompanied by a large, turbaned bodyguard on horseback.

"Militia! Stand down!" Hermeros cried, silently cursing Toutatis. His men drew back, sheathing weapons. The Talons marched into the space between the forces, forming a square around the palanquin. The curtain was drawn aside and the Queen appeared, to the collective gasp of all there. She stepped down and, looking around her, addressed Hermeros.

"Good Captain, you will withdraw your forces immediately. These people are to be left alone. Is that clear?"

"Y-yes Your Highness!" the Captain bowed in his saddle. "Men, gather our dead and wounded, withdraw!"

Within minutes, the Militia were gone, along with their sell-sword allies. The Queen turned to the defenders.

"Which of you is Draccus?"

Draccus, bloodstained and tattered, came hesitantly forward, dropping to one knee.

"That is I, your Majesty"

"I understand you have led these people well and seek only to live in peace in this neighbourhood?"

"Yes, Your Highness. That is all we desire."

"Then I shall make it so"

"Gratitude, Highness. But why, if I may be so bold?"

"Let us just say that I heard of your problems and would help friends of a friend. A comrade of yours who has done me great favour."

"Llorc? You have seen him? Is he well?"

"Yes I have and yes he is. But enough, I must return to the Palace. The situation there remains fluid. There is further aid on the way."

Draccus bowed as head, along with those around who had overheard the exchange. A ragged cheer arose for the Queen as she returned to her palanquin and departed.

Toutatis panted and mopped his sweating brow with a silk kerchief. The sounds of strife and fighting were far behind him, but now he found himself lost in the maze of stinking alleyways. There was no one in sight, though he thought he espied the occasional glimpse of movement in the corner of his eye. Rats no doubt. He had tried to find his way back to the main thoroughfare, spurning the advice of one of the twins. *He didn't need a brainless oaf telling him what to do!* Ahead he could see the glare of torchlight, a welcome sight in this dark warren.

Moving forward he found the alleyway terminated in a deep channel, in which green brackish water rippled. A single plank spanned the channel and Toutatis crossed it, twins following, into the courtyard beyond. Tall buildings loomed on each side, the light coming from a torch set in a wall sconce.

Another dark alleyway showed opposite. Toutatis, glancing around, moved to the centre of the courtyard and sat on a barrel. Taking out a small flask from his robe he took a swig as the twins took position each side of him.

There was a sudden splash behind them and the three men whirled, just in time to see small figure scurry back into the shadows of the alleyway they had entered from. The plank bridge had disappeared from view. The bodyguards drew their swords. A rustle from above caught their attention and they looked up to see several faces peering over the edge of the rooftops. More appeared at the dark windows, many of them appeared to be children. A larger figure appeared, holding a lantern at a small balcony. It was Meg. Holding the lantern aloft she called down to the trio below.

"You two big lads, we have no fight with you, you can go. Reckon fellows such as yourself can jump that channel easy enough."

Toutatis sprang off the barrel and drew himself up to full height.

"Now listen here, I don't know who you are, but I am a Senator! I'll not have the likes of you order my servants about! Now, show me the way out of here at once!"

The twins glanced up and around at the figures surrounding them. They took note of the slings and small crossbows carried by many. They glanced at each other then nodded in agreement. Sheathing their swords, the two large men dropped their shields, wheeled suddenly and sprinted back towards the alleyway. In turn they each made a mighty leap, just clearing the channel, scrabbling on the far side, then disappearing into the darkness.

Toutatis swallowed hard. He swore under his breath then made a sudden bolt for the other alleyway. He made it into the darkness as a slingshot bounced off the wall behind him. He ran blindly, stumbling here and there and bumping into things in the dark. Another twist, another turn and he burst out into another small courtyard. This had two other exits, but as he rushed towards the nearest, a group of youths appeared in it, brandishing weapons. He darted towards the other, robes now spattered with mud and filth. Above, he could hear whoops and cries and the sound of running feet along the rooftops. Behind, there were more shouts, now echoed by those ahead.

He paused to try and orient himself and a stone whizzed close by, then another grazed his forehead. With a shout, he raised his hand up to this head, it came away wet and crimson. He ran again, choosing alleyways at random, sweat and blood stinging his eyes.

Finally, he burst out into a wider area. Ahead, above the rank smell of filth, he could smell the river. He charged onward as his pursuers burst out of the alleyways behind him. *Like a swarm of rats*, he thought. There was a light ahead and he could just make out the docks ahead in the gloom. *If he could reach them perhaps he could find a boat and escape this rabble!*

He came within sight of the docks but saw there was another channel to cross. This one was filled with dark ooze and the stench rising up to meet him was indescribable.

Gagging, he placed his kerchief over his nose and set a tentative foot on the narrow plank that bridged this final obstacle to freedom. It sagged slightly under his weight but held. For now, his pursuers seemed to have fallen back, though he dare not look round for fear of losing his balance. He was about half way across the makeshift bridge when a small, ragged figure appeared at the far end of the plank, a young red headed girl of around nine years old. Toutatis paused, uncertain. Turning his head slowly he saw, in a line along the channel behind him, the crowd that had pursued him. Women, children, youths, faces set in hatred, at their centre the woman who had spoken earlier. *No matter, he only had to make it to the docks!*

He shuffled forward another step and the girl moved to the edge of the channel. Keeping her eyes on him, she kneeled and gripped the end of the plank in her small hands. Toutatis' heart sank and, for the first time that night the reality of his situation hit home.

"No! No, little girl, move away! Be off, I command you! I am a Senator!"

The girl's face remained passive and she strained her muscles as she tried to shift the plank..

"No, listen, I have gold! Here! Take it! Just let me pass!"

Toutatis reached inside his robes and, drawing out a purse heavy with coin, threw it to the girl. As it hit the dirt beside her, she glanced at it, then looking directly up into Toutatis' eyes, straightened her legs and twisted the plank. With a cry of horror the Senator plunged into the black, tarry ooze below. Engulfed in the mire, he threw up an arm and let out a scream for help, struggling, but helpless in the grip of the slime; it felt as though a living thing had him in an iron hold and was dragging him slowly, so slowly, down.

Toutatis' last sight, as the filth covered his mouth, nose and eyes, was of the little girl opening the purse and hurling the gold coins down into the muck to sink slowly alongside him.

CHAPTER 24

Llorc awoke with a gasp and immediately wished he hadn't. There was sharp pain in his side, his guts felt squashed and out of place, his face throbbed like hell and his body ached all over. He was lying on a divan, his armour and clothing stripped away, naked except for a breechclout. Glancing down, he noted his skin was mottled with purple bruises. He sat up with a groan and looked around. An elderly man with a long grey beard came in through the doorway in response to the noise.

"Now, now young man, you just stay there. You have no major injures aside from a broken rib or two but will feel very sore for a few days."

"Who are you? Where am I?" Llorc mumbled, reaching for the water jug on a nearby table.

"I am Thyrenes, Physic to the Royal Family. You are in the Queen's private chambers, you are her guest."

Llorc took a swig of cool water. "But how did I get here? The Prince? Is he -"

"The Prince is well, young man, thanks to you. As to your other questions, rest now. All will be answered soon."

Llorc attempted to stand but the pain in his side brought him up sharp and his muscles felt like jelly. Reluctantly, he sank back down to the divan and closed his eyes once more.

It was the next day, when visited by the Queen and Oresus, that Llorc learnt the full story. The chanting he heard had been Oresus, bursting into the underground chamber reciting a spell of banishment, learnt from one of the many tomes of lore he had been studying. Wit the assistance of a group of Talons, Llorc and the Prince had been carried back out of the Catacombs to the surface. Llorc wondered how they could have found them in such a deep and hidden place. The answer was a simple charm, hanging on a necklace that the Queen had previously given as a gift to the Prince. It had a simple enchantment on it that allowed Oresus to divine the whereabouts of the boy. Llorc also learnt of the assassination attempt on the Queen, the attack on the Ratteries and the death of Toutatis. That, at least, brought him some grim satisfaction.

Within a short time Llorc was back at The Bearpit for a joyful reunion with his friends, though it saddened his heart to see so many faces missing. To his delight Gaios was in the tavern, though pale, bandaged and missing the lower part of his right

Arm.

"It takes more than a few Militia to put me in the ground!" he laughed, then raised the bandaged stump. "Bastards took my hand from me though!"

Llorc clapped him on the shoulder. "What will you do now? Surely this is an end to swordplay for you?"

Meg carried them over a jug of ale then placed an arm across Gaios' shoulders.

"Well, lad," Gaios smiled, holding Meg's hand with his left. "I've been thinking of retiring for a while, maybe running a tavern somewhere. That is if I can find some woman daft enough to have me."

Meg slapped him playfully and kissed Gaios on the cheek before attending to other customers. Draccus and Hespero entered then, to cheers of the assembled. Greeting each, Llorc took Draccus aside.

"I heard Galenna returned, with help?"

"Aye that she did," Draccus replied, "Though she left yesterday."

"Did she say where she was going?"

"Only that she was returning to her family home, there to decide her future. Perhaps you will see her again, Llorc."

"Aye, perhaps, if fate so decides."

Three days later, Llorc, Draccus and Gaios were summoned once more to the Palace. The Queen had taken her place on the throne as Regent. Most of Toutatis' supporters had been rooted out and hung as co-conspirators, fled the city or had a sudden change of heart and allegiance.

In the throne room the three were formally thanked for their part in protecting the Royal Family and the downfall of Toutatis. The Queen granted Gaios a generous pension. To Draccus she gave assurance that the Ratteries would be redeveloped but in consultation with the locals and as long as new leaves were turned over. Then she turned to Llorc.

"And what would you request of me, young man?" she asked.

Llorc, resplendent in white shirt, bright blue silk sash, new boots and fiery red cloak, bowed his head.

"I ask little, Majesty. Some fine food and wine, the company of stout friends and enough room to swing a sword!"

"An interesting approach to life and refreshing in a place where many seek only power and influence. But still, I would give you some reward. Might you consider taking a position in the Royal Bodyguard, or some post in the City Guard, perhaps?"

Gaios nudged Llorc in the ribs and waggled his eyebrows. Llorc smiled.

"That I might, Milady. That I might."

EPILOGUE

The King took another swig from the pitcher, upending the now empty vessel.

"Damn, yarn spinning is thirsty work and the pitcher is dry!"

The young thief sat transfixed, the King's tale vivid in his mind. Eventually he spoke.

"I had no notion, Majesty! I had heard rumours, of course, but none could guess at this, surely?"

"Rumours? Aye, I'll wager you have. Of a bloody handed usurper no doubt. A barbarian tyrant who seized the throne from the much loved rightful King."

"Aye, some of those," admitted the youth. "Though also others, of a King who is fair in his dealings and favours people not purely for their wealth or position."

"Nonetheless, plots are afoot. I never thought holding a crown would be such a battle but, by Dubh, I've found it to be as testing as any field of war I've stood upon, and I have stood upon many!"

"But what of the sorcerer? Was he ever seen again? Is the gateway still below in the Catacombs? And did you meet Galenna again?"

The youth made to ask more questions but the King stopped him with outstretched palm.

"Quiet," he hissed, "there are men outside. It seems this is a night for visitors! Draw your knife, lad but keep aside, I'll not have you harmed for my sake."

As he spoke he glided softly to the wall, taking down a large war axe that hung there. There was nothing ornamental about the grim weapon, scarred and marked as it was but the King hefted it and smiled as though greeting an old friend.

Then he set his back to the wall and turned as the heavy door burst inward. In the lurid torchlight dark figures rushed into the room, each masked and cloaked. Short swords glittered in their hands, their leader snarled.

"So, here is the wolf in his lair! In, men, in and slay the usurper!"

The thief, crouched in a dark corner, counted seven men coming through the door. They rushed towards the giant figure like a pack of dogs attacking a bear. The King did not wait for their charge, but sprang forward to meet them, wielding the axe in a mighty downward chop. It caught the first attacker full in the breast and he careered back with an awful scream, chest shattered. The King immediately turned the chop into a whistling sweep. One attacker dropped like a stone to the floor, the great blade passing over him, but his companion was not so fast. The notched blade took him in the arm, just above the elbow, smashing the bone and almost completely severing the limb. The man's sword clattered to the floor as he fell back with a groan of fear and pain.

But now the remaining attackers were in. Their numbers and lack of space saved the King, as not all could reach him to stab but two did; one attacker crouching low, his sword biting into the King's thigh as another jabbed towards his throat.

The King dodged back with a grunt, shifted his grip on the axe and used the haft to butt the nearest attacker in the face. The man fell back but his place was immediately taken by a fellow assassin. This man, though, underestimated the speed and turn of the axe. The King spun the heavy weapon like a toy in his hand and savagely chopped into the would-be killer's neck. The man staggered drunkenly back, clutching in vain at the blood spurting from his wound.

The King allowed himself a short bark of laughter and began a low war chant that raised the hairs on the back of the young thief's neck. The crouching attacker saw a chance to seize the King's leg, pinning him in place. Vulnerable as the man was, the King was unable to strike him, for fear of giving the three other assailants an opening. For a moment the King was forced to fight defensively, desperately batting away the stabs, though one opened a cut in his arm and another nicked him in the side.

There came a natural pause as the attackers gathered for a final assault. The King, one attacker still clinging for dear life to his leg, laughed mercilessly. Spattered with his own and others' blood, grey eyes glittering in cold fury, that terrible weapon gripped in scarred hands, he presented a fearsome aspect, far from the soft, half asleep King the assassins had expected.

"Who dies next?" he growled.

Though he didn't show it, the King felt the approach of death. Unarmoured and outnumbered as he was, he had little hope of prevailing. But to die without a fight was not in his nature and the blood pounded in his ears as the battle lust rose. The assassins rushed in for the kill. A high slash whistled past the King's head as he dodged aside, the second blow caught him in the shoulder. However, this brought the attacker in close and with a two handed sweep the King opened the man's belly, the assassin falling in a gruesome mess of innards and blood.

The third attacker saw his chance and struck at the King's arm, opening another gash on the bicep. In a last desperate act the King hurled the war axe full in the man's face, where it embedded deep in the bone with a sickening thud. The man dropped on the spot.

Two attackers now remained to face the unarmed ruler, one still clinging to the King's leg, the other gave a bitter laugh and pointed his sword.

"A bloody harvest indeed but no matter if the end be your death! Now die, outland scum!"

The attacker drew back his sword arm, then suddenly stiffened as the young thief plunged a dagger into his back, once, twice, three times. The assassin gave a gasp and fell, sword dropping from nerveless fingers to hit the floor with a clatter. The King drew his poniard and without so much as a glance, slit the throat of the attacker grasping his leg.

Wiping a hand across his face, the King staggered to the chair and sat heavily. Blood flowed from his wounds and, gritting his teeth, he tipped the pitcher up in vain.

"By Morrg, I take it back, slaying remains the most thirsty work of all! Still, lad, we made them pay, didn't we! Ha! I must be getting old though, so many wounds!"

The youth moved to the King's side.

"Is there anything I can do Sire? Should I bind your wounds, or call for someone?"

"Worry not lad, none are deep, just scratches. And with that commotion, I imagine the Guard will be here soon. Listen, best you are not here when they arrive. I know different, but some may suspect you to be in league with these dead men."

"As you wish, Sire but the way I came in may not now be passable."

The King thought for a moment. "Listen, boy. Grab a sackful of jewels from that chest. Go to yon window, open the shutter. If you are as good a thief as you claim, it should be easy to descend the ivy-clad wall. That will bring you to a small, enclosed garden. There is a door on the opposite wall, take that and you can slip out along the main wall. I'll tell the Guards to search the main Palace, so none should impede your exit."

The thief's eyes grew wide in amazement. "You would do

this for me, Majesty?"

"Aye lad, I would. Not only did you prove your courage in coming here tonight, you also saved my life. Such an act should not go unrewarded. But be warned, boy, if I hear of any boasting or telling tales of what has occurred here, I will seek you out myself, clear?"

The young man nodded and grinned. Without delay, he sprang to the nearby chest and scooped a handful of gems into a bag. Tying it to his belt, he unshuttered the window and eased himself over the sill.

"These will buy many a night's revels at the finest fleshpots in town!" he laughed, before lowering himself hand over hand down the thick vine. His last view into the torch- lit room was of the grim, bloodied figure of the King, chin resting on mighty fist, sat deep in thought as the commotion of the approaching Guard echoed down the corridor.

As he lowered himself down the wall, a thought sprung to his mind. *A wolf might run with the watch-dogs but it always remains a wolf.*

THE SAGA CONTINUES!

WOLF IN CHAINS
VOLUME TWO OF
THE WOLF WHO WOULD BE KING

www.innsmouthgold.com

ABOUT THE AUTHOR

Robert Poyton was born and raised in East London and enjoyed a childhood of classic TV sci-fi, Airfix kits and running wild on bomb-sites.

At age 18 he began training in martial arts and is currently an Instructor of Systema Russian martial art. He is also a keen musician, playing in a number of bands and recording projects.

He has long been a fan of Robert E Howard, HP Lovecraft and the other classic pulp authors. The Wolf series is his homage to Howardian S&S fiction.

Robert currently lives in rural North Beds with his wife and a small menagerie. When not writing he enjoys swinging swords and making a noise.

If you liked this book, please leave a review on Amazon.

Please support the Robert E Howard Foundation
www.rehfoundation.org

THE WOLF WHO WOULD BE KING SERIES
THE SAGA OF LLORC MAC LUGHAIDH

WOLF IN SHADOWS   **WOLF IN CHAINS**   **WOLF IN THE NORTH**

WOLF IN THE UNDERWORLD   **WOLF UNDER SIEGE**   **WOLF IN THE WILDS**

WOLF ON THE WAVES

"Great books! One of the better Conan-not-Conan series. Poyton does a much better job of nailing the Howardian vibe than most who have tried." Deuce Richardson

" Action packed and features some solid characters. If you enjoyed the works of Robert E. Howard I believe you will have a fun time with this novel."

" Rob Poyton channels the spirit of Conan, King Kull, and Solomon Kane. Great barbarian sword and sorcery" - Amazon reviews

THE DUNWICH TRILOGY

A MODERN MYTHOS TRILOGY!

THE DUNWICH NIGHTMARE
DC Marcus Hinds and journalist Suzy Bainbridge get
drawn into a mystery following a series of grisly
murders on Dunwich beach. Could there be a
connection to the nearby top secret research facility?

THE DUNWICH CRISIS
The scale of the conspiracy is revealed as Marcus and
Suzy are drawn deeper into the nightmare. Meanwhile, an ancient evil stirs
in the depths of the North Sea and the world is about to change forever!

THE DUNWICH LEGACY
The true purpose of the Geneva CERN facility is revealed and Marcus
plunges into the "world beyond" in order to save his friends and avert global
catastrophe.

*"A must read for all Lovecraftians. Check your sanity at the door to the dark realms of
Robert Poyton's Lovecraftian Worlds."* - Amazon review

All books available via Amazon or direct from www.innsmouthgold.com

INNSMOUTH BOOK CLUB

If you are a fan of Lovecraftian books and films, check out
our podcast the **Innsmouth Book Club!** Exclusive tours of
Innsmouth's cultural sites, including the museum, library
and Gilman house, where we talk weird fiction book, film,
RPGs, and music ,and chat to Lovecraftian creatives.

Also take a look at **Strange Shadows**, a podcast devoted
exclusively to the weird fiction of Clark Ashton Smith!

www.patreon.com/innsmouthbc

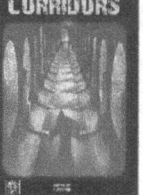

DARE YOU UNCOVER THE SECRETS OF INNSMOUTH?

Decaying New England seaport, creation of iconic weird tale author HP Lovecraft.

But what if it were a real place? What if ripples from that accursed town were to spread out across the world?

Inspired by family documents and photos, this collection brings together tales and poems reflecting the legacy of Innsmouth throughout the ages.

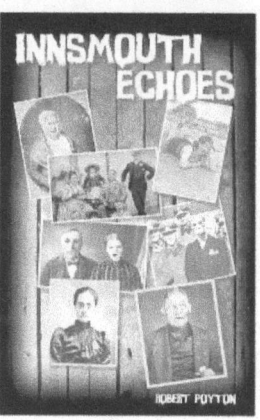

From the loss of King John's treasure in the Wash, to the truth behind Britain's largest earthquake. From secret U-boat missions to the Summer of Love. From yuppie developers to urban explorers. And from the sultry Pacific to the frozen Antarctic. No one who comes into contact with Innsmouth Echoes survives unchanged. Because Innsmouth is not just a place... it's a state of mind.

"Wow, what a read! Here in haunting, pictorial prose, the author conjures up fresh images and fantastic storylines of Lovecraft's Dagon and the Deep Ones a reader's mind." - Amazon review

INNSMOUTH LITERARY FESTIVAL

Annual event with guest authors and panellists, film screenings, traders, readings and gaming room!
Full details at
http://www.innsmouth.uk/